SHARP &POINTY THINGS

ALISON TUITE

CONTENTS

For all the stories that begin after heartbreak and grief.

"De réir a chéile a thógtar na caisleáin."

"It takes time to build castles."

-Irish proverb

CONTENT WARNING

This book contains sensitive material that may be triggering to some readers, including descriptions of:

- Depictions of grief and loss
- Death of a parent
- Graphic violence
- Depictions of Depression and anxiety
- Blood and gore
- Murder
- Stalking/harassment
- Explicit language
- Abuse (emotional and physical)
- Claustrophobia
- Defenestration (throwing someone off of a cliff in this case)
- Explicit sexual references/scenes
- Arachnophobia/spiders

Sharp and Pointy Things heavily explores themes of grief and loss and a character's struggle with depression and anxiety. My intention is to portray these experiences with care and honesty.

However, individual experiences may vary, and reader discretion is advised. If you or someone you know is affected by similar issues, please seek support from a trusted professional and/or helpline.

PRONUNCIATION GUIDE

Irish names/phrases to help guide you throughout the book:

"De réir a chéile a thógtar na caisleáin."
(Dĕ r-ayr Ah ch-ay-leh Ah t-oh-g-tar na Kay-sh-lean)
"It takes time to build castles."

Ciara

(*Keer-ah*)
Dark haired, Little dark one

Sean

(*Shawn*)

Niamh

(*Neeve*)
Bright, Radiant

Saoirse

(SEER-sha)

Gaeilge

(Gayl-guh)

The Irish Gaelic/language

Malahide

(Ma-luh-hide)

Suburb outside of Dublin, Ireland

Sláinte

(Slawn-che)

Cheers, to your health

Lough

(Laak)

Lake

Claidheamh Soluis

(Glaeve-so-lish)

Sword of Light

ALISON TUITE

Craic
(Crack)
News, gossip

Suaimhneas Síoraí Air
(Suave-ness sheer-y air)
"Eternal rest be upon him."

Uallas Jekylle
(Wall-as Jeck-ill)

Slán go fóill
(Slawn guh foh-ill)
"Goodbye for now."

Fearghas Harveye
(Fergus Harvey)

Samhain
(Sow-win)
Summer's end

Sluagh
(Slew-ah)
Hosts of unforgiven dead

Tú mo ghrá
(too moh graw)
"You are my love."

Anam Cara
(AH-nam KAH-rah)
Soulmate

CHAPTER 1

My father's idea of a bedtime story was mostly just nightmare fuel. They were hardly comforting tales of Irish folklore, featuring otherworldly beings who shift into the shapes of various animals, hiding in the woods. Since I was a young age, my father claimed the woods belonged to Satan. Still, I explored them despite the potential dangers, but only during the day.

One misstep in the Floridian woods at night and you may find yourself neck-deep in a marsh and eye-to-eye with a testy alligator, essentially a modern-day dinosaur built for ripping apart its prey. Don't even get me started on the venomous water moccasins that skitter across the tea-colored canals—their bite could lead to internal bleeding and immense pain. Even the plants there try to kill you, like night-blooming jasmine or Queen of the Night. Its otherworldly white flowers bloom only when the world is sleeping and are as beautiful to look at as they are deadly if ingested or even touched. Either of these options is a much more real threat than any of those in my stories.

To this day, seeing those fairy-tale creatures has been a secret desire of mine, especially the Pooka. I'd ask to hear stories about the shape-shifting creatures with white or black fur and the chaos they would cause the townspeople. Every night, my father would sit by my bed and tell a story about a different animal the Pooka turned into.
Some stories he'd read straight from the book, *The Tale of the Pooka,* and others he would make up. My favorite was that of a sleek black horse with glowing eyes that would give people the ride of their lives, though it would most often end up being their last.

Sometimes in these stories, the Pookas would give incredible luck to local farmers, delivering blessings to their crops and land. These types of stories were popular during the Great Famine, to keep people optimistic that the blight on their crops would take a turn in the right direction but only if you came across a Pooka who had positive intentions.

My father always told those stories with such confidence. Now, I couldn't help but wonder if there was any hint of truth in the ones he claimed he had made up, but I was skeptical he would tell me classified information dressed up as a fairytale. One thing was for certain: the Pookas in his stories would always keep you on your toes. You could never be sure of what to expect with these creatures, and I loved that aspect about them.

These days, I would do anything to hear those stories again, no matter how many times I'd heard them before.

A wave of grief washed over me as I grappled with the agonizing reality that my father's stories, and the comforting sound of his voice sharing them, were silenced forever. It's concerning how someone can go through the motions of their day-to-day life and have no recollection of conversations or anything that has happened. If you look up the word "disassociated" in the dictionary, there's a picture of me. I could have robbed a bank yesterday and would pass a polygraph test today, saying that I didn't do it.

The mind's response to trauma is both futile and helpful. I'd finally gotten over my night terrors, finally stopped waking up in the middle of an anxiety attack, drenched in sweat and gasping for air. Stopped feeling like I was being pulled to the bottom of an emerald lake and drowned by some odd horse figure with glowing eyes.

Thanks for the bedtime stories, Dad.

Surely that was his reasoning for the lore: to keep me away from the dangers lurking in the woods at night. To defeat a predator, you must first act like one. Know your own strengths and use that to your advantage. Humans were not built for the terrors that lay in wait at night.

The superstitions that my grandparents and their parents' parents had passed down for generations made us skilled storytellers. In fact, that's the root of our last name, Driscoll, meaning "descendant of the messenger."

About ten years ago, my grandparents moved to central Florida to live out their days in a nursing home.
I used to love spending time with them in the gardens at their facility. The courtyard was full of the bold yellow and orange hues from canna lilies, hibiscus bushes, and bird-of-paradise, as if Matisse himself had painted them.

It was a place where they would tell me stories about when my father was my age. I had tried to visit when I could and I still missed them dearly. Their passing a few years back still weighed heavy on my heart. I thought of them from time to time, and more so when I saw a butterfly on the bright golden blooms of the canna lilies outside our home.

My dad and I lived in the same house just outside of Orlando for my entire life. Our house was your average stucco, cookie-cutter, one-story family home of Florida architecture. He had always taught me the value of a dollar and the labor required to earn it. If I wanted luxuries, there was no sign that we had the means to make it so. I knew my father had a second home in Ireland, but I was always under the impression that it was a small cottage on the outskirts of Dublin, paid for by his years of work within the Irish government. I was only right about one of those things: its location.

In reality, his assets were closer to those of royalty than to the majority of the population's standards.

Despite having lived my entire life in the same house, I was itching for travel and adventure. It was a simple decision to leave behind my basic childhood home and seek my new accommodations in Ireland.

Even though I still liked to imagine that my mother remained in the Sunshine State, I hadn't heard from her since I was a young child.

She was the reason we moved to Florida in the first place, so I could attempt to build a relationship with my mother. I couldn't know for certain if she was actually in Florida, and she made sure the rest of her family cut their ties with me shortly after my dad accepted his position overseas when I was only four years old. This forced him to split his time between us and his work in Ireland.

I didn't think I'd ever forgive my mother for her abandonment. She really missed the mark when they were handing out "maternal instincts" for traits a mother should have. The only thing I kept of her are photos, which I stuffed in an old shoe box under my bed.

Then this big, terrible thing happened, and reality swooped in to reaffirm my worst fears: that my father was not, in fact, soaking up rays of sunshine on a beach, but *was* in fact in a fancy gold and marble jar of ashes awaiting to be picked up at the funeral home.

I was too young to deal with this. At only twenty-four, I hadn't expected to be dealing with my father's death. He was my favorite person in the world, and at fifty-five, his death came far too soon.

My mother left us when I was young. It was a different type of mourning I had for her. One of abandonment, nothing near the finality that comes with death. I never could wrap my head around the fact that she left us so willingly, especially after my father moved us from Ireland to Florida when I was a baby so we could be closer to her family. Her disappearance from my life felt like the worst kind of betrayal, especially now, when I was all alone. I supposed I could find her and reach out if I really wanted to, but why should I put in the effort if she didn't even care to stick around?

My father was gone, and it was up to me alone to fulfill whatever destiny lay before me. I had a legacy to protect. My father's entire life was reduced to a few haunting pieces of paper.

"I, Sean Patrick Driscoll, being of sound mind and body, hereby give Ciara Niamh Driscoll, should she survive me, full ownership of my Dublin estate and all my personal effects..."

Truly, who was this man? Growing up, we never had such extravagances as listed here. My father had played the role of single dad to a little girl with surprising tenderness, often stumbling with the more feminine tasks, but he was always trying his best.

I couldn't help but wonder the reason as to why he thought he had to hide all of this from me, yet here it was, included in his will that I would inherit it all. Everything, including taking over his role at the Irish government's agency he was a part of. After rigorous rounds of training first, of course. Apparently, they don't just hire anyone.

The "estate" turned out to be an actual small castle in a city just outside of Dublin named Malahide. According to the list of my father's personal effects and accounts, I could also live comfortably in said estate for years to come without the need to acquire a job.

Naturally, I was always a daddy's girl, and my mother used to remind me that I had inherited his stubborn streak. Whether my mother loved that about me or despised it was up for debate. I received just enough of the gene pool on both sides that I wasn't fully like one or the other. I had my father's raven black, wavy hair, which I had grown down to my waist; his statuesque height, complete with long, giraffe-like legs; and a personality chock full of sarcasm.

My mother had given me her soft brown eyes, fair olive complexion, and full, pouty lips. I never looked like I belonged at the gatherings on either side of my family. Too tall for my mother's Sicilian roots, yet too Mediterranean looking for my father's Irish side with their deep cobalt eyes and fair skin. I was always just *me*.

At my father's funeral, I simply nodded and thanked friends and family as some of those whom I'd never met before told me they "see his features in my face," whatever that meant. I had never really considered that I favored one of my parents' features or personalities over the other.

From a young age, I have always been independent and forged my own path, never allowing others to dictate my choices or define my identity. I guess it was supposed to be a kind sentiment, to carry on his traits, but I could have done without the forced niceties. Not to mention, I just didn't want the reminder.

His funeral service felt like an out-of-body experience. As if it was just a gathering where we all said kind, impetuous words about him while he was off somewhere, like on a beach with a beer in hand, living the dream and too unfazed to attend the party thrown just for him.

I began the process of wrapping up loose ends with my job, selling the house, and booking my travel arrangements for Ireland. No doubt I would miss my friends here, but this felt like something even more grand, the next level of my *life*. Finally, a chance to start fresh and unravel a few of my father's mysteries. The dead couldn't bury all of their secrets, any crime show would tell you that.

I'd have an entire castle and town to explore in order to unmask Sean Patrick Driscoll. I knew him as a father, a storyteller, and protector. Who did the world see him as? My mind was spinning with all the possibilities.

CHAPTER 2

It had been at least a week since I arrived in Ireland. The unpredictability of Ireland's weather during the first week of September reminded me of Florida summers, with the random rainfall but without the disgusting heat. The summer's tourist crowd had finally dispersed, so now was the ideal time to enjoy the city. I had enjoyed going out for a welcome home dinner with some members of the staff a few nights ago, though the noise level in the pub had been a bit too boisterous for my liking.

My favorite part of that evening was when we got back to the castle and Saoirse and Tara, my kitchen staff, worked their magic making the best chocolate chip cookies I had ever tasted. We enjoyed the dessert while I listened to them all share their favorite stories of my father. They all had a similar theme: he was a hero to them.

On our return to the castle that evening, my steward dialed in a code on the control panel and the black wrought-iron fence mechanically creaked open to accept us. The manicured lawn was artistically mowed in a plaid pattern, roughly the size of four football fields.

At the end of the long driveway was a large circular loop lined with tall, perfectly pruned shrubs resembling cones. Rough-hewn stone bricks formed the extravagant building and viridian green ivy covered the castle's facade. This castle easily had ten times the number of rooms I was used to—forty, or perhaps even more.

Battlements lined the top of the outer walls, transporting me to another time. I could only imagine what it would be like if this castle had once seen wars, its marksmen lining every divot of the wall, protecting the king or queen inside. Ireland was so rich in history–that was evident in the mist-covered grounds and the parts of the exterior that had been built and rebuilt over the many centuries of its existence. Every corner of the castle had a tower; some of them were partially crumbled from cannonballs, left in a state of disrepair to honor the fallen.

The castle's slim, arched windows either had stained glass or were adorned by decorative Celtic framework.

They reflected the purples, oranges, and yellows of the sunset beyond the silhouette of trees surrounding the property. It all made me feel so small and insignificant. The inside of the castle was so grand that I felt like a visitor in my own home. Detailed mahogany panels with cream and gold foiled damask wallpaper lined the foyer. Large crystal chandeliers hung from the top of the vaulted ceiling and sparkled in the reflections of the light. Emerald velvet tapestries lined the floor to ceiling cathedral windows, giving them a touch of elegance.

Now, as I lay down on my bed, my eyes wandered to the grand canopy above me, with its gothic carved mahogany posts and matching headboard. Sheer white fabric curtains gave it a whimsical sentiment. My line of sight trailed down the spiraled posts to the details on the traditional emerald floral carpet and landed on the dark, heated wood floors.

I glanced across the room at one of the heirloom books perched on the boxes that had traveled with me to my new residence, still not unpacked. My subconscious must have been telling me to leave it out, close to my heart: the only familiar item in the vastness of this entire place. The aged, gold flake lettering spelled, *The Tale of the Pooka* on the front cover. It was the closest thing to my father that I could physically hold, remembering the countless times his hands had turned those same pages. Sure, the grounds and even the castle itself were breathtaking—but they still just didn't feel like home to me.

The side wall of my room was complete with a solid, floor-to-ceiling bookshelf, laden with various jewel toned books. A heavy executive desk sat on the opposite wall and held books face down, some half-open; papers were lazily strewn about, frozen in time.

The last time my father used this desk, he was hiding secrets from me.

Despite that, I couldn't bring myself to touch it and disrupt his presence. It was the only sign that he had been here, so leaving it felt right. Maybe one day I would dare to clean it up, but not today. Until then, I'd be perfectly content to explore my new home. However, I was simply drained from all the social interactions today.

I took my shoes off and lay down diagonally on the bed with my arms spread. The bed was so large, that even with me being six feet tall, I barely covered the length of the mattress. Dozens of throw pillows created a cushion for the wooden headboard, cozy and inviting. It was just the right amount of plush and support, much like how I remembered his bed back home in Florida. I took a deep breath and closed my eyes before drifting into a deep sleep...

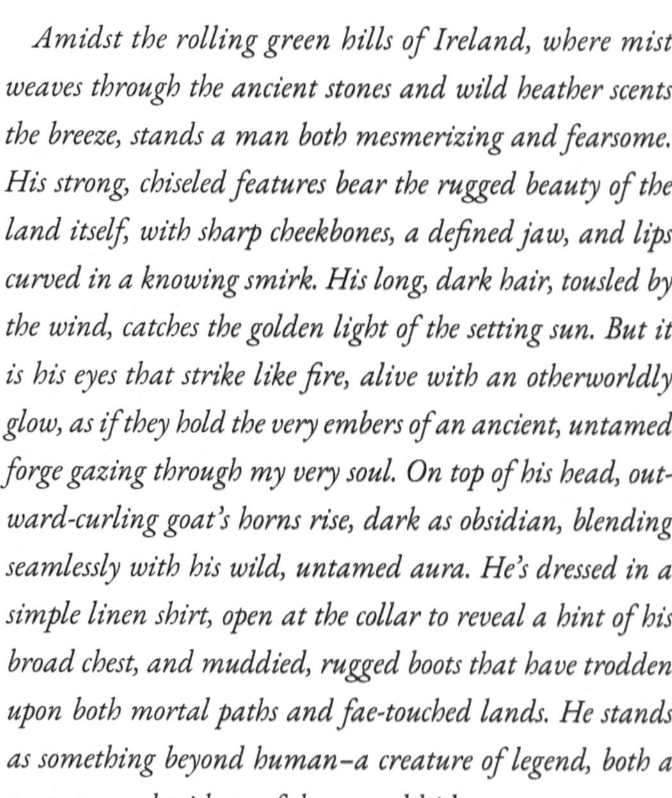

Amidst the rolling green hills of Ireland, where mist weaves through the ancient stones and wild heather scents the breeze, stands a man both mesmerizing and fearsome. His strong, chiseled features bear the rugged beauty of the land itself, with sharp cheekbones, a defined jaw, and lips curved in a knowing smirk. His long, dark hair, tousled by the wind, catches the golden light of the setting sun. But it is his eyes that strike like fire, alive with an otherworldly glow, as if they hold the very embers of an ancient, untamed forge gazing through my very soul. On top of his head, outward-curling goat's horns rise, dark as obsidian, blending seamlessly with his wild, untamed aura. He's dressed in a simple linen shirt, open at the collar to reveal a hint of his broad chest, and muddied, rugged boots that have trodden upon both mortal paths and fae-touched lands. He stands as something beyond human—a creature of legend, both a protector and trickster of the emerald isles...

A knock on my door startled me awake. I shot up from the bed. It took me a moment or two to get reacquainted with my surroundings, until I realized I was safe in my father's old bedroom—*my* new bedroom. The morning sun's golden rays filtered through the cracks of the curtains.

I must have been so exhausted that I fell asleep as soon as I laid down on the bed and remained in the same position all night.

"Miss Driscoll, we have breakfast served downstairs in the dining room," a deep voice said from behind the door.

I was still wearing yesterday's clothes from dinner and the smudged makeup embarrassed me, even though he couldn't see me. I opened the door anyway to be faced with a surprised look on Conor's face as he took in the awful sight of me.

Conor, my steward, was a handsome man. He was always dressed in a sleek and understated black suit accented by a freshly laundered white dress shirt, a matching leather belt that held up his dress slacks and a perfectly coiffed gentleman's cut, his hair the color of wet sand.

I noticed the tailoring of his suit accentuated his broad shoulders and tall physique.

He made every inch of that suit look good–especially his back, with the way those broad shoulders almost formed an upside-down triangle to his waist.

He looked fairly young, not terribly older than me. He always seemed so put together, mentally as well as physically.

At my appearance, his brows pinched, and he ran his palm down his face. Apparently, he thought I'd been up for hours like he had been. I gave a flirty smile in response, despite my haggard appearance. Something about a man in a suit, looking all flustered, was just so satisfying.

"Can you give me a minute?" I asked hastily, closing the door on him before he could deny my question. Immediately, I showered as fast as I could, dressed, and towel-dried my hair.

Once I felt like I looked acceptable, I left my room and was half surprised to find Conor leaning against the corridor wall across from my bedroom door, arms folded. He was the perfect depiction of both patience and arrogance.

"Shall we?" He grinned as he motioned towards the stairway. His smile was devastating. I nodded as he led the way through the halls and eventually into the dining room.

Chivalrous as ever, Conor pulled out a chair for me to sit. In minutes, he returned with a plate of fluffy scrambled eggs, mounds of crispy bacon, and home fries, complete with a crystal stem glass of freshly squeezed orange juice. It was my absolute favorite breakfast. Every Sunday morning back in Florida, our house would be filled with the scent of bacon grease, Dad cooking in the hopes that I wouldn't sleep in.

It worked just about every single time. The memory of those moments made me sigh longingly for the past.

"Enjoy, Miss–"

"Just Ciara," I cut him off. "Please, just call me Ciara."

"Ciara," he repeated, testing the simplified name on his tongue. His eyes glanced down shyly as he pressed his lips into a tight smile. Did I also detect a faint blush?

I speared my home fries with my silver fork. As the potatoes hit my tongue, I couldn't help but let slip a quiet, yet satisfied moan as the buttery cubes melted in my mouth. Not only were they absolutely delectable, but they tasted like memories of home—a small sense of familiarity in an otherwise strange new world.

It was nice to begin to enjoy *feeling* again. I welcomed any emotion that wasn't focused on the darkness of grief. I started to enjoy the little things in life again, starting with bacon. It may not be the healthiest outlet, but I could choose worse coping mechanisms.

Today I thought I'd explore Dublin—the city in which my father's second life existed. While curiosity about my father, Sean, was at the forefront of my thoughts, I also wanted to get acquainted with my version of the city, ideally with fewer crowds.

Tara cleared the plate for me no sooner than I had finished my meal. The abruptness of the attendant made me yelp as I was expecting to just take my own plate into the kitchen to clean for myself. This would definitely take some getting used to.

I rose from my chair and pushed it in before heading out of the dining room.

On my way out, I noticed two crossed iron broadswords etched with Celtic sailor knots above the door frame. They reminded me of the times I'd frequent the local medieval museums. My favorite tours being those held in the weapons room. They were full of forged pieces of various metals designed for the brutality of war before we had any simplicity of modern weapons. In those centuries, if you couldn't be brute enough to hack someone into bits with a heavy sword or mace or whatever was available, you were not ready to be a warrior. It was an extremely barbaric time.

I never realized my father was such a weapons enthusiast, specifically for such ancient pieces. They were all absolutely stunning, but seemed to be an ongoing theme in almost every room of the place. I would bury these questions for a later time, like a squirrel hiding their nuts for winter.

Today, my focus was going to be on what I need. The thing about secrets is that they stay buried until you are ready to dig them up and my shovel was locked away in the shed. I wasn't sure if I was mentally prepared to uncover anything yet, better to get settled in a bit more first.

I stopped a few paces outside the door after I realized that if I were to go anywhere today, it would be Conor who would be the one to take me. What a perfect opportunity to get to know him better over a pint or two. How did a man like him find employment among the silent and powerful, one of whom was my father?

"Conor? Would you mind taking me to the Black Horse Tavern this afternoon? Somewhere I can find a pint, some good food, and some company, if you don't mind."

Did I just ask him on a date? No way—that was preposterous. I'd never been so bold back in Florida, and that wouldn't change here.

Besides, it was his job to be impeccably dutiful to my requests, so I might as well learn to ask for what I want directly. No, definitely not a date, right?

"Yes," He paused, clearly still getting used to removing the formalities from my name, "Ciara. That sounds grand. What time do you think you'd like to go?"

"Two o'clock sounds perfect, thank you."

I couldn't help but smirk at his accent and the idea that getting a pint with me would be "grand." I was looking forward to not having to explore on my own, no doubt getting myself into trouble or lost. The world could seem a little scary, especially with my fragile state of mind.

Conor was someone I knew I could trust, because my father could trust him. For now, it was as simple as that. At his core, my father was always the compassionate man I knew him to be and had associated himself with like-minded individuals, Conor included.

Returning to my new bedroom upstairs, I retrieved *The Tale of the Pooka* from atop my unpacked boxes.

I was confident that the rules of time never applied when you were reading, because the next time I checked the clock, it was already a quarter until two.
I had just fifteen minutes to freshen up and ring for Conor.

After adding the finishing touches to my appearance, I went downstairs to find him patiently waiting for me in the foyer. As if he were trying to give me more space than he had this morning, yet still be available to me should I change my mind about exploring downtown.

His attire was far more casual than when I first saw him at the airport. He'd traded his tailored slacks for faded blue jeans, and his pristine shirt and suit jacket for a charcoal gray aran-knit sweater, which his muscles perfectly filled out. His hair was a bit messier than usual, and his striking green eyes stared up at me optimistically from under his deep brows. He looked approachable, laid back even, no doubt to blend in with the mood of the city in the afternoon. A suit was his business attire at the estate, but this was his own way of self-expression.

I was wearing a pair of my favorite form-fitted jeans, a worn black leather jacket, and a midnight satin blouse, paired with Converse high-tops. I'd styled my long hair in big, tousled waves with looser ends in an attempt at an effortless look.

"Ready for the city, Ciara?" His eyes drifted up my body before they landed on mine and stayed there until I answered.

"Uh, Yes. I think?" I answered shyly, locking my eyes on his just long enough to notice a speckling of brown near his enlarged pupils. I was caught off guard by how the movement of his eyes over my body made me feel. A warm, tingling sensation washed over me, it was nice to be desired in this way. I couldn't remember anyone looking at me like this before. I felt a blush heat my cheeks and I smiled softly before breaking our eye contact.

My intention was to experience the city with an open mind and no expectations.

Conor was already waiting by the back of the town car to open the door for me. Florida boys were never this chivalrous. I grinned broadly and thanked him as I got in the vehicle and we headed toward the Black Horse Tavern.

While we drove, I pressed my forehead against the car windows, absorbing the sights and sounds of Dublin. My smile remained on my face for a decent remainder of the ride. It was a fairly short drive, only half an hour before we pulled up to the tavern.

CHAPTER 3

CONOR

S ir Sean Patrick Driscoll had been the best boss a fella could ask for, especially to someone who grew up with a single mom on the rough side of town. When Ma fell ill, I was eighteen years old, and it was up to me to find a job to not only pay the utilities, but also her lengthy medical bills—with hope for some remaining funds.

It was then that I stumbled upon Sir Sean Patrick, or rather, he found me. It was at the Black Horse Tavern in Dublin those ten something years ago. A hole-in-the-wall kind of dive that probably was one of the very first builds the town had made centuries ago—priorities and all.

He was walking in for a pint and shepherds pie as I was drying glasses with a rag, holding them up to the light to check for fingerprints. Simple as it was, he noticed my fine attention to detail even before his Guinness was sat in front of him. That was when he offered me the position as his house steward.

It was a tad nostalgic coming back here, especially now, with his daughter. He talked about her so frequently that I almost felt as if I had known her before I met her before her arrival at Malahide. She was even more beautiful in person than I had imagined, which made her father's one and most important rule even more difficult to follow.

"If you meet my Ciara, you will not, under any circumstances, have relations with her. Have I made myself clear?"

Those words had been replaying in my head ever since I found out she would be the new heir of the estate, and therefore would be living here, but I knew the security of my job was still concrete. I'm sure her father's reservations were to maintain professionalism at the estate, as I worked for him and all.

Ma had only been getting worse, so I had no choice but to stay. Long-term illness is torture at the mercy of Canta, the god of healing. It was hard enough imagining the day when she would leave this world—the day I knew was slowly approaching.

It must have been incredibly difficult for Ciara, losing her father so suddenly. I shan't have agreed to be taking her to the tavern, especially because my job description was specifically tied to the house, grounds, and car.

I just couldn't say no to the look on her face when she had asked—maybe it was the gleam in her warm eyes that showed sorrow and a hint of hope. The type of gaze they depict in cartoon characters where the pupils are extra large and glossy, and the eyelashes are super long. It was usually depicting the character begging to get their way, and I'd have been a fool not to give in.

To be alone in a new country, without family and knowing no one, and after such a tragic event–the pain and loneliness she must have been going through were unfathomable. So here I was, making a feckin' terrible decision for the girl's sake. It would just be a pint, no relations whatsoever, as promised.

Once we pulled up to the Black Horse Tavern, I immediately went around the back of the car to open her door–but to my surprise, she was already out of the vehicle.

"Thought I'd try something new today!" she said with a bounce and a flirtatious smile. Her eyes scanned my body and I absolutely *melted*. My feet froze to the pavement despite the fairly pleasant September weather. She spun on her heel, smiling wide as curls splayed outward, and headed towards the front door. Of course, she'd wait to have me open the door to the tavern for her.

Confident women were always my weakness, which her father probably knew when he made the rule, the asshat.

"Shall we?" she asked as her almost impaling eyes looked up at me, with no need to tilt up her head like most girls. She was nearly my height—we probably could see eye-to-eye if she wore heels—and jaysus, those legs would be the death of me.

I pressed my lips inward, biting down a silent whimper, and turned around to walk toward the crimson door of the tavern before I let my thoughts wander to a darker place. Those legs, those eyes, those lips...

The door creaked open, and the familiar scent of aged whiskey and peat smoke instantly hit me. Low wooden beams accentuated the ceiling from centuries-old carpentry. A resin-coated slab of oak bar top lined the room, complete with elegantly shaped draft handles. The tavern was just as I had remembered. Some of the same old regulars intermingled with a few fresh faces I'd never seen before. I found us my favorite spot near the end of the bar and pulled out a chair for Ciara before taking my seat next to her.

"They have excellent shepherds pie, if you're hungry, and you *have* to have a Guinness if you're to be a local now. It's on me."

She bashfully smiled up at me through those long lashes and thanked me for taking her here, and for serving her breakfast this morning. I simply shrugged and nodded because it was all part of my duties. At least, that's what I told myself. Ignoring the fact that I'd put in that special order for her favorite breakfast foods so she'd feel more at home here. Based on her reaction that morning, it was a smart move, but I'd never admit that to her.

"Norman, you mucker! Gimme two Guinness and pies for me and Ciara!"

I yelled my order from my seat across the bar. Ciara raised her eyebrows at the slang term I'd called Norman. It took me a moment before I realized she must have thought me a drunkard at how casually I referred to him and placed our order, compared to my prim and proper first impressions.

"Sorry for being so bold, Ciara, but before your father's estate, I worked here as a boy. I started around age fifteen. My ma was ill, you see—still is—and my da was outta the picture, so it was up to me to bring in the money for us. Norman had been working here for ages with me. Even worked his way up to owner from busboy. Previous owner had no living relatives, so he left the tavern to Norman."

I stewed with the reality of that thought for a moment before adding, "I thought you'd like this tavern because it's also where I met your da when he offered me my role at the estate. He was a regular here and one of the town's favorite people."

She glanced down solemnly at the mention of her father and pursed her lips. Maybe I was off to an even worse start, but I didn't know how else to break the ice.

"I know you're here to have a good time and I didn't mean to rain sorrows down on you, but he was a good man to me, your da. I didn't have a father figure, but I admired him. I wanted you to know that I, and this whole town, held him in high regard. And I also couldn't help but notice you both enjoy your literature."

I paused to see her reaction. She was just as still as before, but a hint of a smile tugged at her lips from his memory, so I carried on, changing the subject.

"So, did you know that here in Dublin we have Ireland's oldest library? Or that some of the mountains here are actually hills, the largest of 'em named the Great Sugarloaf? Might be worth checkin' out next time you care to venture out."

A smile lifted one corner of my mouth as I saw her perk up at the mention of a library and "sugar."
Good—more of that, please, and less sentimental ranting from me.
Norman's arrival with our orders of Guinness and pie

saved me from digging myself into a deeper hole with Ciara.

"And *mucker*?" she asked with a huff of a laugh at my slang.

"It means *friend. Sláinte!*" I replied with a smile and lifted my pint up to hers and toward Norman. Norman shook his head at me as if to say, "This boy is clearly up to no good."

After the first forkful entered her mouth, I couldn't help but notice her letting out another little moan similar to the one from breakfast. I couldn't take my eyes off her as I kept eating my meal before I broke the silence.

"Food motivated, eh?" I said the words in between bites of stewed meat and potatoes.

Her eyes widened so I could see the perfect circles of her irises, and she gave me a look like I had caught her doing something naughty–or perhaps *thinking* something naughty. She looked down at her lap and blushed. *Blushed.* What in God's green earth was going on in her mind?

Norman arrived to clear our plates and asked how she enjoyed the food.

I thought the answer was apparent when she cleaned her plate, using the soda bread to soak up the gravy. She must have been famished.

"I—um—the shepherd's pie is fantastic," she said, "Thank

you for showing me this tavern and sharing your story. It's nice to get to know someone here."

"At your service, Ciara! It's nice to see ya again. I hope you'll be a regular here like your da. We miss him terribly and you remind me of him, ya know," Norman took a moment to study her face. "I see it in your smile and your laugh. Well, I'll leave you two alone. Just holler if you need anything from me." He disappeared to the back room to clean the dishes.

"If I'd known food was the way to your heart, I would've fed you sooner," I said.

I couldn't keep my eyes from darkening, making her adjust herself in the seat a little. We both knew I wasn't talking about just food. Why did I *like* the effect my gaze had on her so much? I wanted more of this feeling.

I ordered a round of whiskeys for us. She was an absolute trifler. She was coming on to me as much, if not more, than I was to her. Maybe, if anything were to happen, we could just blame it on the drinks and call it a night. A one time occurrence. It's not like her dad was here to scold us, though I am a man of honor and I should live up to it. I just didn't want to.

She was a brilliant conversationalist, growing more daring and at ease by the minute. We talked about what her old home back in Florida was like, when the best season is for pleasant weather in Ireland (which I couldn't give a concrete answer to), the best places to visit this time of year, and what my ma is like.

But then, when I dribbled a bit of whiskey on my chin, she took me by surprise. She reached over to wipe it off my chin and slowly sucked on her finger without breaking eye contact.

Jesus, Mary, and Joseph, this woman would be the end of me. She knew exactly what she was doing, too—how to make a man weak in the knees with just a gesture.

As we locked eyes, I noticed hers were the same amber hue as Irish whiskey. The warm tones shone through like the sun at dusk. She paused as she searched mine, too, as if she were trying to read my thoughts.

The silence hung heavy, and I had to break it with words before my lips betrayed me with a different kind of expression.

"Hmm. So how do you like the whiskey, Miss Ciara? Is the taste up to your standards?" Despite my efforts to be a good man, her teasing was relentless; I decided to retaliate.

I wasn't referring to just the whiskey and she knew it. I loved this game we played, back and forth with each other, dangling a carrot on a string with our flirtatious innuendos.

Taverns are hardly a place for honor, anyway. Before she

had a chance to agree, which I knew she would, I took the opportunity to role play as teacher and student.

"Part of my training with your father was to become a whiskey sommelier," I began. "There are three categories for tasting it: a super-taster, a medium-taster, and a non-taster. You don't seem like the type to be a non-taster. They're kind of the stick-in-the-mud type, if you ask me. The proper way to taste whiskey is to swirl it around on your tongue, like so,"

I swirled the whiskey on my tongue teasingly, imagining I was between her thighs instead.

"This way you can taste all the flavors—really savor them. Then, pucker your lips into a tight *O* and just take your time. Take note of any flavor profiles you come across. I'm getting caramel...vanilla...oak...Maybe a hint of apple?"

I went through the motions again before swallowing. She watched my Adam's apple dip as she took a sip, mimicking me perfectly.

What was I even doing? I was in trouble, and clearly a glutton for punishment. I was such a masochist for this woman, it was stupid.

"Atta girl. Now swirl it."

CHAPTER 4

I swirled the whiskey around my tongue as I was told. I liked this casual version of Conor. The way this man had shared his story with me and had become his true self was refreshing. This Conor wasn't afraid of embracing his roots, unlike the mask he wore at the estate.

I was grateful that he'd opened up to me about his mom and his life before working for my father. As sad as it made me to hear him talk about my father, it was a relief knowing that my dad had touched so many lives here, Conor's included.

I enjoyed him looking out for my basic needs, like feeding me or giving me a sense of belonging. Welcoming me officially to Ireland in an almost touristy way with a pint of Guinness and a shot of whiskey.

And hearing the Irish slang from his lips was so enlightening and *sexy*. He flirted a lot, and I was impressed with how daring he became with me. I guess I encouraged this playfulness somewhere along the way, too, and now I really wanted to see where it would go.

At this point, we were about two whiskey shots deep, I had been wanting to feel something—*anything*—for a while. I thought a good starting place would be to feel what his lips were like on mine before the alcohol made me numb again.

So I asked him, "I bet you're wondering what this whiskey tastes like in my mouth. Wanna give it a try? You can kiss me. I'm Irish now."

I licked my lips and within a few hesitant seconds, his were on mine, as if he'd been waiting for permission. In an instant, we were a mess of tongue and teeth, tasting each other and exploring. Making out with my steward probably wasn't the best idea given my fragile state of mind lately, but it felt amazing. I'd savor this moment of distraction from my sorrow.

I was only a little buzzed, and we were consenting adults. So what if I needed a little physical pleasure to stifle the emotional pain? I didn't want to admit to myself how easily he'd turned me on earlier, either. I had to rub my thighs together to ease some friction that his gaze alone caused me. It had been a while since I've been with anyone—that must've been why I was so easily turned on.

Given my recent circumstances, now was as good a time as any to seek comfort. Conor seemed willing to oblige, and he was a decent man, from what I could tell.

I wrapped my fingers around his dirty blonde curls and deepened the kiss. How in the hell was this man single? He looked like he belonged on the cover of *GQ* and made out like he'd studied every article on the subject. But the cherry on top? He was a true gentleman.

Because he was so good, I felt like doing bad things to him.

I broke the kiss for a moment to take a small swig of whiskey, savoring it in my mouth as taught. Enjoying a few seconds of its taste to note the vanilla and oak profiles he had described. I was surprised that I could even focus on his words, and not just on what his mouth was doing only seconds before. I gently placed my lips back onto his mouth and then swirled my tongue around his. Just as he'd described earlier, I let the whiskey swish in his mouth as well.

I decided now was a great time to fire his words back at him as I came back up for air.

"How does it taste? Is it up to your standards, Conor?"

He audibly moaned, practically whimpering at the act, like there was an internal battle going on in his mind. I knew I was unraveling whatever shred of dignity he was holding so tightly to, and I think we both enjoyed it equally.

His body language said he was well fucking aware of that fact, too.

The dinner rush was about to come, so it was time to go home. My mind buzzed with ideas for our own personal adventures. Not necessarily of the castle, but just of me and Conor. I was turning this man into a puddle and I was relishing every moment of it.

"You are feckin' delicious," he growled low in his accent.

What had come over us?

Maybe it was the magic of Ireland, but something felt lighter in the air between us. One of the many burdens I carried felt as if it had lifted off my shoulders. Conor was doing something dangerous to me. I could tell he was bringing down my wall brick by brick, but the worst part was he was just being himself—not even trying. I was grateful regardless, and I wanted to show him just how grateful I could be.

"Can we go home, please?" I asked sweetly. "I'd like to request the kitchen make us some cheeseburgers and fries for dinner. You showed me your ways and now I'll show you mine. Honestly, cheeseburgers and fries are the best food to eat if you've been drinking. It's just the rule."

I described my perfect burger to him: medium rare, brioche bun, and all the fixings. He made a call to the kitchen staff about my request and paid our tab. We said our goodbyes to Norman and off we went.

After we exited the tavern, Conor paused just next to the door of the town car, causing me to freeze as well.

"Ciara, I—" Conor started, then fell short of finishing his thought. He lowered his head.

Oh, no, here it was: the speech about how he had to do the "noble thing." But I was so curious to hear what he had to say. I didn't want what we'd started here at the tavern to stop at the tavern, though I'd respect his wishes if that's what he desired.

"Yes?" I coaxed.

"I made a promise to your da when he was alive that I would not have relations with you. If he taught me anything, he taught me to be a man of honor, and my word is my bond. But tonight I just want to be a feckin' eejit and toss all of that out the window. Your friendship is valuable to me, and I never want to overlook that."

I responded by saying I can only offer to start with tonight, and we could see where that took us. But I also didn't want our time together to end right now. I couldn't deny the spark of chemistry that I knew he felt too. After all, my wall was still pretty high, but it was getting more penetrable as the evening wore on.

He nodded for me to sit up front as he once again opened my door. I got comfortable next to him and buckled my seat belt. As we traveled down the road, he placed a hand on my knee and slid it slowly up my thigh, not taking his eyes off the road for one second. I was instantly aware of my jeans holding me together from the waist down. Simultaneously wanting them off and grateful they were keeping me from making poor decisions prematurely.

I rested my hand on his, enveloping our fingers as we continued down the winding roads toward the estate. I rubbed my fingers along his calluses, feeling him innocently. This was a pleasant moment. I felt content in this place.

On the way back to the estate, I noticed a single black goat in an open pasture with strange horns and oddly familiar eyes, staring at me in a sea of white sheep.

Those eyes. They were eerily reminiscent of the dream I had of a man with those same goat horns.

That was strange... Out of all the vastness in the Emerald Isles, the only animals I thought were in the fields were sheep and cattle. They were practically part of the scenery.

But an all black goat? Something was definitely afoot, I could feel it in my gut.

"Can you please at least let me open your door for you when we get home, Ciara?" Conor asked, optimistically sighing with a smirk and breaking me from my thoughts.

I nodded. He was so damn polite. Who opened the door on a date anymore? Chivalry was never dead with Conor.

My mind wandered again as he made his way around to my door. He extended a hand to help me out of the vehicle. I immediately smiled up at him and took his hand like a good girl, exiting the car.

The castle still took my breath away as I stared in awe at its massive size. The heavy reinforced door welcomed us as we entered. He took us straight to the dining room, where our day had started. Moments later, two plates of perfectly cooked, medium-rare cheeseburgers and crispy, crinkled fries arrived.

I was impressed at how he had paid attention to the details as I listed off what makes a perfect burger when he called in the order to the kitchen.

Before I sat down to eat, Conor kissed the area between my jaw and my ear as his large hands reached around to cup my ass. He set me down on the end of the table, mere inches away from the plate of food.

"May I feed you, Ciara?" he asked me while placing his hands on either side of my waist, palms down, as my legs dangled off the table. I liked being taken care of like this.

"Yes, please," I responded invitingly. I bit gently into the cheeseburger he had held in front of me and licked the ketchup off of my lips. He grabbed my chin gently between his thumb and forefinger, then softly kissed some remaining ketchup off my lips that I'd missed. *Fuck*, if this wasn't by far my favorite way to eat a cheeseburger.

Again, his lips found mine, a familiar warmth spreading through me with each passing second. I opened my legs, grasped at the belt buckle on his jeans, and pulled him closer to me. The rhythm of our lips and tongues intermingled passionately.

In one swift motion, he swept plates, silverware, and glasses off the table and onto the floor. Without missing a beat, he took off his sweater to reveal his broad chest and the V-shaped muscles along his pelvis. I couldn't help but bite my lower lip at the sight of him as I took off my top in response, revealing my breasts.

Conor let loose a grunt of approval before taking my pebbled nipple between his finger and tongue. I arched my back into the sensation of his mouth on me as he lay me down on the cool wood of the table, then got to his knees.

I raised my eyebrows at what I knew he was about to offer me. It instantly made me ready and wet for him.

"May I?" He hinted at removing my jeans. I nodded. I usually would be annoyed by him asking, but requesting my consent only made me more excited. He removed my jeans in one swift motion, and then his hands were on my inner thighs.

"Mmm, so soft, Ciara," he purred as he took two fingers and began circling my clit.

A whimper escaped my lips. His touch made me feel like losing control. I wanted him this moment, buried deep inside me.

"So wet for me. I've been curious as to what you taste like," he whispered up at me. He started planting kisses where his hands had been on my thighs, slowly inching up to the bundle of nerves between my legs. Then, he tasted me like the finest whiskey and I absolutely melted in his mouth. There were no other thoughts in my mind besides...

"Mmm—more please, Conor," I begged.

The man was a true artist with his tongue, serving me with skill and passion.

He was truly remarkable. He took the finger he had on my clit and slid it inside me, pumping me into oblivion while licking up my center of nerves. Inserting another expert finger, he increased his rhythm.

My eyes rolled back in my head and I moaned as I let slip a devilish grin. I raked my fingers through his hair and held on tight controlling his face. I let him do his worst until I couldn't take it anymore, then lifted his face so he was looking straight at me with slightly parted, swollen, wet lips. A look of pure bliss was plastered on his face.

"Fuck me, Conor. Wherever you'd like," I pleaded.

I never beg. I usually made them do the begging, but just this once, I would give him everything I had to offer.

CHAPTER 5

"But, Ciara, you've barely touched your dinner," Conor joked from between my legs. His need to satisfy me in every way heated my core.

"You've only had a bite and I've enjoyed a full meal."

His near-translucent green eyes darkened to almost black when he made that declaration. There was that smile again—the one that would ruin me.

My body reacted again in an instant, low in my stomach.

"I'm not hungry for food anymore, Conor... Where would you like to have me in this house?" I said completely seriously as I confidently got up from the table, stark naked. "You know, I still haven't had the full tour." My patience was running thin, I wanted him now.

"You are absolutely magnificent, Ciara. Let's go to the grand library. It's just down the hall. You can be as loud as you'd like."

I bit my lip just at the thought of being fucked in my own library.

"I bet you've secretly wanted to scream in a library. It is yours, after all. You make the rules," Conor said breathlessly, appearing to be in pure awe of the sight of me naked in front of him.

He then picked me up, threw my ass over his shoulder, and carried me all the way to the library. Once we reached our destination, he sat me down on a navy velvet high-back chair in the center of the room.

"Turn around," he demanded as his eyes ravaged my body.

I obeyed, excited at what I knew was coming. From this viewpoint, I could see rows of wooden shelves covering two stories—but now wasn't the time to marvel over that.

Conor licked his fingers and slid them up my slit, then I heard him unzipping his pants. His tip nudged my entrance before I reached around to insert him into me. The initial stretch of him felt magnificent. He thrusted himself in and out at a slow tempo before quickening his pace.

A long moan escaped me as I sensed myself edging toward ultimate pleasure, but I still craved control. I wanted to watch him as he came undone. I wanted to watch the face he made as he came apart inside me.

So I looked back at him and suggested we switch positions.

"Sit down," I ordered, settling myself onto his lap and savoring the sensation of the stretch as I rocked to the carnal gratification of my rhythm. "You said I make the rules, and I want to watch you come undone inside me."

I would ruin this man. I just knew it. The thought had me feral. Just for tonight, I had a feeling we both needed this for different reasons.

The sensation of his girth inside of me coupled with my movements made my legs tremble as I rode him.

"Oh, fuck!" I called out. I couldn't think straight and the word "fuck" was quite universal in the English language. Saying it aloud was almost a release on its own. Conor moaned my name beneath me as I steadied my rhythm.

"Yes! *Yes!*" I said aloud, claiming him with my body. A wave of pleasure overcame me and Conor finished soon after with a groan. The sound of his orgasm was satisfactory enough. A deep rumbling sound that almost had me asking for another round.

I laid on his shoulder for a few minutes, gathering my breath. Soon after, he dressed and brought me back to the dining room to grab my clothes in the same fashion as earlier.

I couldn't help but wonder what else was in store for us tonight. I wanted to continue the evening, and the prospect of a cold bed after what we'd shared was undesirable.

"Conor, will you sleep in my bed with me? Just for tonight. I don't want to sleep alone."

It was the truth. After my dad's passing, I still felt so lonely and having another warm body next to me would help bandage that wound.

I didn't want to be alone, but I also asked because I knew it would be the only time this could happen. He had his mom to take care of, as well as this entire estate. Even though he was so respectable, I knew he was not the type of man I needed in my life, at least not right now. He didn't need another person to take care of, and I couldn't be a distraction for him.

I also had secrets to uncover about my dad, and my grief to deal with, and it would be unfair to rope him into all of that right now. Not to say that I wanted this evening to end. I surely did not, but I was trying to live in the moment—and this, right now, was it.

Who was to say it couldn't be permanent, though? Life was too short to not say what you were thinking. Who knew what tomorrow could bring? To not make a move and therefore force yourself to live with regret was something I could not do.

I wanted to sleep next to him, to share a different type of intimacy than what we shared at the tavern. Or on the dining room table. Or on the library chair.

"Of course, Ciara. Just for tonight," he agreed, even though his somber smile didn't quite reach his eyes. He almost looked disappointed. The internal struggle this man seemed to have around me was becoming melancholy. It was as if we both knew what tonight was slowly becoming, but he also didn't want to come to terms with it.

I changed into my sleep clothes as Conor watched me undress. He stripped down to just his undershorts and slipped into bed next to me. We lay down in bed, facing each other.

I memorized his features for a moment before saying, "Thank you for spending the night with me. I'm not quite ready for it to be over, and I just wanted you here with me for a while."

He brushed a stray piece of hair away from my face and tucked it behind my ear. "I had an amazing time with you today, Ciara. I hope you did, too."

A smile tugged on one corner of my mouth as I searched his eyes for sincerity and nodded. Embracing the bitter sweetness of this moment, I lay him on his back and snuggled into his chest, my other hand roaming over the muscles on his stomach.

"You're amazing, Conor. Maybe if we had met at another time under different circumstances, it would be easier. But I just want to enjoy the rest of tonight with you."

And he truly was amazing—a more-than-satisfactory lover, the most kind human I'd met. And today was the first time since my dad's passing that I actually enjoyed myself. Moments like these could be fleeting. Sometimes they needed to be that way, to keep you grounded. I'd always believed that people come into your life for a purpose, right when you need it—sometimes for a blessing and sometimes for a lesson.

Conor was both.

I wanted to show my gratitude, so I began to kiss his chest slowly, moving lower every few kisses until I reached his waistband. I tugged it down a little, nibbling at his hip bone, looking up at him in a silent request for permission. A low groan of approval escaped his lips as I freed his thick length and wrapped my mouth around his cock.

I moved up and down, inching closer to his hilt, pausing occasionally to wrap my tongue around his sensitive tip. Like a reward for a job well done, I wouldn't stop until his pleasure was released into my mouth. I persisted, moving the tip closer to the back of my throat with each motion. He grasped my hair as I had done to him on the dining room table, directing me toward his conclusion.

With my sex-hazed eyes locked onto his, he moaned loudly while I savored his orgasm. I licked my lips and gave him a pleased hum before falling asleep in his arms.

I awoke the next morning to an empty side of the bed where Conor had been. A note and a freshly cut yellow rose, with its thorns removed, were the only things left behind.

Ciara,

I had a wonderful evening with you. Duty calls. Breakfast will be ready at nine a.m. I have a visit with ma at the the hospital at eight a.m.

-Conor

I inhaled the light tea scent of the rose as I closed my eyes. I placed it in my cup of leftover water on my bedside table and rose for the day. I showered, dressed, and made it to the dining room by nine for breakfast.

Today's menu was a more traditional Irish breakfast compared to my first meal. I sat across the table from the spot from the previous night, staring blankly and reminiscing between bites of egg and hash. I wanted today to start anew, to focus on myself and explore my new town on my own, but I already had yesterday's memories of Conor chasing me. I blinked away the mental picture of Conor sweeping away the contents of the table and burying his face in me.

Dismissing the vivid images, my gaze shot up to the twin swords above the archway. What was with all this weaponry my father had here? Back home in Florida, he was never the type at home to carry such a collection. I never knew that he had even *owned* a gun, but then again, did I ever *really* know him? Was it a secret hobby of his? Did it come with the castle when he purchased it however long ago? My thoughts went wild with possibilities.

Maybe today I'd do a little digging, explore other rooms that Conor and I hadn't tainted so I could move onward. I cleaned my plate of food and took off down the hall, turning left where I had always previously turned right. I roamed the imposing halls, where the detailed Tree of Life runner carpets softened the flagstone floors. Sconces lined the way, casting an incandescent glow. Floor-to-ceiling tapestries adorned the walls, their intricate Celtic knots woven in gold thread on emerald jewel-toned fabric. Everything was so regal over here compared to the other side of the house. Cathedral arches framed in oak lined the doorways along the hall until I came upon a particularly intricate door. It was reinforced with iron branches representing the same Tree of Life featured on the carpets.

Upon passing through the archway, I quickly realized this must have been my father's official study. Dominating the room was a massive, ornately carved mahogany desk.

It made the desk in his—or rather, *my*—room look like a child's play set.

Purposefully placed inkwells, calligraphy pens, and leather-bound folders adorned the polished surface. Floor-to-ceiling bookshelves with rolling ladders lined the wall behind the desk, laden with books that seemed to have tested the existence of time itself.

In the center of the room lay a circular maroon rug with the family crest embroidered on it, also lined with intertwined Celtic knots.

A ship with three masts and a cormorant bird sitting at its peak. It made me think about my summer days in Florida at the creeks, where I'd find those birds drying out their wings before they were able to fly again. Sure, Ireland was my new home, but I couldn't help feeling a little homesick.

I eyed the slightly worn, dark-leather Oxford couch sat near a stained-glass window, making the space feel cozy. It looked like it could have been my father's preferred place to sit, based on the fading of the cushions. The morning sun let in red, green, and blue rays of light that lay printed on the floor.

I could tell that my father spent a lot of his time here as I walked around admiring the space. There was an oil painting on the wall, mounted in an ornate bronze carved frame, of someone who appeared to carry a striking resemblance to me. Upon closer examination, I realized it was me on my twentieth birthday. I recognized that outfit: a sapphire dress with a high neckline, adorned with the silver heart necklace he'd gifted me that year.

Salty tears welled in my eyes at the fact that my dad had this made for his study. Out of all the beautiful scenes or masterpieces of Ireland, he chose to have a picture of *me* framed on his wall. A testament of his love for me. I ran my fingers along the ridges of the carved frame as tears streamed down my face, blurring my vision.

I missed him so much. I was still wrapping my head around how he had all of this here and still found a way to keep me close. Despite not knowing about the castle, there were so many reminders of me here.

I let myself dwell on this for a few more moments. Once the blurriness cleared, I realized I wasn't touching a traditional frame. Instead, it was the edge of a safe made to look like a frame. This was some serious Scooby-Doo shit.

My favorite Saturday morning cartoon growing up, featuring mansions full of ghosts and trap-doors, with villains like Captain Cutler faking their deaths. There was no way my father was like any of the masked villains on that classic show, though. There was no faking this, as classified of a position that he'd held. I'd always thought him more of the Jason Bourne type.

On the far edge of the framed safe, I noticed a small keypad asking for a six-digit pass code. Interesting. Confident that my continued investigation would reveal the code, I made my way back to the desk. I was sure I'd find at least a secret or two there, given its grandeur.

The top of the desk was where I started, sitting in the rolling office chair. I ran my fingertips along the glossed mahogany surface, feeling as close to my father as I'd felt since his passing.
It was an empty feeling but simultaneously filled me with an overwhelming dose of love.

It was hard to turn the page knowing someone you love wouldn't be in the next chapter, but the story must go on.

I started with the portfolios neatly arranged on the corner of his desk, opening one to find his copy of the will. My heart sank in my chest as the reality of why I was here in the first place really hit me. Taking a calming breath, I began to read.

I, Sean Patrick Driscoll, being of sound mind and body hereby give Ciara Niamh Driscoll, should she survive me, full ownership of my Dublin estate and all my personal effects. I hereby give her all of my assets in regards to the Malahide estate, including supervision of all current staff members on the condition that she resides on the property...

My eyes wandered over his signature as the finality his last wishes were in front of me in black and white. I noticed the irony of the black ink on the white paper. I ran my fingers over his signature, feeling the indents of his pen strokes on the paper. A tear escaped my eye again, causing an inked blur on the paper where it fell. Quickly wiping my eyes and blotting the spot on the paper, my gaze landed on a bookshelf.

I approached the bookcase and climbed the ladder until I was eye level with the top shelf, then slid it over to meet an ancient book. Its separation from other older volumes made it stand out among the newer ones.

The Legend of the Solais Sword: Claídheamh Soluis. Immediately intrigued, I carefully removed it from the shelf. It appeared to be an interesting read to pass the time later.

It was a beautiful piece. It had an aging cover with classic golden edges and, a few slightly torn, askew pages. A wobbly spine revealed it as a favorite among many readers over the decades, perhaps even centuries. The cover was once a deep forest green, now faded, with a metallic rendering of what must be the Solais sword—a trefoil long sword with a wide hilt and the same three-circular pattern adorning its edges. It was simple, yet it had all the splendor of medieval elegance.

A folded-up note emblazoned with my father's seal fell out of the binding as I turned to the first page. I immediately opened it to be greeted by a handwritten letter from my father, addressed to me.

My Dearest Ciara,

I hope this letter finds you well. If you are reading this, as I foresee you will be, I'd like to tell you a few things. First, I'm sure you've figured out that not all fairy tales are fiction. With that, I am grateful that you decided to pick up this one in particular.
Second, you've also probably noticed all the weapons, namely the swords, in this house. I only became a collector when I realized I had put my life in danger.
When I decided to have you inherit this castle, it became a necessity to place them in every room for your safety. They are all made of iron instead of steel, for Pookas specifically.

If you haven't already, go find Finn O'Leary and ask for fencing lessons. He is a man of many hidden talents, and he owes me a favor.
Anyway, I'm in the middle of packing my bags to come back home to Florida soon.

Love you always and forever,
Dad

My chest grew heavy and my eyes leaked. Of course, he'd find a way to reach me through books, as he always had. All of those swords were put there, in each room, for my safety. Wherever I was in this castle, he would be with me, always. I wiped my cheek so I wouldn't stain his letter, but the tears kept flowing.

He never did make it back to Florida—at least not in the form I preferred.

Alive and full of love.

That letter was most likely the last one he ever wrote, and it was for me. I ran my fingers along the parchment, feeling the ridges of the indents left by his pen.

He must have purposefully placed the book in the bookshelf so it stood out for this very purpose. So I'd find it in a timely fashion. My father's love of folklore taught me the importance of the rule of thirds.

It applied in real life as well, if you were chasing a goal, you were supposed to feel good about it a third of the time, okay for another third and like shit about it for the last third. If the balance was off, you weren't doing something right.

Not to mention, if three things went bad in your life all at once, you would be out of bad luck with happier days coming.

Three represented life itself: the beginning, the middle, and the end—all of which I'd become all too familiar with lately.

The rule was infinite. No wonder the Irish loved threes. Even their flag was split into three colors: green, white, and orange.

This got me thinking about the password on the safe, triggering a string of memories that I had deemed insignificant in the past. There were a few important numbers my father had told me were sacred to Irish mythology and to our culture.

Three, of course, was the main one.

And five, the number of main roads and provinces of ancient Ireland.

The number seventeen was sacred and often revered as a harbinger of good fortune.

Thirteen, because ancient Celts considered a year to have thirteen months instead of twelve.

Three, five, one, seven, one, three. *Six digits.*

One for each solution to the pass code on the frame. It was just clever enough to fucking work. My father was too intelligent to use specific dates, as someone could easily trace them if they knew where to look.

I carefully typed the numbers into the small keypad on the side of the safe and heard the distinctly satisfying mechanical *click* of it whirring open.

CHAPTER 6

The safe lacked gold bricks, jewels, strings of pearls, and stacks of banded money—unlike movie depictions. Instead, there was a plain manila folder labeled *CLASSIFIED* in stamped red ink, and a sealed envelope bearing the distinct outline of a key.

Sentimental value–*great*. That just raised more questions.

I snatched the manila folder and the envelope, leaving the safe open, and went back to the desk to do some digging. I started by doing what any logical person would do and opened the folder labeled *CLASSIFIED* immediately. A local newspaper clipping was attached to the first page. The excerpt was from a local paper named *The Malahide Craic,* and it was dated maybe a month or two before my father's death. The headline read, *"Residents Warned to Be Weary of Mysterious Black Horse."*

Well, that's not fucking ominous? No wonder it was in this folder.

I unfolded the rest of the article to read, in hopes it would elaborate further.

Many locals recently reported strange sightings of rogue farm animals in the hills surrounding the rural coastal town of Malahide, just outside Dublin city. Commonly reported, has been a black horse with "wild eyes," locals say. Some farmers have even reported rogue farm animals other than their own livestock lingering in the area. There have been a few fierce, brave eejits who have tried to tame the wild black horse and returned in rag order—some not at all, others in pieces. The local Dublin patrol has been searching for the lost persons and asks that locals please do not go after any of these animals. They are considered very dangerous and what they are capable of is still unknown. What is known, however, is that the common denominator of all these dangerous animals is their "wild" and almost glowing eyes. If you see any of these animals that match this description, please keep a safe distance and contact the Dublin animal patrol.

Rogue farm animals? You had got to be kidding me! This was the classified document my father had locked away?

A vision flashed before my eyes of that singular black goat among the white ones on my ride back from the pub. No way was that connected, was it?

I flipped up the article clipping to find an official-looking paper.

This one sounded more like one of my father's stories, not what I'd expect from a pretty damn official piece of paper labeled *Private Information of the Government of Ireland,* with the word *Pooka* appearing sporadically on the page.

No way in hell was this actually happening.

The document mentioned the recent newspaper article and that the cause of the mayhem wasn't "farm animals." It was, in fact, a few of the legendary Pookas that had come out of the woodwork for the first time in decades.

Pookas, meaning more than one.

The document proceeded to say what the newspaper failed to report, which was that these Pookas could shape-shift into humans. However, the tell-tale sign of the Pooka was that consistent and fiery glow of their eyes and how even in human form, they still held onto certain animal features, such as ears or even a tail.

Okay, *now* the label made more sense. They can shift into *humans,* or rather, something akin to one? Creepy.

I had only heard of them changing into animals. The idea reminded me of another rule my dad had always seared into my brain regarding the fairy tales, and I always wondered why he seemed to think it was such a big deal. I would just brush it off as another story to tie into my bedtime routine.

"There are rules when you're dealing with the fae, Ciara... Listen to me closely. You must count the fingers, count the toes, count their teeth, and check the shadows... and under no circumstances should you make a deal with one."

Except this document talked about Pookas, not fae, and there were no rules from what the stories told us. They were just chaos, the masters of mayhem.

The paper behind that one was a blueprint of the castle itself. Blue lines outlined of the entire property, including the atrium in the backyard and, the rose gardens—everything, except for a small room just beside the library, which was outlined in red-orange. It was strikingly different from the rest of the blue lines—but why was it labeled differently?

I opened the envelope and, sure enough, it held an ancient key in a rusted, reddish color. Attached to the key was a velvet ribbon the exact color of the lines surrounding this mystery room.

There was only one thing to do—I took the blueprint and the key, and put the folder back in the picture safe. Following the blueprint's map, I left the study for the great library.

The small room appeared on paper as though it was nestled inside the library, no doubt underground somewhere. Good thing this was already becoming my favorite room in the house, my exploits with Conor aside.

I paused in the corridor before the library, blueprint in hand, key in my pocket, studying the path ahead. There was a cozy reading area in the middle of the library, surrounded by shelves looking down from the mezzanine level. The center was where I needed to go.

From watching mystery movies and reading Agatha Christie, I was familiar with all the typical spots for hidden doors or secret rooms. Given the intricacy of the design of my father's safe, I figured this room would be even more elaborate than that, but I wasn't sure.

Upon entering the library, I spotted the wrought-iron spiral staircase leading to the first floor. It was beautiful. Welded into the bottom of the initial landing was the trefoil shape that matched the hilt of the sword on the book cover. On the railing, a different Celtic knot repeated on every few steps. I recognized them all. The most well known being the trinity knot. The next was the love knot, two interlocking hearts, symbolizing eternal love. Then Solomon's knot, comprised of two closed, interlaced loops weaving under and over each other. They represented the connection between man and the divine. Next was a shield knot, the most prevalent knot throughout the house—for protection, of course. The revelation of why it was repeated so often was unsettling.

I stepped onto the fifth stair, recognizing the Dara knot on my right. Wisdom and endurance...sounded like dad, alright.

The final knot was the spiral knot, a three-sided knot that separated into individual spirals, having a more ancient meaning than the rest. The designs repeated as I spiraled farther down the staircase. I made it to the wooden floor and padded my way toward the reading area in center of the great library.

It had been weeks since I first discovered my father's study and the contents in the safe. I still was not much closer to finding any actual answers.

Sure, I'd discovered Pookas exist and that they're right here in town under the disguise of rogue farm animals, but I never found that mysterious room to which that key belonged. If only these walls could talk, I'd ask them where this stupid secret room was and how to get to it.

I'd been to the tavern a few times since discovering the newspaper article. Norman told me the latest gossip, like animals causing a five-car pile-up just a few streets away from Black Horse. A week later, he told me of a black stallion hanging outside the tavern and enticing those who'd had too much to drink to take a ride on its back, only for them to show back up in town a few days later by foot.

In another instance, a white rabbit chewed through the wires at the local news station, so Norman felt the need to fill me in on all this until they fixed the technical issues. It took them all but the entire two weeks to repair, but listening to Norman's stories was much more entertaining. Regardless, I knew all of this had to be chaos left behind by the Pooka, those devils.

Conor was on a leave of bereavement for an indeterminate amount of time after the passing of his mother, so the castle had been extra quiet lately. He came home from a hospital visit one night with bloodshot eyes and messy hair from running his hands through it over and over, as if it all had been a bad dream, and my heart ached for his loss. Hell, don't I know that feeling?

Despite the size of the castle, it still had a loneliness about it. I felt it lingering in the surrounding halls. Especially with loss so thick in the air here, between my father and Conor's mother and so many others who had also seen such despair within these walls over the centuries. So when I was craving the company of the outside world, I liked to journey to the hustle and bustle of downtown for a little while.

After turning up empty-handed in the library at home, I needed a break from seeking the secret room. Perhaps I'd have better luck if I tried again later with a fresh mindset.

I'd gone to the Black Horse Tavern on my own so many times now that I'd become a regular. I asked Norman about how long he had lived here (since birth), and if he'd heard anything new about the farm animal debacle. It was always the same small talk. He asked me about my day, about Conor and the castle, then he'd tell me how business had been. We'd always take a shot for good health before I placed my order.

Except the last time—he mentioned seeing that black horse again, eyes staring at him like glowing embers off in the distant hills, when he was closing up one night. He thought of it as an omen for the tavern. I thought perhaps it was how the establishment had gotten its name so many years ago, but I kept that to myself.

Don't get me started on all the hours I'd spent in the Dublin library, regardless of my own extensive one at home. I was now a proud card holder.
I loved the extensive antique tomes of fiction, nonfiction, autobiographies... You name it; they had it there.

The unmistakable musk of old pages and the ever-present cloud of dust from countless page-turns filled the air. I adored how the multicolored, jeweled tones on the shelves dotted the entire place, and how the cathedral ceilings made you feel as small as the print on a page. It was magnificent and it was one of the few places that brought me a sense of peace.

People watching had also turned into a game I played with myself. I would create scenarios in my head of why each person was there and what they were thinking about and what books they enjoyed. Everyone had their own story, and reading fictional stories about others, inspired me to make up a few tales about the real people here. There were tourists gaping at the architecture, students from the local university nodding off in textbooks after late nights of partying or studying, business-men and women refining the knowledge of their trades. It was silent, but teeming with life.

However, I still had yet to make it out for a hike on the Sugarloaf Hills, due to splitting most of my spare time between the library and the tavern. Maybe I was avoiding it because of the warnings from the local newspaper and Norman's gossip. That would be the smart thing to do, but I knew that wasn't the entire reason.

I enjoyed hiking, so I had better do it now before the winter came.

The autumn colors of the trees were in peak season mid-October. It was a nice day for Ireland, a little breezy and cloudy, but at least it wasn't bitterly cold and raining. It was a good day for a hike. The foliage never changed colors in Florida, besides green and dead, so it would be a treat to see it for myself.

I dressed in my brown hiking boots, fur-lined leggings, and a matching chestnut-colored heavy jacket. My body was still adjusting to the cooler climate of Ireland. I was definitely more bundled up than the locals.

I called a cab to take me out to Sugarloaf and packed a rucksack, including basic first aid, snacks, water, a flashlight, pepper spray, and a pocket knife, while waiting on the driver's arrival. My father had always taught me to be prepared when dealing with nature.

Once in the cab, I immediately focused my gaze out the

window on the endless green rolling fields, watching the sky for trouble, but finding none.

A bit later, the cab came to a screeching halt before the trail marker at the start of the hills. The driver said something to me in a dialect I couldn't quite understand as I paid my fare, so I just said a simple "thank you" and headed toward the trail.

Sugarloaf was a stunning rocky terrain covered in heather and other wild brush that adorned the faded pebbled trails. I knew they considered it a hill here, but to this Florida girl, coming from where the lands are flat, it was a breathtaking mountain. A light fog eddied the upper region of the hill. I inhaled a calming breath and started my journey to the top.

I was about two-thirds of the way up when I needed to stop and catch my breath. Altitude was new to me, and I barely remembered the last time I exercised without Conor's...help.

I found a fallen tree and decided to rest.

The brush rustled to my right, startling me, and I quickly jerked my head to see a white fox with piercing yellow eyes staring at me. We locked eyes for a moment and I froze in place. Arctic foxes weren't native to Ireland, at least not since the ice ages. Either he was a very long way from home or I was very lucky to have spotted one.

"Hello, little fox. You're a long way from home, aren't you?"

I knew he couldn't reply, but we seemed to be the only ones out on the trail today. The little fox tilted his head at me as if trying to understand what I was saying.

And then he responded.

"I could say the same for you," he rasped, gleaming canines showing.

What the fuck?

Of course, a talking fox would have an Irish accent out here, but his seemed to carry more of an ancient hue than the accents of the people in town.

I backed up off of the tree but then immediately tripped over it with shock.

Foxes don't speak. This must be my mind playing tricks on me.

"D—don't hurt me! Stay back!" I replied, just in case it wasn't only in my mind.

My breathing was labored again, as it was before I took a seat to rest. Adrenaline pumped in my veins, and beads of sweat, despite the cool air, lined my neck and hairline.

"I don't have any intention of hurtin' you, Miss. Our kind have been watching closely, anticipating your arrival."

"Excuse me?"

Did he just say *their kind* were waiting for me? How? Oh...no, no, no.

This was no fox. This was surely a Pooka.

I immediately scanned the rest of his features, remembering the rule my father had told me so many years ago, about the fae. Check the fingers, the toes... no, the *paws* ...for any discrepancies.

Sure enough, his hind legs had an extra toe on each paw. It would be too much of a coincidence for him to be a polydactyl, if that gene was even present in foxes at all.

The overcast sky prevented me from seeing any shadows, even my own.

Make no deals was the last line I remembered from my father's set of rules.

There was no mistaking that this was a Pooka from the fairy tales. Whether he truly had no intentions of harming me was another issue.

"You live in the castle just outside Malahide, yes? We have been keepin' watch over you."

"You're a—a Pooka..." I stammered, barely able to comprehend my own thoughts.

"Well...yes. But you may call me Uallas Jekylle. May I inquire about your name, m'lady?"

"Ciara...What do you know of that castle? Did you know my father, Sean Driscoll?" The words escaped me before I realized how idiotic it was that I gave him my father's full name.

"I have heard of his passing. *Suaimhneas síoraí air*. In your tongue, I suppose it would mean 'Eternal rest upon him.'"

"So you knew my father? How?" Answers, as terrifying as they were, were still answers.

"He was one of the great and few that kept us hidden, so both of our kinds could live peacefully. In his honor, I would like to bestow some luck upon you, if you would allow me, Ciara?"

CHAPTER 7

Bestow *luck* upon me? What in the hell was going on? I'd always focused more on the chaotic nature of the Pookas, never considering the fact that they could also bring you good luck instead of bad. I wouldn't consider myself the type of person who would only focus on the negative, but the folklore I'd always known of them essentially all said the same thing: Pookas were chaotic shape-shifters that dealt menace to whichever communities they resided in. Their name itself—Pooka—was based on the words "demon" or "mischievous spirit" in many Nordic languages.

"Show me your human form first. Prove to me you are what you say you are," I declared, mustering up any valor I still had.

I remembered how the letters from the study declared that Pookas can also shift into a human form, and to be quite honest, facing that form would make it somewhat easier to wrap my head around all this, rather than a talking fox.

"If you insist, m'lady," Uallas said in answer.

Before I could string another thought together, Uallas transformed before my eyes.

A dark shadow swirled around him and then he stood in front of me, no longer a fox, but a man. Well, sort of.

He stood maybe a touch over six feet tall, with impeccably long white hair that reminded me somewhat of Geralt from *The Witcher*. He had defined cheekbones, and a well-chiseled jaw. His piercing gaze translated from the citrine color of the fox form, and his physique was more warrior-like than that of the average man.

Protruding from the top of his head were goat's horns, made of something that appeared to have an ethereal sheen, similar to the likes of moonstone. Pointing out from his mesmerizing locks were his ears, white and fluffy, still in fox form.

He was dangerously alluring. I was simultaneously intrigued and intimidated. He was equal parts fae, Pooka and man.

"Am I more to your liking now, Miss Ciara?" He flashed a darkly charismatic smile at me, proudly displaying his canines. I was breathless.

He was the most beautiful thing I had ever seen. His human voice was rich, making the most casual of phrases sound almost seductive.

"You could say that... Uallas. You are a Pooka, just like from the folklore... But what do you want with me?" I replied, testing his name on my tongue.

"Well, you see, my kind have taken up residence in these isles since what you humans would refer to as the eighth century. But unlike most of my kind, I am one of the few, fair-haired Pookas. I am an Alpeine, so I have white fur and features instead of the dark ones which are mostly depicted in yer lore. As for what I want with you? You are the key to saving my kind."

"What does that even mean, Uallas?"

"Well, all I ask for now is respect, good intentions, the like. So from our encounter thus far, I believe you are deserving. We'll have mutual use of each other," he purred. "I can read your intentions, you know. There's that, and the fact that I know that you have that pointy thing in your sack and haven't reached for it, not even once." He drawled out the last few words and his wink made me blush, knowing he was referring to the knife in my rucksack.

It struck me as odd that, without even seeing my knife, he had known about its presence on me. I didn't dare reach for it now. What good would it do? If he wanted me dead, he would've done it by now, I'm sure of it, but he mentioned he needed me for something. He wouldn't explain why that was and it made me uneasy.

My eyes betrayed me as they trailed down the tuft of hair—or fur, rather—that led from his navel to his lower abdomen, then beneath the seam of his makeshift loin cloth. Why did he also have to be so darkly charismatic? That was one of my weaknesses.

My gaze slowly returned north, following the chords of his muscled arms that also had an ethereal pigment before my eyes caught on his devilish smirk. He was watching me. He was neither human nor animal, but an otherworldly being.

"Good intentions, indeed," he concluded.

My eyes widened, unsure if he could hear my thoughts.

"Yes, Uallas, I could actually use some good luck. No games," I said, grateful for the distraction. I wanted to clarify that I had no intention of making any type of deal with him—he was still a stranger, after all—and that while he claimed to read my intentions, I could not read his.

"I thought you might. And I have a feeling we can trust each other, Miss Ciara. I know the town has talked about our kind out here. Not all of us are as trustworthy as I, y'know. Keep your wits about ya out there. Enjoy the rest of your time on the Great Sugarloaf, Miss. I'll see you again soon," he said with a nod of his head. With that, he transformed into a white rabbit and, with a familiar wink, hopped away.

I didn't know why, but my skin prickled and I instantly believed him to be someone I could trust. Maybe it was foolish to trust him so quickly, but if anything, I knew I could use some good luck these days.

I found it quite odd that he didn't choose to transform into the fox form he'd chosen previously, but into a pure white rabbit instead, almost albino except for those burning eyes. It was then that I remembered what Norman had told me about a rabbit chewing through the wires at the local news station. I wondered if it could just be a coincidence.

I'd read other tales mentioning that a white rabbit crossing one's path signified new beginnings, good fortune, and the importance of trusting one's intuition. Maybe he chose the white rabbit upon his departure as an unspoken message to me, but I couldn't be too sure. He left me puzzled, a million thoughts swirling in my mind.

There were a few things at the forefront of my mind that I knew to be true. That Pooka had actually existed outside of my fairytales. Also, while Pooka existed, not all were bearers of bad and terrible things. The Pooka of this land knew about me and my father and the castle that I lived in.

That last part probably terrified me the most.

Did Conor know any of this existed in this world, or was he as blissfully ignorant about it all as I had once been? That was something I thought would be better left unsaid, just in case he wasn't aware. Not even knowing when I would see him next, it seemed like it would be easy enough to keep from him.

Talking to Norman about this also seemed like a bad idea, given that he thought that horse to be an omen—and maybe he was right about that after all.

That didn't leave me with anyone to talk to about this. I understood the burden of keeping secrets, just as my father must have. I was carrying a secret with me that wasn't my own to keep, but I'd keep it all the same.

Perhaps I could call up Finn O'Leary from my father's note and get some sword training in case more mayhem took over the town. It couldn't hurt to learn. I didn't want to know what could happen to me if I disobeyed the simple request Uallas made me for the respect of his kind.

Before I realized where my feet had led me to, I was back at the bottom of Sugarloaf. I took my cell phone from my rucksack, thankful to have a few bars of service, and called the cab.

The same driver that had dropped me off picked me up from the trail head of Sugarloaf. There must have not been many cab drivers in this rather isolated area or many who were willing to make the drive out here. It was absolutely picturesque and desolate, miles of lush green for as far as you could see. I knew the fare was good money for my driver, based on how much my rate was, so that couldn't be the reason most of the cabs didn't come out this way.

My mind was still reeling from my hike, but at least in the back seat of the cab, I could catch my breath again. Damn, I really needed to exercise more. Hopefully, that training would help.

Once the cab pulled up in front of the castle, I thanked the driver again. This time I asked his name, figuring that if he was one of the few drivers willing to take me out to the hills, then I'd be seeing more of him.

"Me name is Ronan, Miss. *Slán go fóill*," he responded as I left the vehicle.

"Uh, until next time," I replied, recollecting what little Gaeilge I had picked up since arriving here, and walked into the foyer.

Some of my studying in the library was paying off, but his accent was as thick as his midsection.

I walked up the staircase to my room and instantly peeled off my clothes and started the shower, tossing my rucksack on the floor by my bed. It took a minute for the water to heat. I knew it was ready from the steam that trailed up, and I entered to wash myself.

For a few minutes, I just stood there meditating as I let the water fall on my face. I sighed in relief, letting the warm steam wash over me, before beginning to wash my hair with the jasmine and argan oil shampoo I had bought from the city. I stayed in the shower until I'd used up most of the hot water, then toweled off and changed into a comfortable lilac-colored loungewear set and slippers.

I made my way down to the kitchen and prepared the kettle for a cozy cup of tea. When the steam made the un-mistakable high-pitched whistle, I poured the water over some black Ceylon tea leaves and let it steep for a few minutes before adding a teaspoon of sugar. I wrapped my hands around the mug, warming them as I inhaled the delicious aroma, and walked over to the house library.

Sitting in my favorite chair in the center lounge area, I enjoyed my tea while taking in the library's vastness for the first time in a while. I wasn't looking for my next read or a secret room. I just observed the surrounding space, emptying my thoughts from this morning and just living in the moment. I took my first sip as my shoulders relaxed and I closed my eyes.

Except the vision I had when I closed my eyes was of Uallas, in his human form.

Opening my eyes, I let out a frustrated sigh because I could not focus, my thoughts still lingering on the events that took place on Sugarloaf this morning.

I desperately wanted to not let these thoughts consume me to where I might let slip any information regarding what those "rogue farm animals" really were. While it may not have been a nightmare for me, given that I had only met the one Pooka, Uallas, I was worried about any unfortunate meetings with the others that must be in the area.

Maybe instead of trying to sweep these thoughts under the rug, I should indulge in them. After all, what did one do when they met the very subject of their fantasies? There weren't any self-help books in here to help me in this scenario, that I was sure of. My father was one of the few that had helped Uallas and a few of his kind live peacefully, according to the shifter. I knew what dark things the

Pookas were capable of and I didn't want to unleash those demons. This internal battle was just going to stay there, inside my head.

I had plenty to occupy my time, between the tavern and both libraries and that mysterious room I still had not yet found. Just then, an idea struck me. Maybe I was being too close-minded to the fact that the door itself would be in the library. Maybe the door was elsewhere in this castle and led to the room I knew to be down below, and that was why I hadn't found it.

Since relaxing was not in the cards for me this afternoon, I figured I might as well give it a shot before I looked up Finn's contact information. I returned my cup to the kitchen sink and hand washed it before beginning to investigate the many other rooms of the castle.
According to the blueprint, there were forty-five rooms, including the secret one. The chances that the door was in one of those other rooms and not in the library were significant. Even though he wasn't there, my father still managed to send me on a frustrating and pointless search. It would have been easier if he'd been here to help.

I was beginning to understand how simple he wanted to appear to the world though, no doubt, he was a very complicated man under the surface. Maybe that was a trait I was beginning to inherit on my own, taking on this castle.

If these walls could contain the magnitude of these secrets, so could I. I hadn't realized I was inheriting my father's many secrets, but I was starting to understand that this was one of the many assets he included with this new life in Malahide, and why he omitted those secrets from the will. While it was a heavy burden, it was mine now to carry on, as well as many other secrets that I'm sure would surface in the days, weeks, or possibly months to follow.

I'd start today as I made my way down the hall leading to the southern part of the castle.

CHAPTER 8

It took me about twenty minutes to reach the end of the hall, where an extravagant wooden door stood framed by an artistically carved stone arch.

The intricate stonework featured a Romanesque cathedral point with a knotted cross at its peak. The original mason, many years ago, had forged the door handle from wrought iron, preserving the handmade hammering marks. It was simple, yet refined.

I unlatched the door which gave way to an enormous cathedral with vaulted ceilings that must have been as tall as the castle itself.

The surrounding air instantly smelled of aged wood, frankincense, and myrrh. Multiple sconces adorned the posts that lined the center of the room, and oak pews sat on either side. A blood-red carpet lined the aisle, leading up to the marbled altar at the center of attention in the room's front. There were what must have been hundreds of vigil candles on each side, unlit, with white wax dripping down a golden candelabra that was probably hundreds of years old.

The back end of the altar curved into a dome to meet the vaulted ceilings, lined with golden-flecked marble and displaying a mosaic rendering of Jesus on a cross. Thousands of squares and rectangles refracted the sunlight outside into a gorgeous floor-to-ceiling piece of art.

On the far walls were stained glass montages, with colors similar to the windows in my father's study, displaying many of the Irish saints and goddesses that also rose a full story tall. I'm wasn't one for prayer, but this was the most beautiful cathedral interior that I had ever seen. I'd have to come back here to light a memorial candle for my father and one for Conor's mother, as well.

Though thrilled that I had found such a magnificent cathedral within the castle, I was fairly confident there were no secret doors in here. I left the cathedral room, pocketing it in the back of my mind for when I needed help or guidance from a divine power.

I headed back down the hall in hopes of finding another

room with answers. The next door I came upon was more modern, made from simple red cedar.

It almost felt a bit out of place given the lavishness of the cathedral, so I opened it only to find myself in a rather large steam bathhouse, more modernly transformed into a sauna.

Western red cedar completely lined the interior, which featured multiple levels of benches. A wall-mounted switch and dial controlled the temperature. I flipped the switch out of curiosity, and the entire room instantly lit up with an infrared glow. I turned the dial, and the caged hot rocks in the corner started to glow, immediately radiating heat throughout the room.

This was the perfect room to spend time in with the more frigid months approaching—another splendid find. I turned the switch and dial off and exited to another cedar door on the opposite side of the entrance.

Fittingly, it was a changing room and shower. It was sleek, with black marble speckled with glittery mica throughout the entire room. The shower was massive, large enough to fit maybe five people, with jets on all sides of the wall and two shower heads that rained down from above. Marbled benches sat on either side of the stall and everything was encased by floor to ceiling glass doors.

Apparently, I had been using the wrong shower this entire time, because this one was in another league compared to the measly one attached to my bedroom.

A long granite countertop with double sinks adorned the wall opposite the shower. Still no sign of any trap doors or hidden entryways, though, so I left the bathhouse for now.

I just kept coming up short with my search for the secret room, so I decided to pause for the evening. I knew I would find it eventually. I had plenty of time, so for now I thought I'd pay my favorite bartender a visit at the local tavern.

After I called up Ronan again and he dropped me off at the Black Horse Tavern, I spotted an empty seat up at the bar. The tavern was cozy this time of night, less busy than on a weekend but still getting a few odd stragglers blowing off steam from their work days. The crackling fire in the hearth made me feel like I'd been warped back in time.

Norman was on the other end of the bar, cackling with a few of the patrons about something hilarious that I'd just missed before taking my seat. One of the patrons he was talking to was a gentleman with copper hair and beard flecked with white—he must have been around my father's age. I saw Norman's eyes light up as he saw me and then came over to chat and take my order.

"Aye, if it isn't my favorite girl! Are you having the usual today?" Norman asked as he cleared a few empty pints and wiped my area on the counter.

"You know it, Norm. How have things been over here?" I asked, curious if that horse had returned since the last time we spoke.

"Haven't thrown no one outta here, if that's what you're askin'. Business has been good, can't complain 'bout that. I guess more of the town folks have been stayin' local since the Craic came out with that article. What trouble have you been getting into recently, Ciara?"

He slowly drained the tap of Guinness into my pint before placing it before me, the milky foam at the top of the glass barely pouring over the edge before he set it down. I liked that Norman never skimped out on his pour of a beer, a sign of a good bartender. He put in my food order as he awaited my reply.

As tempting as it was to tell him all about the new friend I'd made earlier on Sugarloaf, and my search for the secret room, I already knew what my response had to be.

"Nothing more than the usual amount of trouble, Norm." I curved up one side of my mouth in a devilish half-smirk, insinuating that the normal amount of trouble was more than the average amount of trouble.
"You remind me a lot of your da, ya know. Same smile

when I ask about you and *trouble*. I miss him greatly. He was also my favorite customer. By the way, have you met his colleague, Finn?" he replied, trying to lighten the mood by making the introduction.

It made me feel grateful that my father had touched so many lives that I had no idea about when I was back in Florida—enough for people to miss him and carry on his memory. It made my heart feel full, yet broken at the same time.

"Thanks, Norm. That means a lot to me. I'm grateful he had you to keep him company out here. He mentioned Finn in a letter to me—I'd love to meet him, actually. Did my father ever say much about his work to you?"

Honestly, maybe I was crossing a dangerous line, but I was curious. What did Norman actually know about my father? Or was it just his outside persona that he let him see?

"Come to think of it, he never talked much about work. Always said he came here to escape it, mostly with Finn. We usually chatted 'bout you, actually, and his life in Florida. I'm achin' to see a palm tree and a beach one day. Hold on, I'm gonna go check on your food," he said, snapping back to the present after recalling their old conversations.

I turned to the copper-haired man at the bar that Norman had referred to as Finn and introduced myself.

"Hello, my name is Ciara. My father mentioned I needed to get in touch with you. Glad to meet you here."

"You look exactly as he said you would. My name is Finn O'Leary. Pleasure to meet you at last, Ciara." he held out a hand to give a formal introduction.

"I know this sounds a little crazy, but my father told me in a letter that you were the person to seek for fencing lessons?" I figured I might as well start out the gate strong and get right to the point, before the opportunity passed me by. It seemed like divine intervention that he'd be here, of all the places in town.

"Of course he'd say that. And sure, I guess I'd be your guy. Take down my number and we can set up your first lesson." he put his number into my phone and that was that.

Moments later, Norman arrived with my usual platter of meat and potatoes and I devoured it before we could get more words in. My father was a smart man. It would be far from wise to be telling the town barkeep about anything regarding his life here. While I enjoyed my food and our conversations, I would not find my answers here with Norman.

After Finn and the rest of the customers left, I ended up closing up the bar with Norman, helping him wipe down the counters and put up the chairs. It was getting dark out earlier this time of year. I figured, since it was practically black outside by the time I'd arrived, I might as well stay. I didn't have much else to do at home.

"I'm taking out the trash!" I declared as I exited the back door before Norman could interject.

"Dammit, Ciara!" I heard him call after me as I hurried down the alley to the dumpster.

I was walking so fast that I didn't notice the set of eyes glowering at me in the distance, nor the onyx hooves that pawed the grass so hard they kicked up tufts of dirt, or the huff coming from nostrils that steamed with an intense anger in my direction.

Nor did I notice it was the same stallion that had haunted Norman those many nights ago. I definitely didn't notice the similarities between the fire in its eyes and the midnight sheen of its fur, identical to the black goat I saw on that ride home with Conor.

I only felt the prickly sensation that someone or something was watching me. *They were watching me*, Uallas had said.

With a gasp, I glanced over my shoulder in the direction where I felt the sensation the strongest. I could barely even make out the outline of the trees in the distance. The only lights I saw were the faint glow from the streetlights and those two embers burning bright. Bile rose in my throat as panic began to take over.

No way was that Uallas. This figure, it was black, camouflaging perfectly into the night. Norman was nowhere to be seen, most likely finishing up counting the till inside, blissfully ignorant to the danger I faced out here.

I was utterly alone out here, but maybe at least Norman might hear my scream should things take a turn for the worst. I backed away slowly, never taking my eyes off that piercing gaze in the distance, before running back into the tavern.

Thank goodness Norman was inside counting the till, as expected, and the door remained unlocked.

I threw open the door, a product of pure adrenaline, as it was the heaviest door I had ever encountered. Hyperventilating, I engaged all three locks behind me and rested against the door, attempting to steady my racing heart.

"You alright? You look like you've seen a ghost! I know the rats may be big out there but—" Norman cut off quickly, suddenly aware that my horror and paleness were not because of a rat but something probably worse, and he was right to think so. What I saw was far worse than a rat. "That horse...with the eyes...It—it came back." I formed the words between heavy breaths, still flushed against the door.

"Jesus, Mary, and Joseph, Ciara! I told you that thing was an omen. That horse isn't right. Come away from that door. I can bring ya home tonight—it'll be safer that way."

The offer was too kind of him, but I'd be a fool to refuse the help.

"Okay. Thank you, Norman," I replied, my breath starting to steady.

How had I met a Pooka face-to-face up in the hills, alone, and I hadn't been nearly as terrified as I was in this moment? I couldn't help but wonder if what Uallas said that day had gotten under my skin somehow. Something in my subconscious knew to hear his words as more than just a warning.

Not all of us are as trustworthy as I.

The words he'd left me with must have remained at the forefront of my thoughts.

A warning, but it had instilled a fear of the unknown within me that I was also so curious about. Was there a possibility that the black stallion was trying to warn me about something else? Its gaze was so unnerving.

Whatever it was, I wasn't trying to figure anything out tonight. I wanted nothing more than to be safe within the walls of my castle, my home—but they knew I would be there too, wouldn't they? Would I even be safer there? Maybe if I had no sharp objects or ill intentions for the stallion to read, then I'd be just as okay as I had been on Sugarloaf.

Home would be safer than a closed tavern, at any rate, and certainly safer than waiting for Ronan. Norman finally locked up for the evening and I followed him closely to his car.

Out of habit, I almost opened the backseat when he said, "Ciara, sit up front with me. I want to hear about what exactly you saw back there."

I nodded silently as I opened the passenger door and sat down. I wasn't sure if I'd indulge him in exactly what I saw, or give him the watered-down version he may have already guessed.

Once I clicked on my seat belt and we sped off down the road, away from the tavern, I told him about the horse with the eyes like hot coals that seemed to burn into the back of my head. I told him about the prickly feeling it had given me, and how it had pawed up tufts of soil, and about the steam that came from its nostrils like it was angry or ready to charge. I conveniently left out the fact that I was sure I'd seen the same creature before, but in an alternate form, with the same eyes glaring at me.

"It's all very strange. I hadn't seen anything like this since your father was here."

We kept chatting. I was careful not to reveal too much and before I knew it, we were already at my house.

"Here we are, Ciara. It was great to see you, regardless of how this evening turned out. I hope it didn't scare you away from the tavern for too long."

Norman saw me off as I nodded and said my thanks. Once again, I had arrived back home with more questions than when I left. It was about time I sought some answers for myself.

After tonight's events, I needed some rest. I'd tackle these many questions tomorrow, and I'd start with the black stallion near the tavern. Maybe it had some answers that it had wanted me to know about tonight. I'd have to greet it with noble intentions and be blunt in my questioning, with no sharp objects to instigate violence.

Tonight, I slept soundly with dreams of a man with obsidian horns and those same ember eyes I saw tonight. It was the same dream from one of those many nights ago after I first arrived at the castle.

I awoke to one question answered as I set out to seek answers to the others.

CHAPTER 9

After breakfast the next day, I attempted to see the stallion near the tavern again. The recurring dream of him was another sign that he had something to say, so I would listen. In the daylight and with a satisfied belly seemed like a better way to come across the creature, which I was sure was another Pooka.

Before leaving the estate, I reached into my rucksack. The rough canvas scratched against my fingers as I pulled out the knife. I wouldn't make the mistake of bringing it and risking the Pooka's wrath—the last thing I needed was a death threat.

I had Ronan drop me off a block down from the tavern, like I was back in middle school and embarrassed to be seen with my parents as they kissed me goodbye.

I'd give anything for those brief moments again. You truly never knew what you had until it was taken from you abruptly. I'd give my right arm to just give my dad another hug.

After I left Ronan's cab, I walked out toward the fields that lined the city. The serene view was at odds with the possibility that I could literally be going into the belly of a beast. Despite my nerves, I kept walking forward.

In the distance, I saw herds of white sheep marked with rainbows of paint. They were alongside the oddest company—a black goat. Its back faced me as it grazed with the sheep in the distance, so I couldn't see its eyes, but I was sure they were those familiar embers from the previous night. Its tail gave a little wag as it ate, as if aware of my presence.

On my way home from the tavern that first night, I'd seen it and I will never forget it. This time, because I wasn't distracted, I noticed its horns were a perfect match to the ones in my dreams. Once again, my breath caught in my throat at the sight of it.

Moments later, the black goat finally turned around and trotted toward me, forcing me to halt. Those unmistakable eyes bore into my soul. I tried to muster up some bravery as the goat approached, but I must have left it all in the cab with Ronan.

When it got within shouting distance, I called out, "What do you want from me?"

"Aren't you a long way from home? Perhaps I should be the one asking what *you* want from *me*?" The goat spoke in between brayed words.

My mouth dropped to the floor. I shouldn't have been surprised when it spoke—I'd known it was another Pooka.

"I have no ill intentions toward you, Pooka," I said with more confidence than I felt, "I've come to ask you a few questions."

"Well, go on," he coaxed, his squared pupils looking up at me.

I could have sworn I noticed a brief flicker of amusement in them. It appeared as though he delighted in giving me half-assed answers in the form of questions.

"First, I already know what you are. Could you please shift into your human form just so I can be sure?"

The goat's horizontal, rectangle pupils creeped me out. I knew I'd feel more comfortable speaking to him in his human form, much like I had with Uallas. I only hoped those eyes weren't a feature he'd chosen to keep when he transformed.

"You mean into the man of your dreams?" He chuckled at the double meaning behind his words, knowing he was striking all the right chords with my patience, or lack thereof.

Resisting an eye roll at the cringiness, I took a long blink, staring right back at him when I finally opened my eyes and wishing my glare would burn into his soul.

"As you wish," he purred, if a goat were capable of such a sound.

He then transformed into a black shadow, like Uallas had. When he emerged, he looked exactly like the ethereal man from my dreams. *"The man of your dreams"* echoed in my head again. How in the hell did he know that?

I felt like my privacy was being invaded, but I couldn't help but gawk at him.

His goat's horns remained as a feature of his human form, great swirls of ribbed obsidian protruding from his head. He stood taller than Uallas had in this form, probably six inches above me, his piercing eyes staring down through my soul. Long, dark hair peeked out from behind his ears and my eyes caught on a longer strand falling to his full mouth in the front. A well-groomed beard outlined his stark features and chiseled bone structure.

I couldn't help but gasp in awe at his raw beauty in person. He held a distinct presence, differing from Uallas, besides the fact that they were essentially the same beast. He felt like everything I had imagined the Pooka of my folklore to be: mayhem with a bit of mystique. Just as dark on the outside as their soul on the inside. He had brought chaos to my thoughts in an instant.

For a moment, I lost track of all the questions I'd prepared, as I spotted his hairy, broad chest peeking out from behind that linen shirt. I was curious as to what the rest looked like beneath it.

"You had questions?" He smiled at me, taking note of where my eyes had betrayed me. His words brought me back into the moment, and all my questions came rushing back. One at a time.

"First of all, what is your name?"

"You may call me Fearghas—Fearghas Harveye. I take it you have already met that arse, Uallas."

"That's irrelevant," I spat.

He had a slightly unique accent compared to that "arse" Uallas. It was still old, but not as ancient sounding as his counterpart. Maybe he had adapted better here, closer to civilization, thanks to my father's help, but I couldn't let my thoughts go down that path of sorrow. Not in front of Fearghas because I had no idea what he truly was capable of. What if he had a sixth sense like Uallas? What if his gifts were worse than that?

I couldn't show any signs of weakness. I'd allow for no possibility of him using my weak points to his advantage.

Especially if I didn't want to see my father sooner than later.

It would be hard enough to remain calm, as I was already in a fragile state of mind.

I hadn't dared admit to myself that some of that emotion stemmed from Fearghas ruffling my feathers. Anyway, I wasn't getting anything answered at this rate.

"Why have you been watching me? What do you know about my father, Sean Driscoll?"

"Ah, and you must be Ciara. I know your father was a good man to our kind."

Was a good man... That meant he knew about his passing. But exactly how much did he know and did he have anything to do with it?

Darkness crept over my thoughts, like early morning fog on a lake. The chilling realization that I might be speaking with my father's killer dawned on me too late. I had to shove this thought from my mind as well. I'd much rather be ogling over his muscled chest again. I realized he'd evaded my first question, as he had done to all the others I asked, so I asked again.

"*Why* have you been watching me?"

"To observe," he said flatly, as if stating the obvious.

"What does that even mean? That isn't an answer."

Frustration boiled the blood within my veins.

"*To observe.* To notice something and register its significance. To assess its quality."

He looked me up and down like I was his next meal, making a show of assessing my physical qualities. His stare heated me differently, in a way that I knew was all wrong. Trying to push my thoughts away from their own sinfulness, I attempted to get back at the task at hand—yet again.

No way had he just spewed out the Oxford dictionary definition of the word observe. I got back to the question.

"I know what it means, I just don't know *why*."

I emphasized the "why" part again, just in case that was necessary.

"You won't like my answer, Ciara."

My name on his lips would sound soothing if his words hadn't sent a chill down my spine. I knew that some answers I sought I may not like, but it was still better than feeling lost. Answers meant freeing the burden of my thoughts that were constantly going at a rate of a hundred miles a minute. Answers meant a step closer to the closure I deserved, that my father deserved. The truths may not set me free, but I needed them nonetheless.

"Try me," I challenged.

It was my turn to show off my stubborn grin. Fearghas huffed, clearly annoyed that I was persistent. The emotion almost reminded me of a raging bull in a cartoon.

He seemed hesitant to give me any iota of information I asked for, but his cool exterior was starting to crack. I'd get answers out of him eventually, no matter what cost, no matter how long it took.

He softened his features before he caught my eyes and said his piece: "I've observed you to determine your trustworthiness in carrying on your father's legacy, so to speak."

To see if you are trustworthy enough to protect our kind went unsaid.

"And if you know anything about how your father really... departed this world. It helps that you are also quite easy on the eyes, Sunshine."

I couldn't help but roll my eyes at that last part. That term of endearment he chose for me. *Cocky bastard.*

"See, I knew you wouldn't like it." He looked down at me through hooded eyes, a smug grin plastered on his face. He reveled in provoking me, knowing I'd focus on the trivial statements and ignore his implication about my father's death. Was he doing it on purpose? Of course he was—he was the prince of mischief.

The fact that he called me "Sunshine" was the most irritating part of the sentence.

As much as I knew the other words should have affected me more, they didn't—at least not nearly as much as his attempt at flirting with me. Still, I pressed on, ignoring how it got under my skin. My face turned into a blank canvas of emotion. I was the princess of dissociating, after all, I guess all that practice was useful for something.

"I don't know exactly how my father passed away, but I suspect...terrible things happened." *Way to state the obvious, Ciara.*

I just couldn't think of anything else to say. It was all I knew. The authorities didn't release his official cause of death to the family. I was despising his high-profile position more and more every day. If my father was an average Joe, not only would he probably still be alive, but he would have passed away from more natural causes—perhaps even at the ripe old age of ninety.

No need for what ifs. This was my reality, and I was dealing with it the only way I knew how.

"Terrible things indeed. It is not for me to say how, Sunshine. That is an answer I cannot give you. Uallas might be more helpful, although I doubt he'll share such precious information with you. Have I mentioned how much of an arse he is?"

"You have—though the only *arse* I've met is *you*." I replied audaciously. It was my best attempt to get under his skin, if he was even capable of such emotions. He let out a deep, low laugh at that statement.

The low grumble seemed to reverberate through my chest and I closed my eyes, attempting to shake off the feeling. I just called a Pooka an arse. I'd feel worse about it if he hadn't called me by a made-up pet name and didn't seem to be trying to shoot his shot with me upon our first meeting. What a scumbag.

If he could sense my emotions like Uallas then I couldn't let my feelings get the better of me. If only I could still mute my emotions as well as I had at my father's funeral.

I suspected it was too late for masking my emotions. Humans tended to wear them on their sleeves even if they weren't trying to show them. I supposed Conor had helped me with that. As frustrating as it was at this moment, I'd have to celebrate the fact that my grief wasn't wearing me down as heavy as it had been.

CHAPTER 10

FEARGHAS

Oh, she was a spicy one. I knew I'd be in shambles the day I met Sean's offspring. Shame he couldn't be here to introduce us. He was a pillar of this town, and of the entire country, really. Though most of the country did not know his true significance behind the shadows. My personal favorite place to be.

It didn't matter that his good deeds for the supernatural were under the radar of most of the people here. In fact, that's what made him even better. Sean never did it for the glory or the praise. Most of his work went unnoticed, actually, despite how well loved he was throughout the town. It was solely that quality that made him an excellent human.

He genuinely cared about our kind and believed we could live in absolute harmony one day with humans. An odd sort of balanced way of life.

Even though he kept his daughter almost as much of a secret as our supernatural kind, it didn't mean there weren't folks who didn't have a wandering eye. That was probably why he'd kept her far across the ocean for the entirety of her life.

With her finally here in the motherland, it hadn't stopped them much from staring, amongst other despicable things.

I recalled seeing her in person for the first time. Seeing her with that human on their way back from the pub shouldn't have bothered me that much. I'd had my fair share of maidens throughout the century. Although he wasn't my first pick for her—I would rather send him off the edge of a cliff, if I was being honest.

It was always the same questions. *Who are you, what are you, why are you doing this?* It was just my nature—I couldn't help it. Truth was, there were very few humans deserving of my self-restraint to not chuck them off of a cliff. Ciara just happened to be one of the few.

The other was Sean. Some arsehole felt the need to send his innocent soul into oblivion, so no, I did not have patience for the rest of them. I barely had any patience for others of my own kind, if I was being truthful. Honestly, the less of them, the better. Call me a grumpy old man, but when you'd seen the things that I had over the centuries, you might just have agreed.

Humans and supernatural beings alike going mad over tales or material items. It was always over some stupid quest for some immeasurable prize. Fight the dragon, get the maiden. Retrieve Excalibur, get the power of a kingdom.

Immeasurable amounts of bloodshed were spent, only to find it had all been pointless. Now that amused my cold, dark heart. Play stupid games, win stupid prizes. No one took into consideration that the opposing side simply would never budge on their opinions or beliefs. They'd just fight until no one was left to say otherwise.

Me? I couldn't care less, but some people couldn't leave well enough alone.

Now here I was, on the edge of caring too little and too much. Teetering on the edge of whatever sanity I had to begin with.

My kind don't have rules per se, but more like a certain code of honor. Of course, it was a very brief code, which also added to our appeal. In order to have mayhem, you needed to have a sense of what order was to begin with. A set of rules just to throw them out of the window.

Mayhem was our nature, and it was the one thing I could truly count on. It made my sick little world go 'round. No day was ever the same. The only thing that remained was the code—simple enough.

"For the Pooka-kind, you must stay away from cold iron. Secrets that are not yours aren't for tellin' others, and are always to protect our protector."

I'd done a pretty decent job of abiding by these rules for a time, and I could see why we had them.

Well, first of all, cold iron *would* kill us—that was an obvious one. We didn't get to be bandaged up by a medic if we got cut by one, like our human friends. It was curtains for us instantly, especially for our magic. Everything else? We were conveniently immune to it. I couldn't tell you how many humans had tried to bash me over my head with ale glasses when I merely wanted to give their drunk asses a ride home. I'd been told it wasn't safe to drink and drive in this century, but they all complained about my favor. Screaming at me when they found out that my magic, like an invisible hand, was holding them in place, saddled on my back.

However, that I was able to avoid the cold iron all this time was nothing short of a miracle. If I believed in those kinds of things. It had more to do with the way the metal was forged than anything. Iron had never been kind to the fae types.

The second was just a code of ethics and if you wanted to get technical, it may have been our only ethical code. It helped us stay under the radar enough to carry on our chaos.

It made the mayhem more pure. No cheap blows like telling Patty her husband had been laid up with the town whore for the past two years. Sorry, Patty. It gave us more clever ways to wreak havoc in this world so used to order.

Last but not least, don't bite the hand that fed you. Protect your protector. These rules should have been simple to follow, yet recently someone violated them, endangering our protector, Sean Driscoll. As a matter of fact, they went through all the trouble of not only harming him, but ending his life altogether in the most brutal of ways imaginable—stabbing him in the heart. Remember rule one? What a shite thing to do.

If Ciara proved honorable enough to take on her father's legacy, she would need extra protection, I was sure of that now. I could not sit around and let her demise be the same as her father's.

Knowing that the culprit is still at large made me uneasy. They not only had no regard for the life of humans, but no sense of self-preservation. Not the good kind of chaos.

In no way would I want to cause harm to Ciara by telling her the truth prematurely, but would she become our new protector? If so, I knew who she would need protecting from.

So what if I had been observing her? Damn me if I hadn't been assessing her qualities, of which there were many.

I enjoyed making her squirm with my flirtatious remarks and coy comments. I was the prince of trickery and mayhem, after all. I enjoyed it even more when I caught her blushing at my words and saw how the pet name I chose for her, Sunshine, got under her skin. Didn't she know that was what her secondary or middle name meant? *Niamh*. Bright and radiant, and if she wasn't both. A smart girl who lit up any room or space she walked into. A well-suited name for her.

I'd come to enjoy observing her, ultimately to protect her, just in case.

It was one of the few ways I could honor her father's legacy.

I knew about the dreams she'd had about me because, well, I planted them there. Some of us had these tricks that we played with human minds. Such fragile things, easily manipulated. If you had a gift, then why not use it? So I did.

As soon as I heard of Sean's daughter arriving here in the isles, I infiltrated her dreams in my many forms. I most enjoyed the ones where I was in a human form—I liked how that one felt the best. Mostly because I could tell *she* liked that one the best.

I could tell by the way her heart rate sped up as she slept. It felt like lust. Like a fire that flared up suddenly and demanded to be stoked, a beautiful yet destructive force.

I typically didn't ever let slip a genuine smile that didn't lead to malice, but I couldn't help it when I was around her. I hadn't failed to notice she didn't have any pointy things on her for our meeting, and it made me intrigued. It was bold of her, knowing the tales of our kind, to walk into the fire without a way to extinguish it.

To seek us out, me in particular, was a whole other animal. Speaking of animals, I knew the entire town had been talking about me, or about the "rogue farm animals." I found it quite comical because if they actually knew what the "rogue farm animals" were, they'd all go running for the hills. It was all just a little fun, to keep them on their toes.

To the few eejits that attempted to catch me in my stallion form, I'm not sorry for that. *Survival of the fittest*, I believe that was the term—only the strong and intelligent survived, and they had been neither. I was just helping with the balance of nature.

Ciara kept bringing up what I knew about her father, and there were only so many ways that I was skilled in dodging such a question.

An ache in my chest developed, and it was an odd feeling for me. I needed to figure out a way to evade her questions in a way that she wouldn't keep prying at me to crack open, and then get the hell out of here. Answering questions with questions had always been my go-to.

My first task of protecting her was to withhold information? Great—this wasn't off to a good start. As much as I didn't enjoy this scenario, it was something I needed to deal with. She wouldn't like it, either, but I could be a distraction for her. At least I could only hope.

CHAPTER 11

"**W**hat do you know about the castle in Malahide?" I broke Fearghas's thunderous laugh as his lips curved into a tight line. Now I had struck a chord with him. *Good.*

"Well, that was where it happened, Ciara. With that ancient sharp and pointy thing that he locked away. It wasn't supposed to happen. Shite, I've said too much."

There was a note of sadness and regret in his eyes, like he knew a secret that was not his to share. Then, he vanished without a goodbye into a cloud of shadows, reappearing halfway across the field in his goat form. His lack of manners pissed me off.

Ancient sharp and pointy thing? And it had happened at home, the place that I'd come to recognize as my safe place? It must have something to do with what was in that secret room, the one outlined in the red on the blueprint that I still couldn't find. That would explain the secrets surrounding it all.

Fearghas had said I'd have better luck asking Uallas. What did Uallas know of it? Regardless, I'd have to see him again. I'd start at Sugarloaf, where we first met, to see if he knew anything.

There was still plenty of daylight left, so I made my way back to town and dialed up Ronan.

"Back to Sugarloaf, eh? Great way to spend Samhain, Miss," Ronan said as he started driving. It had completely slipped my mind that the celebration was today. It was a big deal out here: the ancient Pagan celebration that started with Celtic spiritual traditions marking the end of the harvest and the beginning of the winter solstice. The town had the largest night parade in all of Ireland. The name translates to *summer's end* in modern Irish.

Ancient Celts believed the veil between the living and the dead was especially thin during this time, so they built bonfires to help loved ones find their way home. Some said that this tradition was where Halloween was born. Today, participants celebrated with nature walks, feasts, and dancing.

It also was my favorite time of year.

It carried more sentiment this year, now that I was without my father.

"Thanks, Ronan. I'll call you when I'm ready to be picked up."

I made my way back up the gravel path to where I'd met Uallas the last time. Unsure of what form would greet me, I kept an eye out for those telltale eyes so I would know it was him. True to his form, I spotted him as the same arctic fox as last time. His white form stood out starkly against the golden brush.

"Uallas? Is that you?" I asked the fox, just to be sure, though I'd know when he talked.

"Miss Ciara! A blessed Samhain, isn't it?" he declared.

"Cut the bullshit. What do you know about the castle?" I had no time for small talk this time. I needed answers. He changed into his beautiful human form before I could even ask him to. The swift change before my eyes gave me goosebumps.

"Ah, I see you have met Fearghas, haven't you?"

He had a look of disgust on his face before he changed the subject, like the name had produced a foul taste in his mouth.

"Yes, well—the castle where you live, as your father had, and generations before him as well. We will miss them, your father, most of all."

"I have met Fearghas, but I'm not here to talk about him. I want some answers, Uallas, not history lessons," I demanded.

He grinned slyly, ready for a sarcastic reply.

"To get to the other side, outlook not good, reply hazy, try again. What answers do you seek, Ciara? I'll do my best to answer you."

His Pooka-like personality was on full display, a reminder of his dark capabilities. His soft tone as he spoke my name brought me a sense of relief.

"Sorry I was so harsh at first, but I have so many questions that I need answers to. It has been driving me mad. So please, go easy on me, Uallas," I practically begged him. There was only so much banter I could take in a day.

"Yes, dear, anything for you," he replied smoothly, with a brief caress of my cheek.

The term of endearment took me by surprise. It was one my father had called me in the past. It must have been pure coincidence. He couldn't have known that, could he?

"What happened to my father in the castle, Uallas? Fearghas said it happened there... his last moments. What was he talking about?"

Fearghas said my father's last moments had been in the castle gardens.

"Why do you want to know this, Ciara? I don't want to

cause you any more grief than you still are feelin'." It was a roundabout answer to my question. He was avoiding me.

The gardens. I hadn't thought to look there because the weather had been so up and down lately, as I'd heard Ireland's weather can be. My body was still adjusting to the cold climate compared to the heat and nonstop humidity of Florida. I didn't think I'd ever fully adjust to this frigid air.

Uallas was right, though. No matter how hard I tried to mask it, my grief was still there. How could it not be? Who knew if it would ever leave? It was something I wore now, my invisible mask, to hide the pain of my father's untimely death.

I hated that word. *Death.* Every time I spoke or thought about it, it just made the reality of why I was even here in the first place seem so surreal.

Even more surreal was meeting the very beings from my folklore stories.

Pookas weren't supposed to exist—they were just stories, fables that were just words on a paper, bedtime stories. But my father's death and Pookas existing were hard truths I'd have to swallow.

"I... I don't really know. I guess I want closure. Yes, I have grief, but any human would, and I don't know if that will ever go away. But I guess I just thought that if I could get some closure about his... death... then it could help me move forward."

It was so weird, trying to explain my sorrow and having to add that it was a human emotion. It was hard enough talking about it without having to add the obvious hint at the pain because, before this, I was only ever talking to other humans. Having to explain it out loud just reopened the wound.

Uallas being able to sense my emotions didn't help my case, though. If anything, it made getting my closure that much more difficult. He could sense the pain I was feeling, but could not relate any of it to being human. How could he? He wasn't human despite his attempts at transforming into one.

"I am so very sorry for your loss, Ciara," he caressed my cheek again, scanning my eyes to detect the emotion hidden beneath them. The words felt hollow. "You know where you can find me now if you ever want to seek me out. I mostly live by the lake just south of here. The locals call it Lough Guinness. It's shaped like a harp."

I'd heard of it before, when reading some books on Ireland's geography and history at the city library. A vast lake, black as night at any time of day, surrounded by hills and always appearing to have a thick mist blanketing the surface of the water. Reminiscent of the pints of Guinness I'd drink at the tavern.

"But you know where my castle is. You mentioned they were watching me the last time. Would you ever want to visit outside the grounds?"

I knew I needed to exercise more, but I'd be damned if I had to hike this stupid hill every time I wanted to see him. No thanks. Maybe he could show me the gardens, at least. That sounded much better.

"Anything for you, my dear. You can hold me to it," Uallas said.

There was that word again. It almost haunted me. *Dear.*

"Thank you, Uallas. I'll see you around, I guess," I replied, trying to ignore how that word made me feel.

Uallas nodded in silent agreement before shifting back into his fox form and darting off into the forest.

"Hope ya enjoyed your hike, Miss. It's a mighty fine day out today—glad you could enjoy it. Where ya headed?" Ronan said as I entered the back of the cab.

"Let's go to the library in Dublin, please," I replied, not quite ready to go home yet.

Maybe I could find a few new pieces of literature on Pookas that I hadn't already read, or at least I could people watch to distract myself. *Observe them*, as Fearghas would say.

I'd had a lot of interactions with preternatural beings today and I just wanted some normal moments.

As we pulled up to the entrance of the library, I let loose a deep breath, as if I had been holding it in the entire ride there. The outside of the library was just as fantastical as the interior. A multi-leveled rounded colonnade reflected its neoclassical design. Intricate stone carvings and classic motifs with as many tall Corinthian columns as arched windows adorned the entrance. It was all so extraordinary.

The outside of the library also had many students and tourists admiring the fine nineteenth century architecture, or just burying their head in one of its thousands of books. The usual crowd.

I entered the stately, solid wooden doors, a gust of wind helping me along. A few of the front-desk librarians greeted me by name. Yep, we were on a first name basis here.

Smiling, I headed up to the third level. I could get a better view of the people from up there, and the shelves were slightly less crowded than on the floor level.
I passed aisles of classic literature containing the likes of

Agatha Christie, Bram Stoker, and Oscar Wilde, before finding the section I was looking for.

Many time-worn tomes lined the shelves before me that were maybe triple the height of the libraries from home. I couldn't fathom the number of books this building held, nor that the librarians knew most of them and where to find them all. It appeared the Dublin library was home to every book published in the entire world, new or old.

As I approached the end of the aisle, I saw exactly what I was looking for. A few familiar tales of the Pooka and a few dated copies I'd never heard of. I cautiously removed a few of the unfamiliar ones from the shelf and found a welcoming corner with an empty velvet chair, complete with an oak side table and Tiffany lamp.

One volume I picked up was another book on the Sword of Light. Though this tale did not mention Pookas specifically, it mentioned that the bearer of the sword must die by secretive means for a quest to be fulfilled, mostly by the weapon itself. But often, the sword itself was not enough and the supernatural enemy had to be attacked in a certain way by the owner of the sword to weaken its opponent—thus starting the quest.

This story mentioned the significance of animals, or animal souls, along with this sword, as well as the quests being of the bridal variety. A bridal quest? That was such an age-old type of quest. Yet, I couldn't help but connect a few dots here.

A secret room. My father's mysterious death. The Pookas who could shift into both humans and animals. And this book stands out to me not only in my father's study, but here at this massive library as well.

Was some outside force trying to tell me something? Was this why my father died, and so secretively at that? Why Fearghas couldn't tell me the truth, even though I was positive he knew more than he led on? Was that Sword of Light the secret object that was locked in that room on the blueprint?

It must all be true—it had to be.

I already knew that my father had been part of a secret government agency and was close with the supernatural beings of Ireland. Just because he was trying to protect them didn't mean one had it out for him—right? The Pooka would have known enough about him because of his work that they would have known he had a daughter of age to wed...

Oh, no. No, no, *no*.

That couldn't be a possibility. A Pooka killing my father because he was the keeper of the Sword of Light and they wanted me for themselves? But who? Uallas? Fearghas?

That would explain his secretiveness around me... But maybe it was someone or something else entirely?

More answers I didn't like, but they were answers nonetheless.
Though I hoped I was wrong with my deciphering, I had an eerie feeling that I was right.

I shut my book and walked downstairs to check them out and do more research at home later. I called up Ronan immediately to go back to the castle.

Did this mean I was also in danger? Was the sword still there in the secret room, or had my father's murderer taken it with them?

I couldn't imagine a Pooka wanting to have one in their possession, given that it was the only way they could be killed—to risk their own life in that way at all. I couldn't imagine anyone or anything that would risk their own life so greatly as to harm or even to kill another for the possibility of getting me for themselves. As if I were property.

Why did it matter so much? This person, or *being*, who had murdered my father knew all of those things and sought an opportunity for themselves, no matter that it would cost lives. It had been a choice, most definitely not in my best interests. If they only knew that their choice would make me hate them before I even knew who the culprit of such an act was.

Now, only two questions lay at the forefront of my mind. Who and why? I needed to give Finn a phone call.

CHAPTER 12

The next morning, I took my tea and breakfast out in the atrium in the back gardens. As I sat at the iron table and chairs, I took out my phone and dialed Finn's number. He answered on the second ring.

"Hello?"

"Hi, Finn. This is Ciara. Are you available tomorrow to start those fencing lessons?"

"Tomorrow works for me. How does ten in the morning at your place sound?"

"Perfect. Looking forward to it! See you then."

I hung up the phone, a little disappointed in myself for taking this long to set up our first lesson. Better late than never, especially if I was most likely part of some bridal quest I had no idea about. I tried not to dwell on that fact and to just enjoy the nature that surrounded me as I walked out toward the gardens.

I admired the expertly trimmed topiary sculptures that dotted the lawn, along with the variety of native trees. Every type and color of roses you could imagine filled the spaces in between with reds, yellows, whites, pinks, and hybrids of each.

The air was a heavenly mix of roses, blooming wildflowers, and rich soil. Moss-covered statues bedecked the nearby bushes, while multi-tiered water fountains speckled the lawn.

In the very center stood an elegant stone statue carved into an Irish goddess who appeared to be crying streams of real water. Its tragic splendor took my breath away. Aged tear stains showed that because of some phenomenon, her crying wasn't as abnormal as I would've thought. My eyes weren't betraying me.

I took some extra time studying the crying goddess statue, finding it oddly comforting that even if you were as hard as stone on the exterior, it was okay to cry. Though this was quite a literal depiction.

I let my deepest thoughts filter through to the surface. Fond memories with dad at Disney World, or the times when he'd put my macaroni art on the fridge. As I closed my eyes, memories began to flow through me freely, and I let them. Masking my feelings was not the best way to deal with them. It wouldn't change the fact that my father was gone—and nothing could change that new reality. I had to face my grief head-on if I had planned to overcome it. It was healthier to feel the emotions, rather than bottle them up.

My therapist back in Florida was always preaching to me about that, but it was easier said than done. Everyone went through life with their own individual experiences and degrees of relationships, so how we dealt with those experiences or what came from those relationships was as unique as your DNA.

The sorrow over the death of a parent would never go away entirely. You just learned how to manage it as time went on. It was the deepest of wounds and you were left masking the scars. Though the healing was arduous, each small step forward, each fading mark, brought a quiet joy, a testament to resilience. That our human hearts could carry all this emotion and that emotions could heal, just like a physical wound. Everyone may have had a unique method of tending to their wound, but ultimately, it would become bearable one day.

I brushed away the tears I had let fall down my cheek and kept walking through the gardens. The box hedges bordering the castle, which I hadn't noticed before, turned out to be blackberry bushes, full of ripened berries.

With breakfast finished, I walked toward the bush and plucked several berries, their juice already staining my fingers. I licked the juice off before it made a mess of me. To my surprise, all the bushes were abundant with plump blackberries. I practically had an orchard hidden in my backyard. I kept plucking as many berries as I could, using my shirt as a provisional basket. It was a little late in the season for blackberries to still be ripe, so I'd take advantage of enjoying my favorite fruit while I could.

"Ow! Damn!"

On the third bush, I accidentally missed and caught myself on the thorn instead. The blood on my finger that pooled into a droplet was eerily similar in color to the juice of the blackberries—just a touch more red than purple, and thicker in consistency.

As crazy as it sounded, I understood why our ancestors misinterpreted warnings about eating overripe blackberries and said a Pooka could enter the soul of a child who ate them.

During the witch-hunting era, it wasn't a far cry to believe that a berry that dark was not natural, and therefore must be the work of the devil himself. They believed everything and anything was the devil's work—even birthmarks were the mark of Satan.

Disrupting my train of thought, two robins flew from the silver birch tree next to me. My attention snapped to the direction of the disruption, trying to find the source of what had scared the birds.

My blood tingled as I saw Uallas emerge from the rose beds, his human form barely concealing the electricity that still pulsed in the air. I gasped as his presence startled me. He was lean with corded muscles, and shirtless with breeches to cover just the important bits, and show off his muscular thighs. His white fox ears reminded me he was anything but human as they twitched around like sonar, detecting nearby sounds as he closed the distance between us.

"What in the actual fuck? Why are you here, Uallas?"

"Did you not want to explore your grounds with—" he cut himself short as his nostrils flared on the sharp intake of his breath.

"You're hurt," he growled.

Closing the distance, he took my pricked finger and slowly stuck it in his mouth. His amber eyes turned wholly black as he rolled them to the back of his skull. "But you taste divine," he breathed.

"*Excuse* me?!" I was shocked by his audacity. I yanked my finger from his mouth and repeated my first question.

I hadn't remembered whether Pookas drank blood, but honestly, no thoughts crossed my mind except what was happening in that moment. It made me feel so uncomfortable that he just took it upon himself to suck my finger to stop me from bleeding, then reacted to the taste like it was his life force.

I wasn't too squeamish when it came to blood, but there was a line, and Uallas had crossed it.

In an instant, my incensed feelings became mute. Physically, I was present, but my vision blurred and my body tingled all over—this time with lust rather than shock.

My body was reacting to an alien feeling that my mind revolted from. This was a different kind of torture. To not feel in control of your own thoughts, as if an exterior force was at play.

Sure, I thought that Uallas was physically attractive, but I was still getting to know him and in no way was I thinking about acting upon those thoughts. If I was being truthful, the fact that he called me "dear" was a hard pass for me.

The feeling it triggered in me has to do with him not understanding human emotion. Pookas are masters of observing and copying what they perceive, but they are not like us. It was how they were able to get away with such chaos.

It was easy to duplicate features. A horn, a hoof, a paw are all pretty cut-and-dry characteristics. Emotions, on the other hand, were far more intricate, more in-depth than even humans could navigate, if I was being honest. So perhaps Uallas's confusion in the type of emotion he sensed when my dad called me "dear" was out of familial love, instead of the romantic love he clearly wanted with me. It made sense to him in some fucked-up, alternate-universe sort of way.

Wetness immediately pooled between my thighs, despite my thoughts being repulsed by what was happening without my consent. I should have been so turned off by the fact that he licked the blood off my finger and enjoyed it like it was a slice of chocolate cake.

My body was betraying me with a growing ache in my lower center. I'd take being disassociated any day over whatever the hell was going on with me. At least when I was in that murky state of mind, I was still in my own head somewhere, and I had some type of control.

But now, I was a puppet on his manipulative strings.

I didn't know what else to do so I just screamed at the top of my lungs. *How was that for an emotion to read, asshole?*

I was beginning to think Fearghas was on to something when he called Uallas an arse.

He jumped away from me at my exclamation, lifting the veil of lust that had overcome me.

"Stop! Just *stop*, Uallas!" I cried, "Stop reading and abusing my emotions, and for fuck's sake, please stop calling me dear. I never said I liked it, and you never asked me if it was okay to use that word."

Physically exhausted, I lowered onto my knees to keep them from shaking and dug my nails into the soil, gripping fistfuls of dirt to ground myself. Uallas was smart enough to keep his distance this time. He cowered a safe distance from me and apologized.

"I'm so sorry, Ciara. Please, you have to forgive me. I didn't know. I'm not that great with human emotions. I've seen the way you stare at me sometimes, and..." His breath hitched. "I don't know. I clearly read into it all wrong. I'll only call you by your name until you tell me otherwise. Please don't hold it against me forever."

His twin yellow eyes glanced up at me hopefully from under his brows, begging for an apology. I figured he had caught me lost in thought sometimes, admiring the well-cut planes of his human-ish body. Sometimes I wished I wasn't so easy to read, but my expressions gave me away, apparently.

"Uallas, I'll need some time—though forever is probably unrealistic."

I'd do the right thing and give him the benefit of the doubt for the terribly mistaken miscommunication. Believing in second chances, I thought maybe showing him how humans operated would be a good thing. Educational purposes and all.

"Please allow me some space, okay? I'll come to you when I'm ready."

"Okay Ciara. Anything for you."

I nodded solemnly and walked back toward the house, leaving him behind. Uallas watched me walk away as he stood there, still as the birch trees behind him, remaining in his human form. He reminded me of a dog being scolded, tucking its tail between its legs. His fox ears drooped and his shoulders sagged. He looked truly sorry, devastated even, to have hurt me in such a way, but I still didn't believe that he would actually leave me alone for long.

We would have to get past this, but I needed to rest first. An idea struck me.

I went to my room and picked up the new library book I checked out about Pookas and the bridal quest, settling into bed to read. It was the only way I knew to settle my mind, feed it information.

Maybe the book had some other facts I didn't already know about Pookas, as well as whatever this quest was. Even experts don't know everything. I opened the book, an apparent diary, to a random page and started reading:

The Pooka brothers that I've recently met have been created from the pits of hell itself. One brother, with alpine features, is reputed to be a giver of good luck. He also carries a gift that the average Pooka does not have: the ability to read a human's intentions and plant emotions within their minds. This is beneficial for keeping the lineage of Pookas strong, mimicking the thoughts of the human race to wreak havoc on us.

The other brother, the dark knight, or the prince of chaos, often taking the shape of a pitch-black stallion with a wild mane, takes his riders to the cliff's edge for their last ride with his cunning and persuasive personality. His magic traps his riders to his back so they cannot escape. He is also a dream weaver. Unlike his brother, he cannot plant emotions or read them in the literal sense. He can either dispel the worst nightmares or have humans remember the most wonderful dreams that they will probably ever have in their lifetimes. He comes across as jaded, and will almost always be known as the master prankster, forever angry at the world surrounding him.

Brothers? I had to keep reading. It appeared to be a diary from one of the first members of the secret government agency in Ireland. The label clearly misrepresented it as public domain material, filed under *Fiction and Myths*.

It would be safe here with me.

I flipped through a few more pages, scanning the text for the words *bridal* and *quest*, until I finally found what I was looking for:

The infamous bridal quest attached to the legend of the Claidheamh Soluis is one of adventure. Heroes versus the supernatural, pitted against one another for the hand of the fairest daughter and all of the riches of whomever the sword belongs to.

Once the quest is triggered by a supernatural force and the blood of the hero, its wielder is free to take her and the immeasurable amounts of wealth for his own—granted that she has not already been promised to another...

CHAPTER 13

UALLAS

I know some may think it was wrong of me to use my gifts in the manner I had used them on Ciara today. Not only entering her mind to grasp her intentions as I had on that first day, but to make her crave my touch. Part of me had to know that it was only me she truly desired.

I could make any human or animal do or think as I commanded. Perhaps that was why I was one of the few surviving Alpeines of my kind and needed to create more of us.

I just couldn't let her get close to the truth. Not yet, anyway.

For what Sean Driscoll did share with our kind, the best

kind of information he let slip was the fact that he had a daughter of age to wed.

From the moment I heard of her, I did everything in my power to get her close to me, to let her get to know me. The more I found out about her and her upbringing, the more I realized I had to have her for my own. She was an absolute stunner. She had a perfect body and face, and she was fearless around us. Her da taught her well.

Hell, I could transform into her dream man. Any part of me I could adapt for her own pleasure, and by that, I mean *any* body part.

What was there not to love about that?

I hurt her today, emotionally. It wasn't my intention, and truly, I was sorry. I said I would do anything for her, and I meant it. I owed her that much. Maybe I still didn't quite understand human emotions, and I might never.

Human *women's* emotions? Forget that. Far too complicated things. I heard that even human men don't understand their women. How could I even compete with that?

I only knew that I had crossed a line when I heard her scream. A sound that would forever be ingrained in my head, and forever was a long time when you didn't have a mortal lifespan.

But I thought I had scented her arousal, and I could have

sworn that came from her and not my gift. She kept eyeing my body, admiring my muscled chest. I wondered what could be the harm if I just used my gifts to heighten it a little? But I pushed too far.

I can never push her too far again.

The good brother is supposed to be *me*. I am the one that is full of light and luck. That's what the creators intended, after all. We were both capable of bad things, but I swore to myself that was in my past.

I could not go down that path again—I refused. Ciara would be the one to help me, that I was sure of. I don't know exactly how I knew, but sometimes these gifts of reading intentions came with strong intuition about what was to come. The decisions we made today would shape our tomorrow.

I absolutely hated that she met with Fearghas. I scented his unmistakable goat stench on her. The likelihood that he would be a flirt to her just annoy me was significantly high, given his track record. Fearghas was a jaded recluse until it came to anything that gave me an inkling of happiness. By any means necessary, I couldn't allow him to come between me and Ciara.

Once he found out what I desired, he'd take it from me just to fuck with me. Sibling rivalry wasn't supposed to go on for centuries. Siblings were a human concept.

Whoever made me and Fearghas was clearly just bored and wanted to watch the world burn. We were like flame to dried sticks—easy to light aflame. The accelerant of pandemonium. I was sure we actually caused our lands to burn during some fight I'd long since forgotten about. Fighting over which farmer with a torch we'd torture next.

We hadn't always been like this, though—at each other's throats.

I guess being immortal could do that to you. If you didn't die, you lived long enough to watch yourself become the villain in someone else's story.

Sure, I'd give her as much time and space as she needed. I had plenty of that to give. If that was all it took to get her to forgive me, I'd do it in a heartbeat. I'd have to do better by her little by little, even if I didn't know exactly how to get there, or even where to start.

I could at least try. Maybe that would be the best and scariest place to start with her.

CHAPTER 14

I knew time was of the essence for me to try my hand at swordsmanship with Finn. He'd be arriving any moment, as a matter of fact. I donned my most comfortable form-fitting attire, made up of soft black leggings and a long-sleeve turtleneck shirt. My hair was pinned up in a low, sleek bun so it wouldn't get in the way.

I remained barefoot so my feet could get a good grip on the wood floor.

It was my understanding from the tales I'd read that footwork was a major component in the art of swordplay. I'd be ready for anything he'd throw my way.

Well, unless it was a sword. I had terrible hand-eye coordination. Hopefully, these training sessions would help.

Finn arrived with a double knock on the door. I was excited to begin. How many people in the world got personalized sword training with an expert from the Irish government? I'd bet money that it was just me.

"Hi, Finn! Welcome! Make yourself at home. Where would you like to set up?" My voice pitched higher with every statement. If he hadn't already realized if I was an eager student, he'd have figured it out by now.

"Hello, Ciara. I just need empty space with no breakable items nearby." Finn scanned the surrounding rooms for a suitable space but found none within eyesight that were compliant.

"Perhaps it would be better in the solar room? It's spacious and has great natural light as well," I suggested.

"Lead the way," Finn replied with a hand raised palm-up in front of him. I led the way up the stairs, just above the great hall.

We walked down the extravagant hallway, lined with emerald runners with floral motifs. Carved mahogany panels adorned the walls before they gave way to wallpaper that resembled hawthorn branches accented in gold. Short swords with jeweled hilts were displayed proudly on the walls.

I turned the corner into the solar room, a grand room with floor-to-ceiling windows and skylights that made it the brightest room in all the castle. In the far corner of the room was a majestic fireplace with ornately carved white marble. On either side stood two of the largest leather club chairs I'd ever laid eyes on. An oil painting of the Irish landscape stood proudly above the mantel.

It was the perfect space for our lesson, open and with plenty of light. Nothing around for me to possibly break. Finn placed his long bags on the chairs and retrieved a pair of practice swords for us to use. Each one was long and skinny with a rubber tip, wide hilt, and rounded guard.

"These are called rapiers," Finn began. "They're used in fencing and it will be our safest option for practice until we can get you comfortable enough to graduate to the real deal. We'll start with the foundations that every swordsman, or woman, must make second nature when practicing—and especially while fighting. Breath and footwork. Both will ground you and help you think clearly. First, breathe in through your nose and out through your mouth. Hold each breath for seven seconds. Try it. In"—he paused and demonstrated for me—"and out. Good job. Keep going, and be mindful of your breath. You'll notice your body start to relax. Oxygen is flowing freely through your bloodstream. This helps loosen up your body for more complex footwork and keeps your head clear when faced with a stressful situation. Feel free to practice breathwork outside of our practices as well."

I did as he asked. My chest slowly filled with air, as if it were a balloon. When I thought I might pop, I exhaled for the next count. On the exhale, I could feel my shoulders sag and my jaw release its tension.

Subconsciously, I was holding in my stress and nerves to get this session right. My joints felt loose and free. I was ready for the next lesson.

"Excellent. Now keep this in mind while we work on your stance: Your hips are your center of gravity. Too far to one side and you'll be off balance, letting your opponent easily knock you off your feet and either disarm you...or dismember you." He left no room for any possibility of a mistake with that comment, poised to scare me into position.

"Level your feet with your shoulders. Even your stance. Good. Now you're about as movable as a mountain. Note how it feels."

Finn was an excellent teacher. Quite honestly, he was already one of the best teachers I'd ever had. He pushed gently into my shoulder but with only enough strength to prove his point. I wasn't going anywhere.

"See? Your hips, feet, and shoulders are all aligned. If someone was going to try and take you down or sweep you off balance, those are the three points that your opponent would need to make sure are out of alignment to do so. By creating a good foundation for your body, you have the upper hand already." He stepped back and paused before continuing.

"Next is the walking stance. This one is a little trickier to nail. Start by bringing your non-dominant foot out in front of you, just shorter than a pace's length. It should also be the same width as your shoulders, and don't forget to bend your knees slightly. This allows for you to be mobile enough to lunge backward and dodge any strikes from your opponent—or forward to make an attack—all while staying grounded."

He demonstrated with the rapier before he taught me all about proper grips, parts of a sword and the right way to hold it for specific attacks. We practiced basic maneuvers and stances and breathing.

For now, I would start with honing my walking stance. Then, I'd move on to being able to hold a sword for more than a few moves without getting tired.

Today focused on the foundations, and then we'd go from there. I practiced a little while longer before I could feel it in my legs. I'd definitely need to practice before our next lesson.

"I need to take a break, Finn. You're a better teacher than

you realize you know." I smiled up at him to find him matching my emotions in return. Maybe we both needed today more than we'd realized.

"Okay," he said shortly after, with a clap of his hands. "Take a quick break, get hydrated, and then we'll start round two."

CHAPTER 15

The next day I was back out in the rose garden when something odd caught my attention. A slight discoloration of the stones resembling a walled-off entryway was in the far corner of the building. As if someone had rebuilt that section of the stone more recently than the rest of the exterior.

Underneath the newer stone-work, there was a rather plain slab of concrete where every other part of the pathway featured had an intricate inlay of moss-lined brick–an indication that it was put here recently. If only I had come out here sooner, I would have noticed the discrepancies in the brick versus the slab; any later, and they'd have been covered by a blanket of snow.

My years spent grimly watching murder documentaries taught me that poured concrete can hide almost anything. My heart dropped to the floor as my body stood rooted to the ground. Either I would find something completely macabre here, or this was the entrance to that damn secret room that had evaded me at every other turn.

Hoping for the latter, I took a calming inhale, practicing my breaths. My father's stash of medieval weapons hopefully included a heavy iron mallet; otherwise, I would need to find another tool for my DIY demo, which was improbable.

I found the nearest entrance and made my way to the display room, where I had first noticed most of the weapons. I entered the room off to the side of the front entrance, lined with plush emerald runners and illuminated oak display cabinets.

It reminded me of a museum, and I suppose it was. It housed all types of weaponry from different eras. Some made of chiseled glass, some of iron and steel, some fit for a king lined with rubies, emeralds and sapphires. I quickly spotted what I'd come here for: a large and expertly crafted Damascus mallet featuring a wooden handle etched with ivy designs.

While it was too nice for the job I needed it for, it would have to suffice.

I plucked it from the display case, immediately underestimating the weight of the mallet. It was a wonder how anyone could swing this around during battle like it was a piece of rope at a rodeo. I winced when I imagined all the gore it no doubt played a part in over time, and was grateful it had found a happier retirement in the display case of my father's house.

I nearly had to lift it up off of the floor before dragging it back outside to the curious slab. This would not be easy. My many trips walking up the path to Sugarloaf were of no use to me where my weak arms were involved. If I could lift it above my head, gravity would have to be my friend to crack the concrete on its way back down. My body was still sore from training with Finn, and the mallet had to clock in at around fifty pounds. It was just so massive and dense.

I steadied my heavy breathing as I returned to the slab, mallet in hand.

Preparing myself to strike, I carefully swung the mallet above my head like I was chopping wood. When it landed, it made a loud *crack*.

Oh, good. Just about twenty more of those swings and I could break through the concrete. No big deal, right?

Despite being winded after just the first swing, I got ready for another. Soon, I had made some pretty decent progress cracking open the concrete, taking breaks along the way. Those initial swings created a large crack, enough to expose a rusted door handle below.

The more I swung, the more I revealed what the concrete was covering up. After an hour or so of hammering, sweating, and taking intermittent breaks, I finally found what I sought.

Two latched metal doors, chained together with a lock that appeared to lead to an undercroft. The door handle was a rusted reddish color, similar to the key from the safe. I had the key in my pocket, just in case.

Turns out, today, the fates were on my side.

I fit the key into the lock and it clicked open. Satisfied that I was finally about to find some answers, I swung open the doors.

The air was stale and dusty. I coughed at the thick cloud of dust that swirled, disturbed by my presence. The stairs below were about as old as the house, or perhaps even older. There were cracks and chips in the steep stone steps that led to the undercroft.

Silken spiderwebs covered every corner of the entryway. Daddy long-legs spiders scattered deeper into the cellar area. A few seemed to almost vibrate in the webs because of my disruptions. Since I was a daddy's girl, I almost found it ironic that these arachnids were here in my father's castle, though I knew how common they were.

Unfortunately, they lived on every continent, including Antarctica. Maybe it was because my dad had filled my head with the old wives' tale that daddy long-legs have the most potent venom of all the spider species, but their fangs are really just too small to puncture the skin. It was only later in life that I learned how, while they did have a short fang structure, they simply could not produce a medically significant bite to humans—even if their chosen prey was the notorious Red back widow spider.

In reality, the only reason they can kill their infamous prey is because of their ability to cast their lengths of silky webs onto their prey from a safe distance, incapacitating them.

I cautiously trekked through the tunnel of the undercroft.

To my dismay, it was equally as spidery and musky as the stairs. The path was as quiet as the dead, besides the occasional drip of water seeping from the old pipes. As I got far enough into the narrow crawl space, where the light no longer reached, I brought my phone's flashlight out to illuminate the way. The path wound around what I assumed was the length of the castle.

I knew eventually where it would lead to: the small room underneath the library from the blueprint. Finding this room couldn't come soon enough. I was trying to not think about all the mold and asbestos that inhabited this putrid tunnel as I pressed on, and especially not about my eight-legged companions.

In a few more moments, my phone's light revealed a solid iron door with a rusted red doorknob, an identical color match to the key in my pocket.

Despite its wear, it was another perfect fit as I turned it clockwise. As my fingers grasped the rusted handle, a layer of dust and grime coated my skin. Gross.

The heavy door groaned in protest as I pushed against it, resisting the movement after years of neglect. A deep, guttural creak echoed through the silence. Particles of dust and dirt swirled, disturbed from their age-long rest, filling the air further with the scent of rot and decay. Brittle and corroded hinges shrieked as the iron door reluctantly inched open.

At least, the room behind the door revealed itself to me as a hidden armory.

The room appeared to be carved from a boulder, making it fireproof. I noticed that someone had turned off the advanced security alarm, despite the eclectic mix of medieval and modern security measures. Eerily convenient for me, but it was unlike my father to not keep a secret room like this protected night and day. Hell, even the key had been in a safe.

I noticed the room was much cleaner than the underground passages, indicating far more frequent use, perhaps even recently.

Its ceilings were low compared to the rest of the house, yet still more elevated than a traditional six-foot ceiling. Most likely customized so my father could stand in it comfortably, as he stood a few inches over six feet tall himself. I'd inherited his height gene for sure. I would have a difficult time here had he adhered to the classic height of underground ceilings.

My mother, however, would have had plenty of head room, as she was of average Sicilian height, standing around five feet four inches.

Toward the far wall, I noticed a decorated display at the center of the room, but its contents were empty. Very odd. *Extremely* concerning.

I knew exactly what it must've held: the Sword of Light. I bit my lip as I realized why it most likely wasn't there, along with the reason my father wasn't.

On a shaken breath, I took in the rest of my surroundings. Full knight armor was on display in all four corners of the wide room, facing inward, as if phantoms of guards were standing watch over this room. I'd thought the armory in the castle was excessive, but the contents of this room were nothing short of exorbitant.

Flickering warm sconces illuminated the room, mimicking candlelight just enough to show the true art of the weapons and armor in the room.

There were double-headed axes, curved swords, and daggers made from shiny black stone that looked to be carved by hand. Every piece was an absolute work of art and must have held a significant history in order to be displayed here, instead of in the castle's armory with the other beautiful pieces.

Of course, I was interested in the only piece that wasn't in its home.

I was on a frustrating and seemingly endless search for this sword; it had become more of an investigation. However, instead of finding invaluable rewards, I would only find closure about my father's demise.

Closure was comparable to a monster in itself. It relieved you of the demon on your shoulder, constantly nagging at the need to know the last moments your loved one experienced before they left this physical world. Only to be replaced by the endless torture of knowing how they went, and that you couldn't stop it from happening.

But what if you could have?

Closure. A double-edged sword, emotionally similar to many that were on full display in this armory. Instead of imparting physical wounds, no matter what side you spliced, it would only leave emotional scars on my heart. Even knowing that, once I learned of his exact cause of death, it could be so unsettling that it could make me want to throw up, I still sought its closure. No more not having the answers I've been living in the dark about all these years. No more.

If I wanted to take over my father's role as protector of the supernatural beings of this land, I'd need to start here, if only for myself. It was time I put on my oxygen mask before helping others, if you will.

Ultimately, the Sword of Light wasn't here, so it definitely wasn't safe out there. There was another monster that I needed to fight in my quest for the Sword of Light, but for me, it would be the sword of *truth*. I knew that the sword's new owner, wherever they were, would know the terrible truth of my father's death.

For my trouble, I decided to take a small concealable weapon as a souvenir, just in case I'd needed it for my quest. I spotted a beautiful shiny dagger in the far-right corner, next to the ghostly armor display.

I probably picked the most aesthetically appealing weapon over the most functional in the room. Based on the carvings alone, I could tell it was a medieval Irish weapon. It may have been forged from iron in its origin, but the leaf-shaped blade was aged with a darker patina.

Along the hilt and base, a prominent Celtic Dara knot was carved, intertwining with other knots to give some grip to the pommel.

The bladesmith had carved the hilt purely from black tourmaline stone, most likely believing it would protect its bearer. There were no other jewels or extravagant details on the blade, other than the expert engraving on the blade and hilt.

The worn black leather sheath also featured embossed intertwining Celtic knots. Hopefully, I'd never need to use it, but in the meantime, it would serve as a new piece of art to place on my nightstand.

I put the dagger and its sheath in my back pocket. Locking the not-so-secret-anymore room, I exited through the tunnel pathway and back up into the castle.

As I marched through the garden grass and made my way up the stone steps to the castle, I couldn't help but feel a little lighter. Lighter in the sense that a burden I hadn't realized I'd been carrying with me had lifted ever so slightly. Even though the iron dagger at my side was fairly heavy for its size, I had a bounce in my step. I had gotten some kind of closure and that counted for something.

The Solais Sword existed, according to the plaque on its empty stand, and my father had been its previous owner.

According to the bridal quest I'd read about, that had also made him a target.

CHAPTER 16

The following morning, I heard the door knocker pounding on the front entry. I made sure that my newly acquired dagger was hidden under the length of my jacket before answering the door.

The man who greeted me was familiar. Slightly older than my father, and standing just under six feet. He had taupe hair that glimmered a warm auburn hue in the sun, and a traditionally Irish complexion with freckles speckling his entire body. He donned a neatly pressed suit and sported a full beard, just as white as copper. Mirrored black sunglasses hid the color of his eyes, and if I hadn't already known he was part of the secret government agency of Ireland, I'd guess he was part of an alien hunter team with Will Smith.

"Hello, Finn," I said.

"Is now a good time, Miss Driscoll? I apologize for arriving unannounced. May I come in so we can discuss this matter privately?"

"Sure, Finn. Right this way. Should I be concerned? Am I in danger?"

I led him into the sitting area next to the library. Given the secretive nature of his business, I was worried that I actually was in danger. It was quite possible that I'd been so closed off mentally to my surroundings due to grief that I had completely overlooked any potential dangers nearby.

"I don't have reason to believe you are in immediate danger, Miss Driscoll. But we can never be too certain. At this point, I am sure you are aware of the classified sector of the government agency that your father and I are a part of. We have been trying to hold out as long as possible to give you an appropriate amount of time to grieve his loss, as all of us at the office have been doing as well. However, the head of our agency would like to meet with you regarding your father."

He finally removed his sunglasses and hung his head at that statement. This was not good.

"On that note, Miss Driscoll, I would like to bring you into the office to discuss this with a few more members of the supernatural team. Have I interrupted anything?"

"No, it's alright, Finn. We can go, but I have no means of transportation. My steward is on a leave of bereavement and he usually would be my driver."

"My condolences for his loss as well. Don't worry—I'll drive us, Miss Driscoll."

"Thank you, Finn. Please hold on for a moment. I just have to gather a few things upstairs before we leave."

I grabbed my belongings. Wallet, phone, keys? Check.

After I returned downstairs, I led the way out to the driveway.

Sure enough, an all-black BMW SUV sat at the end of my driveway, just past the circle, not too close to the front door.

"Hop in the front, Ciara, and we'll be off. We are traveling to our headquarters near Carlingford. It's about an hour's drive from here."

Carlingford was a quaint waterside town, known for its rich medieval history. It was a perfect setting for a supernatural-focused agency.

After we both buckled our seatbelts, he set off for our destination. The SUV had a smooth and quiet ride compared to the town car. A few quiet minutes passed before I broke the silence with a question.

"How long had you and my father been working together?"

"This year would have made twenty. He was my favorite partner, but I didn't dare tell him that, or I would have heard the end of it. I like to think he knew it, 'cause I'd always bring him his favorite coffee from the corner shop down the street from my house when we'd work early days. I'll never forget when he found out your ma was pregnant with you. He damn near kissed me with excitement and I nearly knocked him out."

 Finn looked absolutely crestfallen at the memories.

I could tell he was heartbroken about the passing of his work partner, my father. It made me angry to think that someone out there could just remove someone from this earth who was so well loved by family and friends alike. Someone who had so much love in his heart that his absence would be missed by many.

I couldn't help but picture them together. My father, all smiles and sunshine and wearing down Finn's tough exterior to reveal his soft warm center, less a punch or two to the face in the process. Their days would have depended on playful banter to lighten the heavy subject matter that was the nature of their work. I tried to remember if there ever was a time that my father had brought Finn up in conversations with me, but nothing came to mind.

 This knowledge, that he had a friendship this strong when he was here on business, and how that was probably the reason why he would look forward to it so much, made me happy. For them both. Friendships like that made life a little more bearable, smiles easier, laughter more freely flowing.

Bonds like that made you feel safe in your skin, where you could let your guard down and feel comfortable sharing your deepest secrets. I could only imagine what other secrets and life events were shared between them throughout almost twenty years.

I looked over at Finn, his eyes still on the road, and my mouth curved up on one side in a knowing half-smile. For the memory he shared with me, one of thousands that he and my father had together, now only one side of the bittersweet story would live on through Finn's perspective.

"Thank you for sharing, Finn. I can imagine him like that with you, now that I've met you and trained with you. I like to imagine him always happy. Thank you for being a good friend to him."

I was truly grateful for him, and also sad for him, now that he'd lost a good partner.

"It was your da that broke me down and was a friend to me, Ciara," Finn said.

I was silent for a moment or two before I spoke again.

"So where exactly are these headquarters?"

Bringing myself back to my initial thoughts, I decided

changing the subject to a less heavy one might be in both of our best interests for the remainder of the drive.

"You'll see. We're roughly fifteen minutes away now." I trusted his estimated time of arrival, even though he had no GPS on the dashboard of his car. Either because it was untraceable, being a secret location from the public, or because he didn't want me knowing how to get there, or both. Time would tell. I wasn't great with the concept of patience, but I was learning every day since I arrived in Ireland.

I cracked the window open to get some fresh air. It must have been hidden in plain sight. There would be no other logical explanation for it. Finn pulled off the road onto a dirt path—I saw why he had the SUV. You needed traction on all four wheels to get through this terrain.

"You know how the agency got started? It was a group of knights in the fourteenth century. One day, while they were traveling across Ireland, they found a creature that was not of this world. It was a fae and it helped aid their path to their destination, obliterating any dangers along the way with their elemental powers. The fire wielders helped keep them warm at night. The warriors kept the beasts that dwelled in the bogs and marshes at bay. However, not every fairy kind had good intentions. The fae protected the knights from those malevolent types, as well. In exchange, they made a promise to protect each other for centuries to come. While the fae kind would outlive the humans, each member was passed down for generations and swore the oath. I expect that is why the president of our agency's sector, Catherine, called us in today."

Wow—that was quite a bit to take in. And it was no wonder my father had left warnings about dealings with the fae. Now here I was, about to swear an oath to continue my father's legacy of protecting the balance between mortals and the fae of the land.

CHAPTER 17

E ventually, the path led to the mouth of a man-made cave. We drove right through it before stopping as soon as the vehicle was completely covered in darkness.

Finn rolled down his window and a biometric authenticator rose from the ground. This was definitely the place. He placed his hand on the authenticator pad and it flashed green to verify our access. A voice spoke through a hidden speaker to welcome his arrival.

"Hello, Finn. I see you have a guest with you. Miss, please state your name and the purpose for your arrival today, then hold up your identification card with the window rolled down."

"My name is Ciara Driscoll, Sean Driscoll's daughter. Give me just a moment to—"

"Welcome, Miss Driscoll. No need for your ID. We have been eager to meet Sean Driscoll's daughter. You will be greeted by Catherine Tierney, our president, in the lobby when you arrive."

Guess I wouldn't need to scrounge through my bag for my identification card.

For them to bypass their typical security routine at the mention of my father was peculiar. I guess they really were anticipating the arrival of the next generation to take over my father's position here.

The hidden lift we pulled up on groaned as we slowly descended below.

In a few moments, we were in an underground parking garage full of high-end vehicles, mostly black SUV's. Finn parked in a reserved spot and I followed him through the tinted sliding glass doors. The hue on the doors was mirrored, similar to the sunglasses he wore earlier. The type of tint they'd use in interrogation rooms, where you can see through from the outside, but the person on the inside couldn't see out.

Finn scanned his retinas, and we were in. We walked down an all-white hallway with fluorescents that turned on one-by-one, with each of our movements. I walked just a pace behind Finn as he led the way to meet with Catherine.

"Don't worry, Ciara—you'll like Catherine. Your father was her right-hand man. He was offered a position as vice president, but turned it down to focus more on family."

"So, he turned down what I'd imagine was a highly sought after position, for... me? Wouldn't she hate me for being the cause of that?"

"I suppose so, if you look at it that way, but she would never hate you for it. Catherine has a daughter who hasn't spoken to her for years because, unlike your father, Catherine prioritized her work first. Her belief was that it would provide everything her daughter could want: a roof over her head, a nice savings account, you know what I mean. But the thing about money is, it can't buy time or love, which was all her daughter ever wanted from her. She sends her gifts every year for her birthday, but her daughter never even calls. Which is saying something, because I believe she is the receptionist at your father's lawyer's office. Catherine may be envious, but she is the most courteous person I've ever met, besides your father. Don't repeat that we had this conversation though, please."

I wasn't expecting Finn to divulge that much information about her, but I was grateful that he had. I was feeling a little anxious about meeting the president right off the bat, especially after Finn caught me up on how the agency got here in the first place. Maybe he could sense my nervous energy.

"It'll be our first secret, Finn. I'm sorry to hear about her daughter, but thank you for confiding in me. I do feel a little better now about meeting her. Thanks."

We rounded the corner to the lobby, a sleek yet stark modern lounge area. It contained basic seating arrangements, no extra frills. A large leather couch with two high-back domed chairs, a coffee table and an end chair, all black in contrast to the white room surrounding it.

A beautiful statuesque woman, possibly in her late fifties, rose from one of the chairs. She had a sleek, bright blonde bob with freshly done highlights. Kohl eyeliner and full lashes framed beautiful jade eyes that displayed slight wrinkles at the outer corners. She greeted me with a broad smile and a firm handshake.

She commanded the space that she was in, not only with her height but with her confidence. It gave an energy to the room that was contagious.

To be a president of a government agency, in a predominantly male territory, must have—ironically—taken balls. To face many years of probably being overlooked for promotions and still come up on top despite it all, was admirable.

She was tenacious for giving her work her undivided attention, even though it inadvertently made her daughter not want to speak to her. I couldn't imagine how hard that must be for her, to continue her work and have it simultaneously crack her heart open. It had to weigh heavy on her mind and her soul.

"It's very nice to meet you, Ciara. My name is Catherine. I'm the president of the supernatural sector of the Irish government, also known as 'The Agency.' I've heard so much about you from your father, and I'm delighted to finally meet you. I'm sure Finn has filled you in on your father, Sean, being my right hand. My team and I are heartbroken by the news. We are so grateful to have you join us today. Why don't we go to my office where we can have the rest of this conversation more privately?"

I got the impression that she was a wonderful mother, regardless of what her daughter may have felt. At least she was trying, which was more than I could say for my own mother. She also seemed genuinely sad about the loss of my father, her coworker.

"Sounds great, Catherine. Lead the way."

I followed her down a hallway at the opposite end of the lobby, fluorescent tube lights illuminating the way. Her stilettos would not be my first choice of footwear, given the length of the halls we walked down, but I suppose you have to keep up with appearances as the president of a government agency.

The size of the underground quarters was staggering. After a few more turns down the maze of hallways, we finally reached her office. It had floor-to-ceiling glass that was likely bullet-proof and soundproof, with mirrored tints consistent with the rest of the building. She used her pass card to gain entry and motioned for us to take a seat at the couches on the far wall. Once we all settled in, it was straight down to business.

"So, Ciara, I imagine you already know a great deal about what we do here. If I know Finn, he's already filled you in on how we came about. I thought it would be best to continue our conversation in the privacy of my office."

That was the same grit that got her here, so I'm not sure why I was expecting her to bring me back here for a simple conversation. That was not going to happen here. She took a seat behind her desk, a throne of power.

"I am so sorry to have to break the news to you, but we have finally received your father's autopsy results. It appears he was a victim of homicide by an outside force."

"Outside force?" I asked her.

"A supernatural being or object. Possibly both. We were only able to ascertain that the stab wounds we found were made by an enchanted object, similar to that of a sword."

The Solais Sword. I was absolutely numb from her words, so Catherine got the preset answer my brain had formatted for all matters to safeguard whatever was left of my heart. At least she'd handpicked *her* words, like she'd done this dozens of times—and she probably had.

I shouldn't have let it irritate me, but grief manifested in nearly as many forms as the Pooka.

Sometimes, before you can get closure, you must first suffer terribly. It was life's way of keeping you in check. If you were taking advantage of every single moment with the people you loved as if every single interaction was your last, then it very well could be. How crucial it was to end every single one of those moments by telling them you loved them and leaving nothing unsaid. It would be a way of life moving forward now.

"Thank you for telling me, Catherine." I mustered the strength to form the words.

In truth, I wasn't thankful. Despite having some closure about it, I felt my heart ripped from its cage all over again, like I'd felt that day I found out my father no longer breathed the same air as I did.

"I truly am sorry about your loss, Ciara. I'd love to meet with you again when you are ready. Finn, would you mind bringing Ciara again, once we set on a date?"

"Sure can, Catherine." Finn finally spoke. He stood from his chair and nodded for me to follow him to his office.

"Catherine, it was nice to meet you, despite everything. I look forward to meeting with you again."

I gave her my best forced smile and goodbye handshake. Something told me it would be the first of many hand-shakes with her. She made her way toward the door and held it open for us to exit. I followed Finn back down the brightly lit hall.

Finn held a quick pace, and it took some effort to keep up. As we rounded a few corners and were far enough from Catherine's office to be out of ear shot. He said over his shoulder, "I know that was a lot to take in, Ciara. How are you feeling?"

I appreciated that he waited until I was out of ear shot to gauge my actual feelings about what I'd just learned about my father's death. With moments like those, it was hard to let my emotions go in front of a stranger.

I didn't say anything and instead began to bawl my eyes out crying.

CHAPTER 18

Someone designed the hallways more to the likes of a labyrinth, not a standard office building. The dead ends held restrooms or offices, and the halls wound around every which way, rarely staying straight for long. If I hadn't kept up with Finn's pace, I'd surely have gotten lost.

We finally made our way back to the elevators. I was grateful that he wanted to get me out of there so quickly. Tears blurred my vision as we exited the building.

"Finn, what's your plan?" I asked through heavy breaths.

"Just follow me and I'll explain later."

Why did I keep getting my questions diverted? This was growing increasingly frustrating. We entered the elevators and Finn pressed a button on the side panel.

I held eye contact with Finn until the elevator doors opened, as if I could read his thoughts the longer I stared. We exited the elevator to the garage level we'd parked on, but I couldn't help the growing feeling in my gut that something else was amiss, besides the autopsy findings. We went straight to his car and got in, then he started the engine.

"Ciara, as you can imagine, inside there is audio *and* video surveillance. We can speak more freely in my car. I apologize if my hasty exit frightened you. I received a notification on my tracking device about one of the Pookas' whereabouts while we were in Catherine's office. The last thing I wanted to do was interrupt. We can look over your father's security system footage anytime, but they are on the move. Buckle up.

He then paused to hand me a tissue. "Let it out, Ciara. That was an intense first meeting.
I wasn't expecting her to tell you about the autopsy. I didn't even know about it before that meeting."

I clicked the seat belt into place and we were off. The tires screeched in the parking garage even though we were moving at a leisurely speed limit, adding to the drama of us leaving unannounced. It wasn't very inconspicuous of us, but we left regardless.

We'd both deal with any repercussions later, if we got caught.

Once we made it up and out of the lift, it was raining outside. *Of course it was.*

Finn smoothly made his way back onto the country road and we were off in whatever direction his tracker led him to.

We trailed through the patchwork greenery that is the Irish landscape. I wasn't too familiar with the roads outside of my primary towns of Malahide and Dublin, but it began to look familiar enough that I could tell we were driving toward where we'd come from.

After about twenty minutes of driving, I recognized Sugarloaf in the distance.

"Ciara, I got word that there have been 'animal sightings'—or rather Pooka sightings, as I'm sure you're aware of by now—near Sugarloaf. That is where we are headed now. Good thing you aren't in heels, as we'll be walking."

It had to be Uallas. I didn't want to see him, but when you left out bits of information, like your friendship with said Pookas, you don't get a say in what happened after the fact. I'd just have to bite my tongue and hope Uallas would do the same. I just stared out the window, trying to comprehend everything that had just taken place.

My thoughts were rampant. I was taking in my quickly moving surroundings as I asked Finn, "Should I be worried? This seems rather dangerous."

"Do you want the truth or an easy-to-swallow answer?" he replied, eyes glued to the road. There was almost a paternal quality to his words—my father must have really rubbed off on him.

No one had ever laid it out like that for me before, instead just defaulting to watered-down truths throughout my entire life, especially regarding my father. Would I even be ready for the truth if I were to ask for it? I had so much to wrap my head around as it stood. Should I just go for the comfort of the easy to swallow answer? When dealing with so many new and discomforting facts, would this be the last straw for my sanity?

Whatever I chose, I had to make the decision quickly.

"I'll take the easy way out this time, Finn. It's all been a lot to take in."

Maybe it was a cop-out, a sorry excuse for me to ask for the easy way out. All of the emotions I've built up these few months since arriving came over me in a wave. The comfort and pleasure from Conor, the curiosity of my father's double life, and the shock of knowing Pooka didn't just exist on the pages of my favorite books. Not to mention the new knowledge that my father had been *murdered*.

I needed the soft, fuzzy coddling in his answer, at least for now. I was grateful he gave me the option, for whenever I would be ready to hear it.

"What if I told you to just keep your guard up when we get to our destination? Is that a safe enough answer for you?"

Super dodgy answer. Just what I asked for.

"Just what I ordered, doc," I said as I leaned my head against the car door frame and closed my eyes.

We still had a way to go before reaching our destination, so I figured a little nap couldn't hurt. If anything, it would help me keep my guard up when we arrived as he'd asked for.

I tried to relax my mind by counting how long my breaths were. Inhale for four seconds, hold for seven, exhale for eight, and repeat. It took me about three sets of those breathing sequences before I drifted off. I knew this because what replaced my thoughts were images of Fearghas.

To be more specific: Fearghas and I.

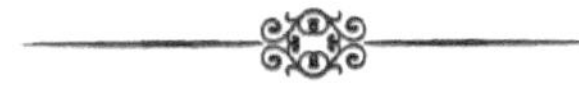

I stared up at him. My eyes roamed over every ridge and plane of his muscled body, up to the very tip of his obsidian horns, before getting lost in the fire of his eyes.

There was a flock of starlings performing a show behind him, like millions of drones in an ever-changing cloud of black, but I hardly paid them any attention. He smelled of spice and ferns, and I drank in his presence in front of me. His usual playfully handsome smirk was absent, and instead, a foreign expression of concern painted his face.

"You shouldn't be here."

The velvety-smooth voice caressed my ears. I felt my heartbeat quicken as my vision narrowed on the expression on his face.

His brows knitted together, studying me. There was a sadness there as he looked me over. His hand reached under my chin and he lifted it slightly, so our eyes locked.

It may have been barely a minute, but it felt like an eternity. Despite the sharp angles of his face, there was a tenderness in his eyes.

"But I always find you here," I replied.

He was a welcomed infiltration to my dreams, ever since that first time after I first moved into the castle. I should be angry he was in my dreams, but I savored the distraction. I'd known somehow we could meet in the astral realm of my dreams.

I shouldn't feel anything for him, especially since I still couldn't count him out as my father's murderer. What girl could resist a man who was potentially a villain, but equally her guardian? His burning gaze said I was both his ruin and his reason for being here.

"Maybe I shouldn't be here either, Sunshine, but for reasons I cannot understand, I cannot stay away..."

His expression of concern shifted into pain as easily as he could change physical forms. I felt my heart-beat pound in my chest as my soul ached for him. Maybe it was because I was emotionally drained, but he appeared harmless in my dreams.

As if that was his cue for an exit, the visual of him dissolved, like sunshine on the ripples of a pool. My vision went black, and he was gone...

I awoke with a gasp, feeling lonely, regardless of the fact that Finn was right beside me.

"Bad dream, eh? I'm not *that* scary," Finn said, a slight tone of amusement in his voice. I appreciated his effort to lighten the mood, but it wasn't working.

"No, no. It wasn't that. How far away are we now?"

I just left it there, as I changed the subject. Typical Ciara move. A moment for just me to indulge in and ponder over. My heart was still racing after my interaction with Fearghas in my sleep. I furrowed my brows trying to make something of the conflict I saw in his face without raising an alarm to Finn.

My eyes darted out the window to gain a sense of my new surroundings.

"About ten minutes out now, Sleeping Beauty. Are you ready?"

I chuckled at the impromptu nickname. I could only imagine how many nicknames he'd given my father over the span of their partnership. It made my heart ache again for all the good times they'd shared, knowing there would be no more nicknames or banter between them.

I smiled grimly, because I had a feeling that would be another thing I hadn't expected to live up to, taking over for my father. It was probably a comfort for Finn to start the banter early on, so just because I'd taken a nap in the car, I was now labeled a fairy-tale princess. If only that was all it took to become one.

"As ready as I'll ever be, Finn. I'll be keeping my guard up, as instructed. You take the lead."

The corner of his mouth rose in a grin, and I couldn't help but wonder if I reminded him of my father at that moment. His eyes remained planted on the curve of the road ahead as he followed the turn toward Sugarloaf. It was gradually growing larger in the distance. I couldn't help but wonder exactly what awaited us and where our destination would lead. Would it be Sugarloaf or another undisclosed location Finn knew of?

But what use would it be to mull it over and over in my head when we would arrive there in a matter of minutes? These were just my anxious thoughts coming to the surface to taunt me. They'd always been the devil on my shoulder, making any situation intolerable.

My nap wasn't as calming as I'd hoped it would be either. When can a girl catch a break?

Unaware of my new surroundings, we came to a halt on a gravel pathway surrounded by golden aspen, the Sugarloaf hill behind us.

I took note of the surrounding landmarks. The dense forest, full of varying shades of golds and reds and spots of evergreen, opened up in the center to an inky body of water. It could only be...

"Lough Guinness." Finn continued my thoughts aloud. "I've seen a bit of activity here lately, but was never close enough to investigate, like I was today. Stay close, Ciara."

I nodded in agreement as Finn awaited my confirmation before exiting the vehicle. He headed off toward the forest, mapping the tracker on his phone in the palm of his hand like a compass. I stayed a few paces behind him, peeking in between the scattered rows of tree trunks to see if I could spot Uallas or possibly Fearghas.

It would be no use. They could be in any of their many forms, likely not in the familiar human forms they reserved for me. If so, they'd risk sticking out like a sore thumb in the middle of the desolate wooded area. Humans rarely came here; it was part of the protected lands. Not to mention, the glowing eyes and horns would probably have given them away as something other than of this world.

They'd have far better luck blending in at the comic cons back in Florida.

There were no set paths near Lough Guinness. We weaved in and out of trees, over downed stumps. Wherever Finn went, I followed. I wasn't exactly wearing hiking boots, but I made do. Leaves crunching under our footsteps told us we were the only ones here. Silence filled the space around us, except for the occasional sparrow chirping in the trees or squirrel darting around the dirt that was covered in leaves and sticks. We pressed on deeper into the forest, the lake displayed on our far left.

Finn stopped abruptly, holding his hand up in a fist to have me take a pause as well. About twenty yards away, a pure white fox peered out from behind the telltale reddish bark of a yew tree. He slowly inched toward us with his back arched and tail curled, yapping at us in warning. His eyes were glowing yellow.

He was unmistakably Uallas.

"Ciara. Don't. Move," Finn warned me, but I was already one step ahead of him.

Even though Uallas wasn't in his usual human form, he was no less terrifying as a fox. Especially when he was clearly upset that I'd brought company.

It struck me as odd that the presence of Finn made him so on edge. Finn was one of the good guys. He sought to protect the Pookas so we could all live in harmony.

So why was Uallas all but baring his teeth at him, as if we were a threat?

"Finn, I know him. This Pooka. Why is he angry at you?"
I questioned carefully, aware that Uallas could hear me, too.

"Angry at me? We've protected them for centuries. What is the meaning of this, Uallas?"

I figured Uallas was aware we meant him no harm. Hell, he'd been able to read my intentions from day one, and now was no different. Maybe Finn's intentions were less than pure according to Uallas, or maybe he always carried a knife on him. The latter seemed the more accurate reason for the hostile greeting.

"You have the pointy thing on you, dontcha, Finn? Keep it away from me, you hear?" Uallas vocalized in his human voice, but it almost had a duality in its tone. As if two voices were speaking at once. The sound was enough to make my bones shiver.

I'd never heard him speak in that way before I made sure to keep a safe distance from him.

I could only speculate as to the source of his frustration: Was it the pointed item in Finn's pocket, or my now rather hypocritical request that he stay away from me after our previous encounter?

Either way, if I remembered one thing from my father's stories, it was that it was ill advised to upset a Pooka, should you ever come across one.

CHAPTER 19

UALLAS

What in the blazes was she doing here? Especially with *him.* Finn wasn't my favorite. Far from it, actually, but seeing him there with her just made this scenario a lot worse. I didn't like obstacles in my way.

I didn't think she'd sorted herself out from our last interaction, and it was fucking with my plans. He must have dragged her out here in search of me. He was always on the defensive. Meddling in my business.

Finn acted as if he could never do wrong. I thought The Agency was all about peace between our kind, yet he couldn't just leave me the hell alone. Ever since Finn first joined the human's government agency, he always made it a point to stick his nose in my business.

To study me, perhaps, but he put me off. He was never like the others, always well prepared in case of an altercation.

I despised it, I liked my targets easy.

It was as if he just assumed the worst in us, instead of trusting our capabilities of doing good. I had never once met him without him having at least one cold iron knife or dagger on him.

Not that he didn't hide it well, but I knew when I was in the presence of such a hindrance to my well-being. Finn always impeded my grand plans, and today was no different. He was truly a thorn in my side that I could not pluck out.

Irritations aside, it was so pleasant seeing her face far sooner than I had ever anticipated. The one thing that I would ever be grateful to Finn for, would be that he brought her here to me. I'd wager that Ciara left out every detail about our interactions recently, or he wouldn't have dragged her along on his little side quest to hunt me down. I'd even go as far as to say that she had left out the part about our little acquaintance altogether.

Why would you do that, dear? What an interesting creature you are, Ciara. But who are you really protecting? Us or yourself?

I wished I could have her all to myself now that she was here, but I'd still respect her wishes. She didn't seek me out on her own today, so I'd respectfully play along with her little games. She didn't know me well enough yet, and I didn't know her as well as I'd like, but that didn't matter.

She just knew my kind existed, at least. Otherwise, Finn wouldn't be here with her.

I had to know what she was feeling, despite a little voice in my head telling me not to go down that rabbit hole again with her.

You would think I'd be able to tell how these gifts work by now, but it's simply too hard to track in the infinite forms I can choose from, or to venture into the depths of reading emotions. No two souls are alike. This time, I wouldn't be planting an emotion on her, but rather feeling the emotion she currently had. This gift had helped me survive this long, through the savagery of when humans forged the first weapons against us.

Long through the bloody wars, the angst and disease of the famine and beyond. A lack of nourishment enraged humans. It made them unpredictable. Pookas didn't eat for sustainability, not as humans did, so that was a learning curve for me to sort through the intensity. If emotions had colors, the spectrum would never be fully complete.

I knew I still had a lot to learn about human emotions, not only because of what happened in the garden with her, but after all this time, I still made many mistakes regarding matters of the heart. It wouldn't be easy to explain to her how my gifts manifested, as I was still figuring them out centuries later. If I could try, it would start with me entering a room: the human mind. Within, I was either figuring out what kind of room I was in, given the decor, or the feelings I was given. Or it was up to me to do some redecorating of my own, planting the feelings there.

That would be my best analogy of these gifts.

My creators gave me this for ultimate survival, and here I was, still kicking. So it must work to some degree. If I came across someone who feels rage, I was supposed to plant calming emotions to diffuse the situation, but where was the fun in that?

I preferred to let the rage burn and would gladly add the accelerant to the flames. The thing about still being alive after all this time is that you got bored. What if I didn't plant those calming emotions as I should? I seldom did. What if I wanted to see what kind of fight they can give? They ended up begging me for their life. So, sometimes I let those thoughts win. Just for the fuckery.

They hadn't though about the irrefutable nature of the Pooka when they created me.

So then, to ensure balance, they created the other biggest pain in my arse: my brother, Fearghas. Besides the pointy things, and possibly Ciara, he was the only other one who could destroy me. Even unnatural things are created with a balance of life and death, good and bad, in mind.

Power could not surpass a certain threshold. However, even our mayhem had a limit. The rules of the Pooka.

I'd always thought of them more like guidelines, anyway. I could not get sidetracked here—*focus*, Uallas.

What could you possibly be feeling, my dear Ciara? I'll allow myself a little peek.

I channeled the part of me that could reach into her emotions. In my fox form, it caused my fur to rise as though electricity were coursing through my body. Maybe that was how this worked.

Electromagnetic waves of energy passing from being to being. Exchanging the transfer of emotions from one to another. My fox form chittered and snarled in warning but all that faded as I felt her thoughts. Tight tremors skittered down my body in response to sensing her emotion.

She was... scared. Scared of me?

I had to prove to her that she should not be scared of me, while politely getting Finn to fuck off. So, I did the only thing I could think of to put her at ease, while hopefully causing Finn to shite in his pants.

I closed my eyes and embraced the shift. Swirls of onyx shadows completely engulfed me. I always thought the shadows were a showy effect, until it came time for my bones to warp and snap, and for my organs to shift.

The shadows not only created a sound barrier, but also provided a curtain for the horrific view that was occurring for those not accustomed to seeing the shift. How polite.

The shadows subsided and before them stood my manly figure. I was quite proud of my form. It kept Ciara's eyes lingering a little longer on me than if I'd remained a fox form. Good. We were making progress.

Finn looked flabbergasted, practically tripping over up-turned tree roots at the sight of me. Of course, this time I'd shed my clothing and I was now standing before them, completely bare. It was much more of a nuisance to shift into a human form in clothes. Not only was it restricting when you were used to the animal form for so long, but it was extra work I didn't care to do.

To my relief, they both reacted as I'd hoped. The look on her face at the raw sight of me was absolutely delightful. I'd address it to her later. I had to have some fun and games with Finn first.

"Finnegan O'Leary, do you not find the sight of me as appealing as your associate does? Would you rather I have a goat head to go along with my horns? I think I quite enjoy every aspect of my—*form*..."

I looked down at my human male parts pointedly, enjoying how the sight of me on display was making both parties blush.

Except she did not look away. *Naughty girl*. She enjoyed the sight of me bare as much as I had enjoyed how easily it had turned her scared emotions into lustful ones. Maybe I could finally master this trick, after all.

I turned my attention toward Ciara.

"What about you—anything you'd like me to change for you, darling?"

She raised her eyebrows as she looked away and shook her head in reply.

Hmm, nothing to change. As I had anticipated. *Perfect*.

I paid extra attention to not call her dear and opted for darling instead. Hopefully, it was the right choice and my new pet name for her would suffice. I chuckled at how easily I had affected her.

"So, what brings the two of you to the secluded area of Lough Guinness? Unfortunately, ye see, I'm out of pints and the lake is just mere water. So please, enlighten me."

I felt Finn's anger begin to bubble as Ciara hid her laughter under a smile at my comment. Good—I was getting somewhere now. Piss off Finn enough that he gave up on whatever brought him out here in the first place, but not too much where he uses his daggers against me.

Do whatever it takes to get Ciara back into my good graces again. The plan was working. Finn remained unimpressed that my body was still exposed, likely feeling insecure because mine was superior to his and he knew it.

Finn asked me to cut the crap, and what I was up to, along with another string of varied, boring questions. I dodged them gracefully and efficiently. It wasn't much longer before the golden rays of the sun setting hinted at them that it was time to depart, and I was thankful for that, despite wishing Ciara would stay with me.

I remained in my nude human form to keep Finn uncomfortable and make sure he wouldn't change his mind and stay if I'd transferred back to my cute and cuddly fox body.

It proved fruitful once I heard the rumble of the vehicles ignition in the distance, then the sound of tires peeling off down the gravel road.

I felt relief at their absence at that moment, so I decided to remain in my human form, knowing it was just me and nature here now. I wanted to revel in this body, enjoy the feelings of the crisp wind, of the earth between my toes. I walked toward the lake and slowly dipped my body in. Cool yet refreshing water hugged my body as I let it slide up my thighs. A few more steps and it completely covered me from the waist down.

This body had no fur, besides some light hair in very specific areas on my skin. My legs, arms, chest, and my balls, which had caused such a ruckus during today's meeting. The hair was nowhere near enough to insulate me from the temperature of the lake, but I was a Pooka, after all.

I wanted to feel it, though: the cold. In hopes it might dampen whatever was making me stand at attention. The sight of Ciara, I'd imagine. Human bodies were so quick to get turned on.

I walked in a little deeper, up to my chest now. The tips of my long hair flowed around me as they got wet. Taking a deep breath, I submerged myself under the blackness of the water. I opened my eyes and could barely see my own hand in front of me.

Dark as a pint of Guinness, indeed. It was a nice, quiet moment under the water, but when I was ready, I rose back to the surface. I ran my fingers back through my wet hair and glanced around the perimeter of the lake.

I was the only living creature here now besides the birds and that sparked a devilish idea in my head.

CHAPTER 20

The ride back home with Finn was awkward and silent. I still couldn't believe Uallas had decided to conveniently neglect his clothes this time when shifting into his human form. I knew he did it on purpose to make Finn feel uncomfortable because of some kind of past feud they seemed to have.

He hadn't done that to me before, ever, out of respect, I imagine. I did believe he *was* capable of such a thing. I hated to admit that it had been quite a pleasant yet unnerving surprise, seeing him in such a pure form. It was very bold of him to do so, but something about that turned me on. I couldn't put my finger on it. It must have been the establishment of dominance that I had such a weakness to.

I kept my face forward, focused on the road in front of me, but took a glance over at Finn to see how he was doing. His face was still red from the fury and embarrassment that Uallas had caused him in the woods. I felt bad for him, but I also couldn't help but wonder what had caused such conflict between the two. Finn and The Agency were protectors of the Pooka kind, so why would Uallas appear to be out for blood? Something didn't add up here.

"Finn? Are you alright? What happened back there? I want the truth this time."

He let loose a deep sigh before answering me. I was in no mood for sugar coating anything at this point. That whole interaction today in the woods was ridiculous. I'd hit my tipping point for truths with the safety still on.

While I didn't know Finn that well just yet, I'd grown fond of him as an associate. I didn't like that Uallas had wound him up this tight, and I had to find out why.

My father would be disappointed in me letting the truth slip through my fingers so willingly. He gave me an entire castle with many things to uncover. I had to find that little girl in me again—the one who loved to dance with danger in search of the real world around me. Who longed for a reality of her own. Life was easier then, especially with dad around. But I wasn't a little girl anymore, and my father was no longer around to save me. I had to do that on my own now.

"Ciara, I'm alright now. I appreciate your concern. If you must know, I met Uallas way back when I started at The Agency, years ago, when I was thirty-four. As you've probably already noticed, we aren't on the best of terms. You see, he was my first big assignment with the partner I had before your father."

A tear slowly trickled down his cheek at the mention of that previous partner, and I feared what came next.

"The reason I was assigned to your father, and the reason why I always make sure I carry an iron knife or dagger, is because Uallas was the very reason for my previous partners demise. He gave Pookas the benefit of the doubt. Fiercely believed that peace was easily achievable, and knew that Uallas can detect intentions and emotions. He disregarded warnings and never carried any protection. One day, Uallas taught him a lesson that would be his last. Uallas put him in a coma and your father instantly became my new partner. As much as I appreciated your father's friendship over the years, I always made sure we had the proper protection on us wherever we went, during our work or not."

Finn paused to take a heavy breath.

"I was certain I'd never lose another partner if I took those precautions, but I was wrong. I cannot emphasize enough how sorry I am for bringing you here. Clearly, it was a mistake. I was being reckless to seek out this lead, but I'm just thankful we're both safe."

Wow. That was a lot to handle, but I needed to hear it.

That's why Finn had been trying to warn me about Uallas earlier. I hadn't realized Uallas was capable of such things. I just watered it down to a Pookas true nature.

"Me, too. Thank you for sharing, Finn. I'm so sorry to hear about your other partner."

That was why he always carried that knife on him. My dad had concealed one, on a belt clip under his shirt, as if it were a gun. Was that why my father didn't have any guns or 'other 'modern' weapons in the house, but had left least one blade in almost every room of the castle he gave to me?

Jesus, Mary and Joseph. Thank goodness I'd kept that knife from the subterranean armory and stuck it in my room. He was protecting me, even after his death, just in case it took me a while to figure everything out. My eyes welled at that thought.

Honestly, I couldn't wait to get home and do some reading in bed. The long day was drawing to a close, which was a relief. I had a lot to think about regarding the events that had unfolded today. The new information I was finally unafraid to ask about.

The truth, at times, isn't always meant to have a tightly sealed lid. Objects under pressure tended to explode. I'd ruminate over it and allow myself to feel whatever emotions I needed to once I got home.

Finally, after a silent car ride, we entered my driveway. Finn drove around the roundabout and came to a halt at my front door.

"Ciara, you have my number if you are ever in trouble. And I'm sure your father kept a few iron daggers around here for your protection. Please use them. Hear from you soon for our next practice," Finn said with a quick nod. "Good night."

After I made it safely inside, Finn left my driveway. It took a few minutes for him to finally leave the property. I locked my door and went upstairs to my room.

I immediately took my new dagger out of the drawer and rested it on my nightstand before I changing into my sleepwear. For good measure, I also locked my bedroom door. Maybe I was being a little paranoid after of today. Or maybe I was just the right amount of cautious.

Whatever it was, I'd err on the side of caution to ease my mind before going to bed tonight. I brushed my teeth and hair and snuggled into my comforter, my new book on the

Solais Sword in hand.

I opened to the page where I'd left off and started to read:

In the mist-veiled hills of the isles, there lived a princess named Aelia, whose beauty rivaled the moon and whose heart burned for more than just palace walls and polished suitors. Her people whispered of her kindness, her cleverness, and her peculiar dreams—dreams of stars, peace, and a silver sword glowing with sunlight itself.

This sword was no ordinary blade. It was the legendary Solais Sword, forged by the first light of dawn and a touch of magic. It was buried deep within the cursed forest of Heywood, guarded by creatures with claws and sharp teeth. Legend said only the one with a heart forged in truth could wield it—and whoever did would bring an age of peace to the realm. But Aelia didn't seek it for peace. She sought it for freedom, which is tranquility in itself.

On the eve of her arranged marriage, she slipped away in the dead of night, clad in traveler's leather, instead of her usual silks, with her hair bound back and destiny in her hands. In the thick shadows of Heywood, where even the birds didn't sing, Aelia met a fox.

Not just any fox. He was a fox of two faces.

One side of his face was golden-eyed and handsome—noble, even. Trust radiated from it. The other face, when he turned his head just so, was sharp-fanged and shadow-eyed, flickering like smoke. His eyes were too clever, his smile too cruel...

Maybe reading before bed wasn't quite as helpful as I thought it would be.

I marked my spot in the book with the attached ribbon to save for another time, and put it back on my bedside table. I laid back on my plush pillows, closed my eyes, and thought about today.

My mind started with the most recent events before working backward toward the morning. Of course, my mental image hesitated on the picture of Uallas, bare, in the woods, now calling me *darling* because I'd asked that he not call me *dear* anymore.

It wasn't a creative new pet name for me, but anything was better than that other word.

I let my mind wander and think of all the dirty thoughts it had accumulated but was too shy to show during our meeting in the woods. I still had to be professional, after all. Except here, alone in my bed, I could let my inhibitions run wild. Objects under pressure exploded, so I thought maybe it was time to relieve some pressure of my own.

I kept my eyes closed as I slowly slid my hand under my waistband and into my underwear. My two fingers explored my sensitive bundle of nerves as I brought my other hand up to caress my breast. The mental image of Uallas shifted in my mind wandering to Fearghas from my dream in the car.

An attractive body is nice and all, but the way Fearghas was pining over me in that dream was a force to be reckoned with. It was hard to choose one thing to focus on at this moment, but I kept my hands busy until it was time for my release. Pleasure built into bliss as I realized maybe sexual interaction was one of my ways to deal with my sorrow.

After a few minutes of touching myself, I let out a whimper of satisfaction. It was just the type of release I needed after a day like today. A chemical reaction occurred in my brain to release the stress and promote pleasure. Though I didn't have a willing partner this time, my hand also never did me wrong. I would surely sleep like a baby tonight.

I got back into bed and turned off my lamps after cleaning myself up. Staring up at the ceiling, I let the day's thoughts filter through my mind. After each thought, I dissected it, assessing how it made me feel before moving on to the next.

I hadn't even gotten to all the events of the day before I drifted off to sleep.

A wave of calm numbed my body. My sleep became even

deeper. It was then that I began to have one of my new favorite dreams. A crisp image of Fearghas in his human form entered my mind.

He was in the field with the sheep where we'd first met in my dreams, a beautiful sunset behind him that rivaled even the most beautiful cotton candy colored sunsets of Florida.

"I told you that you shouldn't go there, Sunshine. When will you ever learn?"

His voice was both a warning and an acknowledgement of my presence at Lough Guinness and the surrounding forest with Uallas.

"I hope you at least enjoyed the rest of your evening?" His eyes darkened knowingly at that remark and he laughed. It was a deep sound that hit me low in my stomach once more, and I swallowed at those feelings rising to the surface again. Of course, he knew what I was doing tonight. What a prick.

He smiled widely, showing a perfect set of pearly whites at the expense of my embarrassment.

"It was alright. Could have been better."

Truthfully, the only thing that would have made my evening better would have been the real thing instead of my hand. Whether he understood what I meant or not was up to his own discretion. At the very least, I hoped it would rattle him up a bit.

"And what would have made it better, Sunshine? My hand or yours?" he purred, eyes boring into my soul, teasing me. He knew damn well what would have made it better, but he was such a flirt. He couldn't do a damn thing about it in my dreams, could he?

"Nothing you could do about it here... Why don't you ever seek me out in person, Fearghas?"

It was an honest question. I'd seen him more in my dreams than in person. If he wanted to observe me, he was doing so from the confines of my mind instead of from a physical standpoint. I didn't exactly want him stalking me again, like he had on the drive home from the tavern that night I was with Conor.

"I want to be respectful of your boundaries. I prefer to observe from afar, anyway. I told you I can't seem to stay away..."

There it was again: that look of internal conflict regarding me.

"And why is that, Fearghas?" I asked.

He just shook his head, unable to answer, or not wanting to. "That is an answer I'm not ready to give you. Sleep well, Sunshine."

CHAPTER 21

FEARGHAS

The more I infiltrated her dreams, the more I knew I was in trouble.

Connecting to her this way was like having a tether into her thoughts, but only in a dreamlike state. I wasn't nearly as bad as Uallas, though. I didn't seek to add her to my collection like a trophy, or to force her hand to repopulate our species.

For one, my intentions were pure. Well, mostly. I'd only been trying to keep her nightmares at bay. That was my top priority with Ciara. I knew her purpose for going to The Agency's headquarters, and I wanted to distract her from learning about what happened to her father. Anything

I could do to help ease her pain, I would do it without question.

I didn't want to invade her space in the process. I enjoyed my time alone and I found personal space sacred. If she wanted to seek me out, I knew that she would.

She certainly did so before, that first day we officially met.

Yesterday had raked on my nerves, ever since I wove myself into her dreams during the first nap of her day. It didn't take me long to realize she was headed to Lough Guinness with Finn to meet with Uallas. Uallas wasn't much of a threat to her on his own, but add any company and I knew how hostile my brother was capable of being.

That was another reason why I wanted to give her space. Fuck dealing with Uallas and his gobshite antics. When he set his mind to something, he got tunnel vision. He turned into a dog with his bone, protecting it at any cost, and usually with his teeth for anyone who got too close. The bone in question was Ciara, and his stupid idea that she would be his, as if she were property. A prize to be won.

Hate was not a strong enough word to describe my feelings on the matter.

So instead, I used my charm and let her decide what she wanted. I didn't need to stay in her dreams the other night. I knew after entering her astral plane she was handling it, and then, after realizing what activities she had participated in prior to dreaming, that she would sleep soundly.

While I was there, it couldn't hurt to push a few buttons—maybe flirt a little.

I couldn't leave well enough alone when it came to her and the last thing I wanted was to come across as a possessive arsehole.

The idea that before I entered her dreams she had been pleasuring herself to the thought of me was so delicious. After I left her dreams last night, I had to take care of myself just to stop thinking about it. It took three rounds before I finally felt satisfied enough to settle down and relax. By relax I mean find a loud, drunken idiot from the tavern I was named after and drop them off in some desolate marshland, giving them time to walk off the ale from the previous night's shenanigans. I was really doing them a favor.

I could not remember a time when I'd been so turned on. Needless to say, it had been ages. She consumed my waking thoughts so much so that I hadn't been tormenting the town nearly as much as I usually did. This woman was making me soft.

Today, I needed to change that by giving someone my signature ride over the cliffs of Howth. My favorite place in all of Ireland. The chunks of green land were absolutely beautiful; they appeared roughly cut off where they met the sea.

In most seasons, except winter, the cliffs were lined with hearty evergreens and vivid yellow gorse flowers that scented the air with a hint of vanilla.

I wasn't completely heartless. I showed my special riders a glance at true beauty before I sent them to their maker. It was about time to see if the vanilla-scented hills were still lined in yellow.

I closed my eyes as black clouds swirled around me, bones warping, intestines shifting, transforming me from human to one of my many desired forms: my stallion body. My stallion form was probably my favorite, other than my human body. It was muscular, and the midnight-black coat had a wonderful luster to it in the daylight. My mane was long and as wild as I felt. My hooves looked like polished obsidian pounding the ground as I galloped through the patchwork greenery of the lands.

I started toward the outskirts of Dublin city. It was likely too early to find a drunk stumbling along the streets who was bold enough to take me on, but the landscape was beautiful, and maybe I could spot Norman at the pub. I tried not to frighten him anymore, for Ciara's sake, but the general consensus for human reactions when spotting a horse with glowing eyes was not a welcoming one, especially since the papers ran that article about us.

Maybe if he were to spot me in the daytime instead of during his nightly rounds of trash duty or locking up the joint, I'd alarm him a tad less. It wasn't every day that you got a pub named after you because of how often you'd visited said establishment over the centuries.

Luckily, I always kept it consistent in this stallion form. Hence the favoritism.

Black Horse Tavern was a favorite of mine as well, home to many eejit passengers who'd had too much to drink since its establishment around the fourteenth century.

It was a staple of the town, both visually and as a well-established business. Another one of my favorite tidbits about the pub? The fact that, throughout generations, they'd kept the door painted red in homage to the color of my burning eyes.

No one had altered it, not even once; perhaps a slight tonal shift occurred over the years as it weathered or the paint chipped. The irony of the missing persons posters featuring my latest cliff divers being posted just outside, on the telephone poles, was almost humorous, come to think of it.

In the field, I found the recent flock of sheep I'd been mingling with as a goat, and made my best attempt at camouflaging into the scenery with other animals. Because I wasn't feeling up to changing into my goat form again, I stayed as the stallion.

I remained a safe distance away from them, though. I had to pretend I was a wild horse, after all.

Keeping a close eye on the door paid off when I saw the first arsehole stumble out the door and trip over the step, pushing a woman out of the way and shouting loudly into her ear. I could just barely make out what he said from this distance, but judging by his intensity, he was very aggressive.

Suddenly, the sky opened up and water fell from the clouds.

If Ireland's weather was anything, it was dependably wet and frigid throughout the entire month of November. It had been like this every year, consistently, since I could remember. The late afternoon was far too early in the day to be in rag order for this bloke, especially if he was sloppy and angry when drunk.

It took me a minute to realize that the woman's long dark hair was oddly familiar. She stumbled a bit as she walked up to the door when the little shite shoved her again. She was trying to hide from him and his stank breath in her face, searching for the best opportunity to flee.

I only caught a glimpse, but it was sufficient for me to make out the profile of the woman in question. It was Ciara.

As soon as I laid eyes on her, I could feel the pace of my heart quicken. Like the beats of a drum in battle.

If I had hands right now, they'd be turning into fists, but instead, my hooves pawed the earth.

I flared my nostrils, huffing out tendrils of steam, and pinned my ears straight back. I was ready to charge. I disregarded the risk of being seen as a Pooka; this man was physically threatening her. I focused my sights solely on this arse and Ciara, everything around me blurring black as night, and I charged toward them.

I must have missed seeing the gate before the tavern entrance as anger engulfed my senses, because suddenly, splinters of wood were crashing around me. I pushed forward, straight to the threat, knocking him on the ground.

I got there so fast, it was almost as if I had teleported from the field to her.

"Are you hurt?" I managed to ask her between huffs. Her eyes grew wide in shock and she shook her head. She looked up at me through glossy eyes and bit her lip at the sight of me.

I wondered what could possibly be going on in her mind.

It felt as if she was taking forever to answer my question. Time didn't feel real at this moment.

"I'm alright now, Fearghas. I'm not hurt. Thank you."

The sound of her voice was almost angelic. I was elated that she wasn't hurt. The sound of her saying my name was the cherry on top and it caused me to produce a nickering sound through my muzzle.

"If you'll excuse me, Sunshine, I need to take the trash out. Don't go gettin' into any more trouble, yeah?"

I didn't hesitate before what happened next. My teeth latched onto the back of the feckin' gobshite's collar and I flung him onto my back, my magic holding him there like invisible cuffs. I resisted the urge to shake him up like a rag doll in front of her, choosing to run off instead.

I tried to calm my breath but it was still going a mile a minute, in rhythm with my hurried heartbeats and hooves.

Back to the cliffs of Howth with the plaything. I couldn't gallop fast enough. Patience was not a virtue of mine, especially when her safety was on the line.

I was overdue for the thrill of sending a deserving human over the cliff's edge. Tourists came to visit and all you heard about was how pretty the cliffside was.

If they only knew the real reason creatures like me loved the cliffside, they might back away a step or two. In a way, it was a team effort to keep the balance of nature going strong.

A vanilla-scented breeze flooded my senses, and I knew I was nearing my destination. Gaining momentum, I hastily turned my trot into a gallop and beyond. Before long, I was racing at a breakneck speed, jostling him awake.

Next came the screams and questions, which I ignored until we got closer to the edge of the Howth.

"You know damn well why we're here and what I am!" I bellowed. I had no time for games. He was grinding on my last nerve. In truth, I needed no explanation.

I held the title of the land's most fearsome creature, the dark, chaotic Pooka; the prince of mayhem, a reputation that struck fear into the hearts of many. A well-earned title through the ages.

There was some truth to the tales that had been passed down for generations. The stories claim that Pookas in horse form go on a rampage, taking the townsfolk for the rides of their lives where they were forced to stay on by unseen forces. But none of the stories said they actually killed their unwilling passengers. They just gave their riders a terrifying high-speed ride and dropped them in a bog or marsh far, far away.

I just happened to enjoy it with a bit of a twist. You see, the sea washed away and cleansed many sins, so why not do it my way?

I continued onward regardless. I was going to do this my way. He was more than deserving of this fate.

"You are the scum of the earth! How dare you lay a finger on another, let alone a woman? A woman who, even on her worst of days, is still infinite leagues above your own. *Who am I?* Who are you to touch her, shove her, abuse her? Heaven forbid your manky mouth ever utters the words reminiscent of an apology. It's no one's fault but your own that you're a sorry excuse for a drunk. It's too late for you now to learn your lesson. How does the phrase go? Once an abuser, always an abuser? Or maybe that was in regards to other things you have done—but why take my chances? Care for a lift?"

The man's eyes bulged out of their sockets, either from what I'd said or because he'd just heard a horse talk. Bonus points for me if it was both.

Silent tears streamed down his face and his perspiration was so heady with the odor of liquor, it was practically giving me a buzz. I skidded to a stop, right at the edge of the cliff, with him barely hanging on.

"It appears we've reached our destination."

CHAPTER 22

I never made it inside the Black Horse tavern. Just my luck, when I was trying to talk through my pain with my friend Norman without my day going completely awry. I immediately wondered where Fearghas was taking that drunk asshole who attacked me. As soon as he trotted off with him, I remained a safe distance behind, trailing him.

Because the open countryside was absolutely vast, it was extremely difficult to trail someone unnoticed. Ancient dry-stone walls separated the end of Dublin city and the beginning of the untouched patchwork fields of rural Ireland. Using them to my advantage, I crouched behind them. Not until I almost lost sight of Fearghas and his new passenger, did I leave the safety of the wall. I was now using the rain as my leverage to remain unseen throughout the grassy meadows.

Luckily, Fearghas was keeping a quick and steady pace, so I was still able to keep a decent distance behind him. What on earth was he doing with this guy?

I doubted he was taking him on a joy ride into the field.

I had no idea what was about to happen or what was going on with Fearghas and this jerk, but I needed to know where he was taking him and what he had planned.

I wasn't even sure why I felt the need to find out.

One minute, this random stranger thought it was okay to put his hands on me, push me, and yell at me for no reason whatsoever. Then Fearghas was taking him away in a split second. I should be satisfied with the knowledge that I would most likely never see that dipshit again.

Instead of stalking Fearghas in the rain, I should be warm and dry in the tavern with a piping hot bowl of stew and chatting with Norman. I guessed once I'd gotten a taste of some of that unfiltered truth from the other day, I'd become addicted. The little girl was back—who never gave up on herself.

Fearghas picked up his pace to a full gallop and I found a lone tree to hide behind. He was just far enough away that his words were still within ear's reach. I heard it all. Every word that he practically yelled at the man was...

I gulped, my throat dry despite the weather.

He was standing up for me, to a stranger, when no one was around to witness it.

In all my years, I'd been told that integrity was all about what people said when no one was looking was what truly mattered.

My hair was now sticking to the sides of my face. My clothes had become completely soaked.

It seemed as though his speech was coming to a close, but then he bucked and the asshole went flying. Straight over the edge of the cliff. I raised my hand up to my mouth to muffle the scream begging to be released.

Sure, that man was a complete asshole, but maybe sending him over the edge of the cliff was a bit dramatic. I could attest that getting shitfaced and making stupid decisions was not worth a death sentence. Heaven knows I'd made my own dumb decisions involving alcohol, though they were perhaps the opposite of violent. I choked back the rest of my silent scream. My body froze in place as still as a statue.

Twin flames in the distance narrowed on my presence. No use in hiding now. Fearghas had caught me snooping red-handed. A light puff of steam escaped his nostrils at the sight of me. Honestly, I was surprised that he didn't sense my presence here earlier with his powers, however they worked.

I should have been terrified, I should have run away, but my feet remained planted firmly in place.

Dark smoke whirled around him as he came toward me.

In a matter of seconds, the dark stallion was gone, and in its place was Fearghas, the almost-human. He was bare from the waist up, trousers low on his hips, showing off every decadent muscle. His messy black hair was soaked in the rain, dripping at the ends. His horns stood regally atop his head, adding an heir of dominance and wickedness to his demeanor. It made sense now.

He stopped walking half way to where I stood, allowing me to come to him first. I had just seen him throw someone off the cliff in my honor. I'd only read of the violence that Pookas were capable of; I'd never actually seen it before. Nothing to this degree.

He was right to pause and take note of my nonverbal cues before approaching me first. Uallas could take a note from Fearghas's playbook for that. I took a few steps toward him, closing the distance between us to silently tell him it was okay.

"Did you just...?"

He nodded, head lowered, like a dog in trouble. I could only imagine that his animalistic mannerisms were second nature, given that he could change into just about every other animal in the forest.

"Well, I don't approve of what you did, but... thank you... for standing up for me. I can't remember a time when someone did that for me."

It was the truth, though it felt a little awkward and vulnerable. I let it out.

This feeling was genuine and I'd embrace it.

"So, do you give everyone a speech after you give them a 'lift'?" I nodded toward the cliff behind him.

"If you *must* know, no, I do not give all my passengers a speech. No one has ever tried to harm you in front of me before." His brows scrunched together, eyes looking at me as if I held the answers he sought. I couldn't be the sole reason for him to display such acts of violence.

"So why did you do it, Fearghas?"

"Because who has helped *you* lately? There is a reason I just cannot stay away from you, Sunshine, and I *absolutely* intend to show you why you are worth it and more."

A thoughtful smile graced his face. Thoughts appeared to be ruminating in his brain. Perhaps they were listing all the ways he intended to show me why he could not stay away, even though he had tried on many occasions. He had a point, though. Who *had* helped me lately? Who made my heavy days feel a little lighter?

Conor was probably the last one, and even that was just situational and had an expiration date. A pleasant distraction. No one really had helped me face my grief head on and navigate the messy emotions that I battled daily.

One might have thought that, as an only child, I'd be used to being alone, but no one deserved to go through this inevitable experience that way.

The sorrow of watching your parents' age is something no one prepared you for, yet it was an honor that I wouldn't get the privilege to experience.

"Ciara?" His deep voice shattered through my reflections, bringing me back to the moment.

"Well, um, I guess...no one. I am my father's only child, so it's solely on me to wrap up his life's work and wishes. Business first, emotions later, I guess. I've just been avoiding that last part..."

It became easy to put your feelings aside when you had loose ends to tie up. Something to distract you as your heart shattered over and over, every day, into little fragments. Everyone around you expected you to already have made the decisions following a death in the family. Wrap up the estate, notify close friends and family, plan a funeral service. It felt like a second job, and the mental strain was unbearable.

Most families had multiple members willing to delegate

these tasks, but seeing as I was the only one, it all rested on my shoulders. Who had time to cry and scream properly when your days were full of making these arrangements and pretending to love everyone's casseroles?

"Let me help you, Ciara. With anything you need. Just say the words," he uttered.

I searched his eyes for any degree of truth. I was confident that I'd know the difference between someone telling me what I wanted to hear, rather than what was genuine. He closed the distance, eyes still lingering on me, waiting for my response.

"Would that be alright?" He moved a soaked piece of hair away from my face and tucked it behind my ear before I could answer.

"But how could you know anything about human emotions and grief? Uallas hasn't learned anything after all this time." It was a valid question.

His brother admitted to not knowing much about it, even though he could read intentions. Maybe these Pooka brothers were gifted with these talents to gain better knowledge of their human counterparts and how we would react to different circumstances.

His hand moved slowly from behind my ear and he fisted my hair gently, tilting my head back. His lips were a mere inch away from mine as he spoke.

"This," he breathed, panting heavily. "This is desire. To want something badly."

His lips caressed a sensitive spot on my neck, planting the softest kisses there, tickling and teasing me.

"Lust. A strong desire for someone." His kisses traveled lower, just to the rise of my breasts through my jacket. Before I could process what was going on, he ripped open my coat, revealing part of my nipples, which were instantly tightening from the cold rain.

"Now, it appears we are both exposed. Do you trust me enough to explore more?"

I didn't mind that I was exposed like this in his presence. I just stayed there, waiting for him. I wanted to explore our connection. I wanted more.

My heart pounded in my throat, and an electric current thrilled the nerves between my legs. I could still sense the phantom feeling of his lips caressing my neck. I brushed my fingers against the spot, trying to hold on to that desire.

Do I trust him to explore more? Yes. It was as simple as that, despite what I had just witnessed. He was right, in a way: we were both exposed. The need for him to protect me and prove that he was not like his brother was overwhelming. I shifted my glance back up at him and nodded in response to his question.

"Fearghas, why do you feel this need to save me?"

It had been at the forefront of my mind in the field today. I was a grown woman. I could manage myself. I wasn't going to entertain that asshole—I was just going to slip away and find Norman inside. Tell him the town idiot was on the loose.

But why did Fearghas constantly feel the need to protect me? Whether it was through messages in my dreams or with situations like today. Wasn't I the one in charge of protecting his kind now? Family business and all.

"You're gorgeous and you've got a heart of gold to match. No words can describe how wonderful you are. You are collectively all the best qualities of your father, and then some. No one should go through life alone, Sunshine. A life worth sharing is a life worth living. All those other eejits who haven't stepped up are just frightened of you. I'll thank them later that it led me to you."

The words he spoke were so genuine, I could feel it in my bones. It was a relief to know my emotions were not being manipulated.

I was sure living for hundreds of years would give you a vocabulary as vast as a dictionary. He had explained the definition of one of many such words to me as he did now as well to prove he was well-versed in human emotions.

"Ciara, I need to tell you something that has been grinding on the insides of my mind." Fearghas broke my reverie.

I'd never heard him plead with me in such a way. The desperate undercurrent in his voice had me on edge. He'd been infiltrating my dreams more and more frequently since we first met, especially since that ominous warning whispered during my nap in Finn's car.

He could have told me multiple times since then, during any of my dreams lately, so what could have been so important that was holding onto it?

"What do you need to tell me, Fearghas?" I asked him.

Trust had to do with transparency on both sides. A feeling of relief mixed with anxiety crept up. The kind where you felt comfortable to open up with the other person, or Pooka, in this case, no matter what manner of information you were holding onto.

A life worth sharing is a life worth living. His words haunted my memories again. He was so right. I hadn't been living lately because I hadn't let anyone to be close enough to share it with.

Most people here, save for Norman and Finn, were just placeholders for the genuine connection I'd been seeking after the loss of my father. I couldn't share my deepest secrets with them—well, not really.

Granted, most of my secrets were just that: secrets. Fearghas had his own set of secrets, as well.

Maybe it would be nice to have someone to confide in to lessen the load.

Maybe we could be that for each other.

CHAPTER 23

FEARGHAS

How was I supposed to tell her that when it came down to the instinct to protect her or save my own flesh and blood, I would not hesitate to choose her?

Every time, without a second thought. I hadn't wanted her to witness the extent of where some of my riders ended up, the fact that I'd happily kill anyone who threatened her to ensure her safety. I would give anything to be someone she could trust, someone to lean on when the road got rough—and it has been treacherous for her lately.

Against my better judgment, I knew she was better off living in Florida. Far away from our kind and the destruction we could cause here. Her father's life was the price she paid for my brother's malevolence. And to her, he had been her everything. A rather large price indeed.

I knew that I could not completely fill that void for her, but I'd do my best to make her days more bearable. As long as she didn't shy away from me, I could be that for her.

Fuck the rules. She had to know about the dangers she put herself in whenever she was near Uallas. I needed to tell her, not only for her safety, but to build her trust. Uallas and I were cut from the same thread, but unlike him, I had evolved.

He had been given every opportunity in this extensive, immortal life that we were given to not only do better, but to use it to co-mingle with the humans of the land. He was given the gifts from our makers so he could be the one to be able to share these lands together so we could both live harmoniously.

He was the Alpeine, the pure one. Made for peace and understanding between the species. I was the dark one, in all aspects of the word. I was here for balance, to bring the chaos, and to test him along the way. I was never built for speaking truths, but then here she came: the very ingredient I needed to make this world more palatable. I wondered daily since she had come into my life if I was meant for something greater. The only way to find out for sure was to be what she needed.

So I kept a close watch on her, infiltrating her dreams as a means of getting to know her deepest thoughts. That was when I found out that one day, she was taking a nap on the way to the forest and Lough Guinness. I had to warn her without frightening her of the dangers of going to that place, of seeking out Uallas there.

I remembered it like it was yesterday, when her father was going there to make peace between him and Uallas. That was when Uallas found out about the sword Sean owned, and its magical properties.

Despite its obvious dangers to us, he turned into the likes of a rabid animal at the prospect, knowing what magical properties came with it. The knowledge that it simply existed flipped the switch in his brain that made him go after the Solais Sword by any means necessary. That was the day I lost everything I had known about my brother.

The threat he made against our sole protector was frightening, even to me.

I should have told Sean to leave it to rest, because Uallas wouldn't stop until he had what he wanted: the sword and Sean's daughter. I should have said that he would stop at nothing to obtain it, and whoever was standing in his way would see the wrath he had bottled up all this time, waiting for its inevitable release.

Maybe if I had, he would still be alive, and Ciara would have her father, and they would both still be living in the land of sunshine. I never understood the appeal of the sword to Uallas, but maybe that was also why we were so different. I was never one to care about such trivial items.

To me, it was more about the collective moments that life had to offer. Uallas was no different from those I pitied over the years, fighting for nothing of actual value.

Sure, the Solais Sword could probably have been appraised for millions of dollars for humans, but what he failed to notice was the value of friendship or true love. Something he never understood throughout our entire existence. It wasn't like he was a treasure hunter, either. Human currency was of no use to us. The only thing Uallas ever sought was glory and power.

Every step of the way, when I was sure that there would be a moment when Uallas would finally grasp the concept of emotional connection, he would utterly fail us—though he had never broken any of the cardinal rules before.

Maybe I should have predicted this happening, though—that he'd go so far off the deep end that he'd break the rules and do anything in his power for something as lame as one of those pointy things, and the type that could kill us, too. If only I knew where he hid it. If only...

No, I couldn't do that, could I? Well, sure I could, but *should* I?

She already knew that I would do anything for her safety, so the thought of killing wasn't out of the question entirely. There were two types of evil in the world: the evil that killed for the fun of it, and the other that killed in an attempt to purify the world.

When exactly had I jumped from one kind to another? Possibly, it was about the same time that Sean left my world and Ciara entered it. It was a trait I was born with, this evil.

How I went about it was what I had to figure out on my own. It was why they put the word "Fear" in my name. Only it was now apparent that I was not the one who should be feared.

My brother and his many faces were aptly named, however, with a secondary name like "Jekylle." The only thing I feared now was what would happen if Uallas were to have Ciara meet a fate similar to her father's if she denied him.

So many words on my mind—she was still awaiting my answer. How could I explain all this, or better yet, put it into words for her to understand without shattering her heart all over again?

"I don't want to admit that I care for you because if I do that, then it puts your life in danger, Sunshine. It becomes this tangible thing. I would throw the entire world into the sea if it was what gave you peace. I am the fearless, the prince of chaos and mayhem. I'm not supposed to be the good one, but I would do bad things for the best reasons."

In a nutshell, it was the utter truth. I just refrained from divulging what my sadistic brother was up to. I would tell her, but not today. I could only hope that it was enough for her to open up to me in the way I knew that she wanted to. That was how humans built trust. Shared secrets, heavy with unspoken implications, exchanged between two people that the other would never share. A silent understanding that the other would never betray them with the knowledge they had just acquired. Trust was the foundation for everything. It was found in anything from love to friendships.

I had left her speechless with my words.

Her innocent eyes gazed up at me under raised eyebrows and slightly dilated pupils. Attraction. I knew she felt something, too. I flashed one of my infamous smirks at her. The one where I realized I'd been making the thoughts scramble around in that pretty little head of hers ever since we met. I may have been honorable enough to let her make the first move, but I'd be damned if I didn't coax it out of her.

She kept opening and closing her mouth like a fish out of

water, picking her words carefully but unable to find the right words to reply.

Her eyes scanned each of mine before settling on my mouth, and before I knew what was happening, her lips were on mine. Rain continued to pelt down on us, dampening the kiss and making it all the more delectable to savor her.

Occasionally nibbling and sucking on her lip, I was enjoying every taste of her that she would allow. I let out a deep growl when she ran her tongue along my lips.

She was a magnificent kisser. I couldn't get enough, my new addiction. I took it as an invitation to taste her more deeply when she opened her mouth for me. So willing and curious, my radiant girl.

Within several minutes of us intertwined, the rain clouds started to clear.

The timing couldn't have been more impeccable. All the shadows of doubt scattered away to clear skies. Sunlight illuminated the field gradually, as if nature nodded in approval at our coupling. I knew fate was on our side—if not mine, then definitely Ciaras. I broke our kiss momentarily when the sunlight illuminated us.

"Sunshine," I smiled, looking toward the sky and then back down at her.

She was glowing, and it wasn't from the rays of sunshine alone.

"You are radiant, Ciara. Always the sunshine to my rainy days." I could not get rid of this smile from my face. I was elated to simply have her in my arms. I would cherish this moment forever, no matter what the future held. I would make sure that no more cloudy days were in her future, as long as I was involved.

Beyond the physical chemistry we clearly had, everything about her just felt right. Hell, the clouds cleared for us in our favor, and if that wasn't a message enough, then I didn't know what else could be.

She matched my smile at the sentiment about her being my literal and figurative sunshine. It made me feel as though my heart was going to burst out of my chest. I had it bad for her. I was in far too deep now to go back. Way past the point of no return—not that I wished to go back; I just don't think I ever could now.

Nevertheless, I couldn't shake this nagging feeling that the clouds clearing so the sun could shine down on us wasn't pure coincidence. When her father's voice could not speak his approval of her decisions, he had to show her in signs sent from the heavens above.

Sean moved the clouds for his daughter to see the light, so I could move mountains for her. Simultaneously, he told me that I was worthy of his daughter's love. My eyes welled with tears at the realization of his significant message to us. I hoped she'd come to the same realization I had—I'm sure she did.

"Fearghas, I know this sounds crazy, but I feel like the sky clearing for us was a message sent by my father. I've been hoping and wondering constantly what he would say about my decisions lately, and I think it was his way of responding. I think he approves of whatever path I've started to lay for myself... you included."

"Never crazy. Take it from someone who lives within this realm and the dream realm. He approves, Sunshine." I wiped her tears with the back of my forefinger before our lips met again.

CHAPTER 24

I was still in a lustful haze from being with Fearghas yesterday evening.

When I woke up this morning, I couldn't remember how I got home, or anything after our kiss, really. I checked my phone to see if I had any missed calls that may help me piece together the rest of my evening. A little red notification displayed on my cell phone, showing that I had a new voicemail.

"Ciara, this is Finn. I was calling to set up another fencing lesson with you. Give me a call when you're ready."
Just the other day, I'd planning to pick up some roast from the tavern to bring home after talking to Norman, but the rest of the day's events took me by surprise, to say the least. Butterflies were still fluttering in my stomach, as I thought

about Fearghas. The idea of my father sending me signs from beyond would linger with me forever. I'd constantly be on the lookout for more of them now.

I dialed Finn's number to set up our next lesson.

"Hello, Finn? This is Ciara."

"Hello, Ciara. How are you?" His friendly words met mine on the other end of the line.

"Hi! Yes, I'm doing okay. I'm returning your call to set up another fencing lesson. Are you available later this afternoon?"

I couldn't help but wonder how on earth was this my new reality. Was I really taking fencing lessons, and actually enjoying it? It would definitely be a useful skill to have here with all of the weapons plastered on the walls.

"Sounds like a good idea, Sleeping Beauty. I'm working remotely at the cafe now.
Would you like me to bring a cuppa tea or coffee for you?" Finn asked.

"How kind of you, Finn. I'll have a black cream tea with sugar, if you don't mind. I'll see you around two o'clock?" I suggested.

"Sounds like a plan." Finn ended the call.

Perhaps it was about time that I checked out the camera feeds from the subterranean armory, which started all this mess in the first place. There had to have been cameras—some kind of footage of the break-in and theft.

My dad would be pissed if I just left it all alone, after how far I'd come. I just couldn't give up, even if I thought I should. It would be easier to deal with the fact that this weight on my soul would never quite go away.

Closure. That's what this was all about.

Wrap up all the loose ends my father had laid carelessly about and tie them up into neat little bows. I made my way over to the study to get the blueprint. I punched in the digits on the picture frame's keypad and the locks whirred open again.

This time, the red-orange lines that marked the subterranean armory mocked me.

I'd have to look over that map again to even get an idea of where a surveillance room could be. It would take me a while to memorize the dozens of rooms in the castle. It was so vast.

I scanned the parchment for the words *surveillance room* or something similar.

I spotted the room I was looking for next to the stairs that led to the cathedral. Realizing I'd avoided that holy place since discovering it, I took a deep breath. I shoved the blueprint back into the safe and closed the frame. I decided to make a stop back inside the cathedral and light two of the candles that still had wicks: one for my father and one for Conor's mom.

This corner of the house was just as extravagant as I remembered. Its beautifully sculptured altar took my breath away, the stained glass masterpieces shining colored light on it. I said a little prayer for them both and blew out the candles before I left the room, hoping luck or something even greater was on my side.

Walking toward the surveillance room, my palms began to sweat with the possibilities of what could be on the tapes. Wiping them on my jeans didn't prevent my nerves making them clammy yet again.

 I finally came to a matte-black metal door with the shield knot printed above it. It held a plaque with gold lettering spelling out the word *Security*.

I entered the same six digits as the safe on the keypad and waited.

Good guess. The door unlatched for me. The room was rather simple except for the fact it contained hundreds of screens displaying different areas of the house in live action.

One screen in particular caught my attention. Instead of it being a clear live-action shot of whatever its paired camera was recording, it showed black-and-white static, as if the camera was offline entirely. I was sure it very well could have been, but the screen hadn't been turned off inside this room. That must be where the footage from the armory was.

I searched the console for the corresponding tape and, sure enough, there it was in the slot. The tape had numbers that matched the ones displayed on the screen.

The possibility that this recording held the answer to my father's fate and the sword—or even a clue of its where-abouts—was both terrifying and hopeful.

I checked for any signs that the tape had been tampered with, but found nothing. A silver lining to an otherwise strained situation.

At minimum, the tape would depict reality.

I knew Finn would arrive momentarily, so I went back to the sitting area in the front of the house. His arrival was announced by a knock on the door.

"Your favorite delivery man is here," Finn said through the front door.

"Hi, Finn! Come in!"

I opened the door and stepped aside so he could enter. We made our way back to the sitting area to enjoy our refreshments before getting down to business.

After my last sip of one of the best teas I'd ever tasted, he asked me how I was feeling. In truth, my emotions were all over the place, between learning my father had been murdered by something magical or supernatural, and kissing Fearghas in the rain after he saved me from that man outside the bar. I had also just found the security footage of the armory. On one hand, I was relieved to have a little more closure on who stole the sword from my father's armory. Yet the harsh reality of someone breaking into what had appeared to be a well-guarded castle where I now lived was very unnerving.

Anxious would be a good place to start, but before I could dwell too much on everything, I told him what I found when I was in the security room.

Fencing lessons could take a break for now.

"Okay, so here's where I found it. It was the only monitor that was cut out, but the tape was in there," I pointed to the now-empty slot.

"I hope whatever it recorded beforehand, you'll able to recover. Would you have any idea where he kept a tape player?"

Finn stopped paying attention to me mid-sentence upon discovering the very thing I was curious about. Off to the side sat a touch-screen monitor, paired with a complex hard drive and various vacancies for whichever technology he required to view.

Finn slid the tape into the corresponding spot and played it from the beginning. For hours of recorded time, there was nothing except the view of the armory door and hallway. Ominously still and perfectly normal.

Until it wasn't.

"There! That shape, is that...?" Finn's words cut short as we both stared at the blurred white shape on screen.

It was in the form of an albino rabbit. Its eyes smeared the footage like motion-blurred headlights from a photographer's lens. Its ears twitched like sonar searching for any nearby resistance as he gnawed through the wiring on the alarm system. Then the rabbit paused as if waiting for the hum of the electricity to still.

 A strange familiarity washed over me, tingling the blood in my veins with fear.

My heart sank to the bottom of my chest like an elevator with its cords cut. I'd seen that rabbit before once, although it usually appeared to me as a fox.

Uallas.

That cunning bastard. Taunting me with smooth words and the symbolism of what foxes represented, all the while betraying my family in the worst way possible.

"Uallas. It's him, I'm sure of it, Finn. He shifted into that same white rabbit one day when I saw him up on the hill."

So much for peace and understanding between us, only to

be paid back in deception. I needed to see more, just to see the true extent of it all.

"Keep it playing, Finn. I need to see what else he does." Finn pressed play in response.

After Uallas chewed through the rest of his desired cords, he shifted into his human form. He grew one long nail before our eyes and then used it to expertly pick the lock.

The one saving grace of watching a centuries-old Pooka break into my father's armory was that he had completely forgotten about the cameras being in place. He never learned, despite being given all that time about everything humans could create. Such as the ability to replay the tapes.

With both of our eyes glued to the screen, we witnessed Uallas leave the room, the Solais Sword clearly in hand. For someone who thought he had expertly dodged all the security measures my father had in place, he was very sloppy. He paused just under the doorway when he realized he was being watched. He was just tall enough to knock out the camera, and then the screen went blank. It was safe to say I could piece together what happened in the aftermath, when the recording turned to static.

"When I went down there that first time, the lock on the door was still intact. Uallas must have locked the padlock on the door again in an attempt to cover his tracks."

I told Finn this in hopes that he could help me piece together the rest of the information that wasn't readily available. Now that we knew who had the sword, the next task was finding out where it was hidden.

For now, I'd learn to put up a good fight.

CHAPTER 25

Finn and I agreed that he could take the tape back to the agency to be reviewed again for evidence. Then, I needed something to take the edge off what we'd found. Fencing lessons would be the perfect vice.

After getting ready in my room, I went to sweep my hair into a sleek ponytail but realized my hair elastics were nowhere to be found.

With my fist temporarily securing my hair I searched my room for one, but the book of the Solais Sword caught my attention instead. I picked it up with my free hand to check underneath it and, luckily, spotted my lost elastic under the book. It all came back to this sword and the fairy tales surrounding it... I'd have to continue reading after practice.

Something in that book was important to this case, I could feel it in my gut. Finally securing my hair, I went to the solar room where we'd practiced last.

Finn entered the room, placing a large black canvas bag off to the side, near the wall. He cracked his knuckles, readying to begin his lesson.

"Show me your fighting stance," Finn said.

I got into the stance with one foot behind the other, as asked. I had one hand to guard my chest and the other out in front of me, as if holding an imaginary sword. I turned my attention to an intricate steel sword on the wall, focusing as I counted my breaths and adjusted my center of gravity.

"Excellent, Ciara. Good breathwork. Our goal is to incorporate holding a real sword. Today, we'll do a few exercises to warm up first. Your body needs conditioning before being able to swing around a sharp, heavy object."

We started with a series of stretches and fifteen minutes of running in place for cardio. Stretching was easy; it was the cardio I despised, even though I knew I needed it the most. I had to take multiple breaks within that timeframe to catch my breath. I was out of shape, despite the slim appearance of my body. There was no way we'd be graduating onto using an actual sword for this lesson if this was how it was starting.

"I'm not ready, Finn. I'm so out of shape," I said, hands on my knees, panting.

"Ciara, do not let those thoughts win. If anyone is cut out for this, it is you. Your mind is the most underrated muscle. You are strong—a *warrior*," Finn said to me. "This is the purpose of conditioning the body. It's why we train: to hone your muscles until they make these moves look easy. Every expert was once a beginner. Get some water and then we'll begin."

Finn pulled a heavy wooden sword, probably weighing a few pounds, from his case. He got into a fighting stance, holding the wooden sword with both hands directly above his head and slicing it downward so the tip of the sword was just at his knees. He repeated the movement with ease.

"These are practice drills," he explained. "They'll work your arm muscles so you gain muscle primarily in your triceps. The purpose of the wooden sword, or the waster, is to condition your muscles without over straining your body before you pick up the real thing."

He grabbed an identical wood sword from his case and handed it to me so I could mimic him. After a few reps of the motion, I started to feel the burn in my triceps. It was a satisfying feeling; it made me feel like I could do this with a little practice. I was far from perfect with my form, but it was a start.

After a few more reps, we continued with other similar drills, moving the sword diagonally and then, shoulder to shoulder. We then held it out in front, making a small X in the air in front of us. Finn explained how the slight change in movement after every sequence was meant to work other muscles in my arms.

Boy, did I feel it. We continued these drills until my arms felt like cooked spaghetti.

How would I be able to hold a real sword and do this in a fight if I was so tired after just using the waster? Practice made perfect, I guess.

"How are you feeling, Ciara?" Finn asked.

"Like jelly," I replied honestly.

"Good—that means it's working. Keep that one for yourself for practice. I expect by the next time you'll be ready to hold a real sword, if you make the time to incorporate the drills into your daily routine. Don't let that self doubt creep into your head, either. You've been making remarkable progress, Ciara. That's all for today."

I drank some more water as Finn packed up his bag.

"Thank you, Finn. You're the best," I said after taking a large gulp.

After Finn left, I went straight to my room and opened the ribbon-marked page of the Solais Sword book. The feel of the aged, battered pages caressed my fingers as I found the sentence where I had left off:

Aelia kept trudging through the forest, her destiny not far off. The fox wouldn't trouble her today, she thought. After several days of trailing through the Heywood Forest on foot, she came across a body of water. It was so vast, so dark, and the dense mist hovered just above its surface in a curious way that raised the hairs on her arms. The lake seemed to be an entity in its own right, its presence as bold as Aelia's dreams. A metallic glimmer in the water close to the shore caught her gaze. She waded into the lake up to her hips before diving under to retrieve the source of her distraction.
There it was, in all its glory, as if calling out to her–she now possessed the Solais Sword. The very object of her freedom, for if she held the sword, no suitors could use it to claim her. Although she had royal duties and responsibilities, she was an unfettered woman, not a possession; a prize belonging only to herself...

Pieces of the mystical puzzle were slowly coming together.

The description of the lake near the Heywood Forest was strikingly familiar to what I knew now to be Lough Guinness. The dark waters, the heavy mist. This meant that the forest surrounding it must be the ancient Heywood woods. I recalled what I'd read earlier, of Aelia's mention of a fox and creatures of sharp claws and teeth.

It reminded me of the recent betrayal of Uallas, and how he previously had me fooled with his apparent kindness. A fox with two faces.

I slammed my book shut and sat there stewing in what I'd just discovered, unsure of whether to share this information with Finn just yet.

Quite honestly, I wanted to be more sure of myself before he talked me out of it. I also wasn't particularly eager to go back and meet Uallas in the forest again.

In truth, I was scared of what Uallas could be capable of. Maybe the concept of it all coming together was just as frightening.

For months, I'd been so comfortable seeking the right answers that I never thought about what I would do if the fruits of my labor actually panned out. Now here I was, answers in hand, and all I needed to do was reach out a little further. I was doing this for my father, so his death would not be in vain.

If anyone is cut out for this, it is you.

Finn's words replayed in my head like a broken record, but he was right. His words went beyond just practice. It wasn't that no one cared to solve my father's murder, but certainly no one was as invested as his own daughter. I needed to find the truth. I needed to hear it.

That this was because of a Pooka, that Uallas was both dangerous and highly manipulative. Which face did he show to the princess? Was he the golden-eyed, noble fox I once thought him to be, or was he the sharp-fanged, shadow-eyed one I saw him as now?

CHAPTER 26

I continued reading, hopeful that I'd get my answers within these pages. Anything would be helpful...

The sword hummed in her fingers. Her destiny lay in her hands in the form of a shiny iron sword. To the untrained eye, it was a plain piece of scrap metal. Sure, there were more extravagant pieces of varying designs belonging to kings and queens in kingdoms unknown, but none held such a tight grasp on her future. She would be a pioneer of her fate. Someday, she would save herself for true love if it were to ever stumble upon her doorstep.

Today, she'd earned her freedom in the thicket of the Heywood Forest. She defied the legends of the monsters that resided here, both of lore and of man. An optimist in her own right...

This only confirmed my theory that this fairy tale in particular was set in real places around Ireland. Places I'd seen with my own eyes, and the monsters mentioned, as well. It left me wondering if the events were true as well, regarding the Solais Sword.

I recalled all the ancient swords displayed in the library, free from their cases.

I hadn't put much thought into it before, as my main goal was to search for the secret armory. One at the beginning of each bookshelf section. A plain yet shiny one for nonfiction, one that looked as though it could've belonged to a pirate for fiction and fables and so on. Each blade looked as though it belonged in each corresponding section.

Now that I knew the purpose behind their naked mounts, I loved each piece a little more. That was my father: always paying attention to detail. I remembered his letter that I'd found the first time I picked up this book, where he mentioned that not all fairy tales were fiction—this one in particular.

I had a hunch that Lough Guinness and the surrounding forest were actually the Heywood Forest that the princess had mentioned. The letter all but confirmed it for me. It opened my mind up to consider the possibility that the fairy tale could have been an adapted version of Aelia's diary.

The author wrote it largely from her point of view, recalling events that happened around her specifically. It was only labeled as fantasy to keep the truth of this magical world a secret from the general public.

It made me think about that last time I was there, with Finn and Uallas.

With so much on my plate, now was a better time than any to call him. My mind was distracted from our lesson and I wanted to be sure that if he found anything else on the tape, he'd let me know.

After a few rings, his muffled voice came through his car audio: "Ciara, wasn't expecting a call so soon. Everything alright?"

I smiled through the phone, even though he couldn't see me. Who knew if it was hope or desperation that was keeping me going at this point. Better yet, a volatile combination of both. Hope that it would help me protect myself and my home from however Uallas might betray me next—among other unimaginable threats.

From what I knew about this crazy world that I inhabited, swords, especially iron ones, were a must. I wasn't simply reading fairy tales; I was living one.

"Yes, Finn. I know you're still on the road, but I just wanted to ask if you'll keep me in the loop with anything you find on the tape."

I concluded our conversation after he assured me that if anything else was amiss, I'd be the first person he'd inform.

The rest of the book was waiting on my favorite chair for me to finish it.

Hours passed before I made a noticeable dent in the story. It had ended the way I'd had feared: that while Uallas was the cunning fox of two faces, he preferred the one of deception and power.

The clock above the mantle showed it was roughly one in the morning, my favorite time of night. Anytime between midnight and three felt like being transported to another realm when all the world was quiet.

I took the opportunity to practice some of the fencing drills in the dead of the night. My breath and whip of the air against the waster were the only sounds in the entire castle. Letting the movements ease my mental pains, I didn't stop until my heart was pounding in my chest.

After I cleaned myself and went to bed, I stared up at the ceiling, thinking about what I'd just read. The only thing that could break the bridal quest was true love, which Aelia never found. I interpreted the rest as a road map to what the next few weeks, or even months would have in store for me.

Hopefully, history would not repeat itself.

CHAPTER 27

It had been a week since I finished The Legend of the Solais Sword.

Finn didn't find anything on the tapes that we didn't know already. It gave me a strange sense of relief, but still didn't fully ease the constant dread in my gut.

I continued practicing my drills and stances every day, just as he had asked, and I could feel the strength building in my body.

I needed to get the ball rolling if I wanted to wield an iron sword, so I asked Finn for another lesson. We began with our usual warm ups and he praised me on the progress I was making.

After an hour or two, he invited me to remove the short

sword from its lodging on the wall. He seemed to trust me more than I trusted myself.

"Even though it is shorter than the standard sword, it will still be much heavier than the rapier or waster, or even than what you may be used to carrying, weight-wise, in one hand. Swords are seen as an outdated means of defense, but as you know, we may sometimes encounter things that modern weaponry cannot kill or defeat. The hilt will always be the heaviest point of the sword, and every sword has a different purpose. Short swords, as you may have guessed, are for close encounters, and are also easier to carry and conceal. They give you an advantage in smaller spaces and increase your agility, with quicker thrusts and slashes."

He had me practice against an invisible target, occasionally correcting my form. Though I hadn't expected to be perfect right off the mark, a part of me felt like I was letting my father down with every misstep. The heaviness of the sword dragged down my movements, making each stroke feel even more wrong than the previous one. Dramatic sighs gave away my frustration.

"Ciara, it's okay. To be sure of the right ways, you also need to learn the wrong ways. Go easy on yourself—you will master this before you know it, with a little more practice. You have already come so far. To understand the feel of a sword, you must use a real one instead of a practice one. Use the mirror here to check your posture."

He used the rapier as a pointer to adjust my balance. "Your hips are too far outward—tuck your behind in just a little. There, feel that Perfect posture."

That was all I had to do? So close from giving up and all I had to do was make the smallest of changes for it to be perfect. It was a fitting paradigm for the majority of my life. It was time for me to make a shift in my life, to make some changes to become a better version of myself. To quit talking about it and start doing the little things. Everything would eventually add up. Finn was right. I could become a master of my destiny.

"Let's try a few more combinations. Slash, slash, stab. Just make sure you really lean into it on the last stab. Lead with your front foot for momentum and exhale for better mobility. Aim for the sternum." He pointed to the center of his chest and backed away, leaving more than enough room for me to practice the moves with the short sword.

The sword was much different than the wooden one, so I wasn't so sure I'd be able to manage these movements, but I had to start somewhere. I had enough faith in Finn that he wouldn't suggest something if I wasn't ready for it. So I attempted it.

With my focus more on where my hand movements were, my feet stumbled into place naturally. I slashed and slashed, and stabbed the air where my invisible rival's chest would be.

"Excellent, Ciara. You're a natural. Your father would be proud."

He paused, waiting for my reaction. But he was right—this is what my father wanted. I would give anything in the world to have him here, witnessing this on the sidelines. He'd probably be giving me advice or bickering with Finn about the best way to teach me. I slouched, making my body smaller at the thought.

CHAPTER 28

That night, I slept like a rock. Sword training with Finn had proven to be very draining, despite all the practice I put in. I loved the breathing exercises, however; they calmed my mind. I practiced those between bites of food at mealtimes, in the shower, literally anywhere I could think of.

After breakfast, I went back up to the solar room. I stretched to relieve some of the ache in my muscles and then practiced my stances. Every movement had a breath; every stance had a purpose.

Keep practicing, a voice in my head told me. *You're already getting so much better.*

I smiled at the voice in my head as I studied my form in the mirror. I altered my position to make sure it looked and felt right. Closing my eyes, I breathed in for a count of seven, chest rising gradually. Then out for another seven, a slow exhale, as if waiting for the air to be released from a pool toy.

I was almost at an ultimate calm when I realized the voice had not been my own, but it *was* one I recognized. My eyes shot wide open and I searched the room, my eyes falling on the mirror and landing on a shape out the window.

A reflection in the mirror revealed the figure.

Far in the distance, near the edge of the birch trees, stood a familiar face with silken white hair and iridescent horns gleaming in the midmorning sun.

Uallas, infiltrating my mind and rattling my calm.

How *dare* he think that a kind pep talk would help me forget the fact that he stole from my father, the very person who sought to protect him? My nostrils flared at the sight of him on the edge of the garden below.

Every rational thought left the building as I stormed downstairs and threw open the doors to the yard. Rage had me ignoring the brisk winter air biting at my nose and ears. I'd barely enough time to work up a sweat with my practice, and not enough sense of mind to put on a coat or boots before I left the house.

Frozen, crystalized blades of grass crunched like broken glass under my bare feet as I stomped toward Uallas. At least he had enough sense to back up a step or two after sensing my angry arrival.

"What in God's green earth are you doing here, Uallas? What makes you think you will *ever* be allowed in my presence again after that stunt you pulled down at the armory? Don't think for one second that I don't know it was you who stole the Solais Sword from my father!" I berated him, and he deserved every last word I threw at him.

"I thought it might come to this, Ciara," he said as if he was bored, but his face twisted into desperation at his next words.
"It was never my intention to hurt you. In fact, quite the opposite. Gaining access to that sword meant that I'd ensure your safety above all others who might wish to... gain access to you," he practically cooed.

His arrogance grated on my sanity. It made my blood boil. At the very least, I knew that in my currently pissed off state, my emotions were still my own. Real.

"What do you mean, 'gain access to me,'" I asked cautiously, not giving him any reason to think that I had an upper hand with my knowledge of Aelia and how she described the sword's singular qualities. Of how it granted her freedom of choice for a suitor when she held it in her own possession.

"Oh, I don't take you for a fool, Ciara. I think you know very well what the Solais Sword means for me and any other bastard out there who could've gotten their paws on it, or what that would mean to you. You would be theirs to do with as they wish, but their intentions are not as pure-hearted as my own, you see."

He cautiously closed the distance between us, as if these words would be enough to get whisked away by him forever. As if it were as simple as saying a few words to control my rage.

He should have known better, but he was foolish.

"The only bastard I see here is *you*, Uallas," I spat, halting his steps from coming any closer. Good. Maybe those words would make it clear how I truly felt about him. To me, he was the same as those slimeballs he believed to be out there in the world. No matter what words he spewed at me, he had proven it time and time again.

Closing my eyes, I focused on breathing exercises to calm myself.

I would no sooner call him mine than give him any reason to sway my emotions in his favor. I had control over them. The conversation was over, and I'd had the last damning words.

With my anger subsiding, I realized my ears and toes were numb.

I needed to go back inside for warmth, so without another word, I turned around and left him. So much for his claims of "protecting me" if he couldn't even see that I was about to be frostbitten out here without the proper attire. I ignored him calling out for me, pleading for me to return to him and settle the conversation. Like hell if I'd give him the power of returning to be his little fool.

I bit my shivering lip to refrain from letting the anger fuel me again with words I knew would be pointless. Vapor from my exhale clouded around me; the warmth from it was welcome on my frozen face. Once I made it back through the double doors, I locked them immediately and drew the curtains.

I went straight to the kitchen and put on the kettle for a comforting cup of tea. The ritual was as relaxing as the breaths I took.

Kettle on, wait for the whistle, put a spoonful of tea leaves in the strainer, and watch the water transform. Once satisfied at its deep color, I made my way over to the sitting room and turned on the fireplace with a switch on the wall, wrapping myself in the thickest blanket I could find.

I stared mesmerizingly at the licking flames coming to life in the fireplace. The glow of the flames drew me into a trance. I let the conversation with Uallas from earlier ebb from my mind.

The more thought I had given to him, the more authority I gave to him.

Did it matter if what he was speaking was the truth? That if, in stealing the sword and breaking into my father's armory, he was in fact saving me from the world's greater evils?

If Pookas were real, I could only imagine what else could be lurking in the nearby woods. I thought of the other nightmarish creatures of my father's stories, the sluagh. Evil spirits of the restless dead, some tales depicted them as dark, shadowy winged figures with malevolent intent.

I remember them being the main cause of my night terrors when I was merely six years old, and the main reason I was terrified of the dark. Why my father thought those types of stories were appropriate for a child, I'll never really know.

Yet here I was today, having a standoff with a Pooka on the lands of his vast estate.

I suppose I should have asked him, but I always thought we'd have all the time in the world together. That he'd grow old with me through this life. That once he was a grandfather, I'd be able to make an excuse to ask him then. Maternal instinct surging through my soft exterior so the stories wouldn't scar my future child as they did me.

It was a moment I knew I would never get to have. Uallas stole that future from me.

My eyes stung, but I was plenty warm sitting by the fire with my cup of tea in hand. I let the tears flow, giving in to visions of a perfect future that would never exist. Knowing that if I had a child, they would only know their grandfather through my memories. They would never fully understand hearing the sounds of his joyous laughter filling a room, his clever jokes that left everyone howling, or the theatrical manner in which he would tell such stories (if I let him).

I allowed my mind to wander, because grief was a better emotion than anger, if only slightly. At least, with his memories, it was a way to hold him close.

CHAPTER 29

My cup of tea heated my hands as I sat in my favorite leather chair, curled up with the softest sheep's wool blanket I could find. My thoughts were spiraling due to the previous events, and I just wanted a moment of serenity. It seemed as though a lifetime's worth of secrets had unraveled within such a short time frame, and I could barely catch my breath.

Powdery flakes of snow were starting to collect on the window panes outside, a stark contrast to the remote-controlled flames I had turned on in the fireplace. I found the licking flames enthralling, a captivating spectacle that hypnotized me before the world around me faded to black.

It was just me, the chair, the tea, and the flames. Simple.

If I could go back in time, would I still seek the answers I had now?

The saying "the truth will set you free" is purely subjective. In no way did I feel "free" knowing the truth of my father's betrayal by Uallas. It felt more similar to having an itch that needed to be scratched. Once you scratched that area, and felt satisfied, the itch simply moved to another area. Never leaving you genuinely satisfied.

It was the honorable thing to do, that much was for certain. To commemorate my father's life so I had no regrets, regardless of this rugged trail it had led me on. I closed my eyes and took another healing sip of the black tea, both hands warming on the mug.

Between that and the radiating heat of the fire, I almost felt as if I were back home in Florida on a late spring day, with the summer heat trying to intrude prematurely. I figured at some point I'd miss home, but no matter where I went, the unbearable weight of what had happened would forever be in the back of my mind.

If my years of living with anxiety had taught me anything, it was that the mind was one place no one could escape from. At least, not forever. Moving forward was just a narrative you played over and over to make it more palatable.

A knocking at the door grabbed my attention, as I wasn't expecting anyone this evening. I took the closest sword off its mount. I hadn't had enough practice yet to wield the weapon in an actual fight beyond my drills, so hopefully, whoever was about to step foot over that threshold was a friend and not a foe.

Couldn't a girl catch a break?

A figure with disheveled hair and recognizable, somber green eyes cracked open the front door warily.

"Ciara? It's Conor. I apologize for coming in unannounced. Um, can you please put that down so we chat for a moment?"

I released the breath I was holding when I realized it was just him. Thank goodness—I didn't think I had any fight in me tonight. I instantly dropped the iron sword and ran over to give him a friendly hug. The clatter echoed throughout the halls as I released him.

"Please, come in! I'm so grateful to see you. What did you want to chat about?"

I motioned for him to take a seat next to my spot near the fire and eagerly awaited whatever he had to say next.

"I'd like to start by saying thank you for giving me the time I needed for my ma. I just put her house on the market. It held too many memories for me to stay there all by myself. I was wondering if it would be alright if I lived in the guest quarters until I find my own accommodations when I return to work. I promise not to trouble ya unless you ask."

I couldn't deny the desperation in his voice. He had done so much for me in the short time we'd had together here at the estate, it would be the least I could do. I definitely had enough rooms to where he could live comfortably on the other end of the castle, and we'd likely never run into each other. Whenever he was ready to come back, I'd welcome him with open arms, much like I had tonight.

But first, I had a few lingering questions that I needed answers to before I could make an official decision on the matter.

A tiny voice in the back of my head only grew louder upon his recent arrival. It started as a whisper of what he *really* knew about my father. For someone to work so closely with him, Conor had to have some kind of knowledge of what had happened to him.

Everyone deserved their own time to mourn, especially for their parents, and if I was being honest with myself, it was rather nice not having him around while this mess was happening. It gave me time to think—until he walked in. Another moment that Conor caught me off guard.

"I have something to ask you first, before I can make my decision."

I took a sip of my tea to stall the inevitable question stuck in the back of my throat. "Do you know anything about the theft in the subterranean armory?"

No need to sugar coat it—better to keep it simple and straightforward. I couldn't look at him without memories of that one night infiltrating my thoughts. I just continued to stare straight into the flames. It took nearly all my emotional strength to look at him, but I finally broke my gaze from the fire to look him directly in his eyes.

I observed his body language to detect any uneasiness or awkward eye contact that would tell if he was lying. Conor started fidgeting and running his hands through his hair, much like that one time he came home from a visit at the hospital when his ma wasn't doing so well. I clearly remembered his hair, messed up from his own fretting, just as it was now under his stress. He was understandably still distraught over his mother's passing. I was eager to hear him speak.

"I know of it. I'm so sorry for letting you down, Ciara. Uallas threatened me to make sure I'd keep it a secret. Doesn't matter much now—his threat is meaningless now since ma is—"

Gone was the word that didn't have to be said for me to understand the implications of why he held that information from me. Uallas didn't need to use his gift of toying with emotions in this way. Conor was absolutely, positively, beyond a doubt, just plain manipulated.

"So, what exactly do you know?"

Maybe this time, Conor had entered my life at the most opportune moment. Maybe this time, he would help me out with something other than an orgasm. It was about time for another break in my investigation. I wrinkled my face into my best *pretty please* pout in one last attempt to get him to spill the figurative tea.

"Uallas was one of the Pookas that your father sought to protect and make peace with for our community here in the isles. Part of my many job descriptions was being well enough versed within his world here. I don't know everything—just enough that he would allow me to learn, before you ask that."

He swallowed and continued, "As far as the break in with Uallas, he made me show him where the subterranean armory was and how to get in. He never forced me to tell him about any video surveillance, so I conveniently left that information out. I asked him what he planned to do with whatever he was seeking down there. He kept dodging my question and just kept repeating, 'When it is done, it will be in the bottom of the abyss.' He kept speaking in riddles. Dodgy guy. I didn't think much of it until after it cost your da his life. I'm so sorry, Ciara. Do those words he spoke mean anything to you?"

My jaw was on the floor the more Conor dragged it on. Anger and betrayal bubbled under my skin. He consciously decided on a course of action that ultimately led to my father's death. One better, he let me believe he was a good and honest man, someone my father could trust.

In order to save his mother, he cost me my dad and his boss.

I didn't want to wrap my head around where he knew the implications of what he was doing or not. If the roles were reversed, would I not do the same?

Of course, I would.

When it is done, it will be in the bottom of the abyss.

I never thought only four words would be enough to completely crack me open. "When it is done." He was referring to the murder of my father, no doubt. Especially because I already knew his death was caused by outside natural forces.

Despite the warmth the fire gave, I was completely frozen. Everything around me felt unreal, as if this was the worst dream and I couldn't wake to make it stop. I couldn't cry or scream. The shock of this holding me down like invisible hands suffocated my emotion.

The bottom of the abyss? Not too many abysses I knew of had a bottom, unless it was a body of water of sorts. The only bodies of water I knew of were the sea near the cliffs and Lough Guinness. The coast would be much too far, though.

Was that it? The sword had to be on the bottom of Lough Guinness. How could you tell how deep one of the blackest lakes in the country was?

I tried to recall what I'd read in the library about the lake and the surrounding area, but all I remembered were a lot of confusing numbers.

Despite my love for reading, I was never very competent at memorizing numbers or stats. I vaguely remembered reading about a series of numbers for the square footage of the lake and the forest, and that the number representing the depth of the lake had one comma attached to it. Too deep for humans to free dive, and definitely not with my measly lung capacity. Conor had no idea that he had inadvertently told me where Uallas had hidden the Solais Sword—the weapon that killed my father.

"Conor, I appreciate you telling me all that, but please understand why I can't trust you living here with me. Even if we may or may not run into each other. I just need some time to think, okay? If you need, I will set you up in a hotel for the time being."

He lowered his gaze, unable to maintain direct eye contact. He seemed either guilty of finally relaying the truth, or bitter about my response.

"I understand. I'd better get going, then. Good to see you again, Ciara."

With that sentiment, he got up and walked out of my life. Again.

CHAPTER 30

I tossed and turned endlessly that night. So many thoughts from the day swirled about in my subconscious. Once I finally fell asleep, I entered the nightmares from the stories my father had read to me. I dreamed of the feared sluagh, coming to take me as his wife into the land of the unliving.

A dark, winged figure, made up entirely of shadows and smoke, sliced my father through the heart with the Solais Sword. His wails were ear piercing and shattered my heart into millions of pieces all over again. My screaming matched

his, a symphony of love and death. The sluagh was claiming me as his own as his shadows wrapped around me in a bitter, deathly coldness and his wings lifted us away.

Uallas was cackling on the ground. "I told you, Ciara, but you would not listen, would you? Now look at your fate"

A kiss from the sluagh would seal my fate as his own. I would no longer be in the land of the living, but with him, forever, in hell. Eternity separated me from my father, even after my own end. There was no hope for me to live out my days happily.

I'd forever be in this state, young yet miserable. A bride stolen against her will. I was trapped by the fate Aelia sought to free herself from. It was divine retribution for ignoring Uallas's warnings. The sluagh sucked the very soul from my body, chaining me to him eternally...

My scream jolted me awake, body drenched in sweat. I was gasping for air, as if that had been stolen from me, too.

I took note of my surroundings. I was safe in my room, in bed, despite the chokehold the dream had on me. No shadows or trace of Uallas in sight.

I acknowledged four things I could see, touch, hear, and smell. It was a grounding technique seared into my mind from my therapist back in Florida, meant to ease my anxiety. Desk, damp sheets, birds chirping, and, on an inhale, I detected the light musk of pages from the bookshelf.

One thought that persisted was that the nightmare would have been the perfect moment for Fearghas to intervene in my dark dreams—but where was he?

Come to think of it, he hadn't pursued me at all after that day in the fields.

I was sure he had some great excuse, as they all do for leaving me high and dry.

After my breathing steadied, I got up and took a hot shower, letting the steam soothe my body. Lavender and mint shampoo eased my nerves and the scalp massage was exactly what I needed to start my day refreshed.

Today was noticeably warmer than the previous day, as if my dreams of hellfire had held some eerie truth about them. The ice had melted away and reset the world from its wintry wonders. Today was the perfect day to check out Lough Guinness before it froze over again. I may not get the opportunity again so soon and I would not make the same mistake of being caught outside without the proper garments. I opted for my fur-lined boots, fuzzy socks dad had gotten me last year on Christmas, and the warmest attire I could find. It was still cold out, but not enough to freeze the lake.

I'd had to scour the town once I got here to find some proper clothes for the weather. Ireland had all four seasons. Being a Florida girl, I'd never owned a proper winter jacket. Our seasons consisted of two options: hot and bug-infested, or hurricanes.

I grabbed my mittens and matching tartan scarf and called the kitchen to whip up a quick breakfast of bacon, eggs, and buttered toast. I made a call for Ronan to pick me up and he was here within the hour.

"Oi, Ciara. Nice seein' ya again. Where are ya off to today?" Ronan said with his thick accent. It was an oddly comforting sound.

"Take me up to Lough Guinness, please," I'm sure it sounded like an odd request given the weather was still crisp, but I had tasks to do.

Surprisingly, no questions were asked. He just nodded as we departed the driveway. Maybe he's grown used to my unusual requests. I maintained my usual spot, staring out the window in awe of my surroundings.

I was blessed that this was my new home. It had, in fact, become home to me over the past few months here, both the people and he places I'd become acquainted with, Ronan included. A hint of a smile tugged at my lips at the thought.

We were finally approaching Lough Guinness and the surrounding forest that I'd come to realize was the ancient Heywood Forest. The cab screeched to a halt at the edge of the thicket near the path to the lake.

"Thanks, Ronan. I'll give you a ring when I'm ready to be picked up," I smiled back at him.

"Already waiting," he said as he lifted his phone.

I turned around and he was off to pick up his next passenger. I stared up at the tall trees in front of me. They were now bare of their crimson leaves I'd seen in autumn. They reminded me of skeletons having lost their skin.

A whole army of them made up the forest. Visibility was a bit easier, given that I didn't have the leaves blocking my view. Easier for Uallas to see me, harder for me to hide. Good thing my attire wasn't bright, save for my mittens and scarf. I tried to stay on the path with thicker trunks so I could hide at a moment's notice if need be.

I didn't want to risk Uallas knowing I was here in search of the sword, or especially obliging myself to speak with him if he presented himself. I kept my eyes ahead of me, in pursuit of a clearing with a mist-ridden obsidian pool.

Aelia claimed the blade had "called out to her" in the book, and I couldn't help but wonder how much of the fairy tale was myth and how much of it was truth. Time was of the essence.

Just a little further.

I'd been here before, but everything looked as if it was part of a dream. Yet, I knew the sword was nearby. Maybe this was what Aelia was feeling. A sensation of familiarity.

A connection with the sword.

I steadied my breaths: seven counts in, seven out. It took me five full sets of breathing before I saw it. A permanent veil of mist hovering over the stilled black water, oddly reminiscent of the trademark pint.

I'd finally made it. One task achieved, now onto the next. The sword. What would I even do when I found it? I couldn't dive in—the water was still ice cold.

Sheets of ice still clung to its borders, though the majority had melted away. Even if I dipped my toe in, my blood was still too thin to adjust to the cold.

I would get frostbite, or worse. That was if I didn't fall through the ice. Who knew how deep it reached in those spots? Doubt started creeping into my mind, pilfering my hope.

I hadn't put much thought into the logistics of it all until now.

I released a defeated sigh. As I turned around to the clearing behind me, I swore I saw a shimmer in the darkness, but it was not the sword.

CHAPTER 31

Fearghas entered the space, the swirling shadows behind him adding an air of drama I couldn't help but gawk at. It had been a while since we shared that tantalizing kiss in the rain. Why had he stayed away from me?

Especially the previous night, when I needed his soothing words or pleasant dreams. I had spent many nights wondering about this very moment, trying to dream of them. They'd only been blocked by some external force I could only imagine was him.

He hadn't even sought me out in my sleep. Did he get what he wanted and decided to leave, like those brief one-night stands I had back in Florida?

He'd seemed to have a lot to say to me that day in the field. Had his words run dry now?

"Ciara, what a pleasant surprise to see you here," he crooned, interrupting my thoughts.

Seeing his perfect face in person was a far cry from remembering these past weeks. No words in my brain surfaced to answer him in return. My gaze just traveled along his human form, noting his bulging muscles, his full-lipped smile at my presence. A tease. My throat bobbed, taking note of the watering that had pooled in my mouth. I had almost forgotten how beautiful he was and how it affected me. What had he called it? Lust? Desire?

I couldn't help the thought that it felt more than that. I should have been elated to see him here, but I couldn't control the words that spewed from my mouth.

"Is it?" I scowled.

Judging by his actions the past few weeks, it seemed as if seeing me here had been anything but pleasant and simply just a surprise. He deserved my anger.

All those sweet nothings he whispered about being there for me, only to flee. The tears he'd wiped from my face reassuringly. Had he thought I'd come crawling back to him simply because he was the most delicious-looking man I've ever seen? His broad chest rose and fell with a heavy sigh, but I didn't miss the swell of his muscles with it—against my better judgement.

"I have only been distant for your safety, Ciara."
He sounded exhausted and hurt, but continued, "As you know, Uallas can read emotions. I have a brotherly bond with him, so I couldn't allow him into any part of me or us. It has been absolute torment every waking minute, believe me, to know that my brother betrayed you and your father that way—"

He'd slipped and revealed too much, but I deserved to know everything.

"You knew?! How long have you known, Fearghas?"

Oh, if I thought I was angry before...

"Ciara, please. He has become dangerous and the laws of our kind forbid me telling you sooner about his indiscretions. If he could get into my mind and understand what led to your current–" he hesitated before saying the next word, "emotion, you have no idea the wrath he could bring upon us both. I am so sorry I kept this from you. You have no idea how much it has pained me to harbor this knowledge."

"How long have you known, Fearghas?" I gritted out, anger clouding my rational thinking skills.

"Since you arrived at the castle," he said with his head down, balking.

"Are you kidding me? This entire time, you knew? That bullshit you told me about doing anything for me? This is *not* it. Pretty damn far from it, actually. You two really are cut from the same cloth."

The words tumbled out of my mouth, meant to cut deep.

I released my resentment toward him that I had been bottling up for so long. If I was honest with myself, that last bit was only said to see how much he'd actually fight for me, or if he'd just accept my words as his truth.

"Don't you *dare* compare me to that filthy excuse of a brother." He closed the distance between us, trudging over while holding his finger directly in my face. "I have already killed for you, Ciara. Tell me, what else do I need to do to prove you are everything to me? Your safety is my top priority. I'm sorry if how I make sure of it doesn't fit your standards."

We just stood there, suspended in each other's furious glances.

Words shared were meant to slice on both sides. Despite his finger in my face, that was one hell of an apology, truthfully. He *had* killed for me, for my safety.

Even though it was a little late, his confession of what he knew of Uallas's theft was there. He confessed it without being asked, unlike Conor.

"Everything I said in that field that day was the truth. You are beautiful, you are radiant, you are my obsession, you are the sunshine on my—"

I shut him up by sucking on the finger he was holding in front of me. I didn't know what came over me—I just wanted him back.

The pain I'd detected in his voice after the anger started to soften, transforming to desire. His words were like a cool breeze on a warm summer day. Maybe I shouldn't have been so bold. A simple kiss would've been sufficient. But damn it all when I missed him like I had. His thick brows rose, and he let out a soft whimper at the act.

Our eyes locked as I slowly removed his finger from my mouth, suggestively closing my mouth on his fingertip. His eyes widened at the sight of it.

Good. Maybe that would shut him up.

But my plan had backfired when he kissed me. He put such passion into his kiss, as if making up for all the weeks that had passed. As if this immortal being had been counting down the days or minutes until he'd be by my side again. He'd given into breaking his rules for me. Crumpled at the pleading, simply because I had asked him.

So I opened my mouth a little further, inviting him to taste me.

He deepened the kiss as if under my command. We flowed together, completely intertwined in each other's ecstasy.

I hadn't realized just how much I had missed him. My skin began to feel electrified, an aching building up low between the apex of my thighs.

My hands gripped his buttoned neckline. My fingers blindly undid a few buttons, leaving his chest bare for me. We didn't missed a beat of the kiss as he took this as his cue to squeeze my breast through the jacket. It was still too far away, so he removed my scarf and started trailing kisses down my jaw, around my ear, and on the soft spot on my neck, causing shivers that had nothing to do with the weather. I hummed in pleasure, trailing my hand lower down his abdomen.

I hated to admit it, but he really was my dream man—in more ways than one. I'd never hear the end of it if I told him, cocky bastard he was. He was such a pleasant distraction from what I came here to do.

Speaking of that—

"Wait." I had to push away from the kiss or else I'd never return to consciousness. "If you know of Uallas and the sword, are you able to retrieve it from the lake? Being immortal and all that?"

I made an excuse to revel in his form making note of the planes of his chest and his muscled arms. He watched me do it with feline curiosity.

"Hmm. I suppose my immortality would aid me with

breathing underwater for extended periods of time and not freezing to death. These clothes might be a hindrance, however. If only I could change…" he smirked suggestively at me.

"What an odd way to tease a girl," I replied. It was hard to hide my laugh at his remark and its double meaning.

Sure enough, shadows swirled around the middle of his body. With a seductive wink, the swirls dissipated and he stood there, naked and at full attention. My throat bobbed at the sheer sight of it, of him. He was a perfect size. His entire body was in full view for my pleasure, as if carved from stone. He was a masterpiece. Completely unaffected by the crisp air as a human man might be.

"Show off," I snickered as soon as I mustered up enough brain cells to speak.

"I would still do anything for you, Ciara. I always will. Let me start by retrieving your sword."

Before I could reply, I heard a modest splash that would make an Olympic diver envious, and he was off to the bottom of the lake.

Seconds turned to minutes, and he was still under the water. I wondered, how deep really was Lough Guinness? I had to keep reminding myself he was immortal and him spending this much time beneath the surface was okay. *He was fine.*

Time kept passing and I kept my gaze on the rippled area he'd made when he leapt in. It was now smooth as glass. I couldn't help feeling as though something went wrong. It was only human of me.

Suddenly, as if answering my silent prayers, the water broke the surface on the other end of the lake. I audibly sighed in relief when I saw Fearghas, the Solais Sword raised above his head. I put my finger to my mouth to make sure he remained silent as I motioned for him to hurry back with my other hand. It took him much longer than I had anticipated to swim back to me with the sword in hand. He threw the sword up onto the land before pushing his cold, wet, naked body onto the ground before me.

"As you wish, m'lady." He showed off his body, yet again, accompanied by a flawless smile, "You know, Pookas aren't known for their swimming. Need I remind you, the lengths I would go for you are immeasurable?" His voice was a caress.

He picked up the sword from the forest floor and handed it to me, hilt first. I took it, purposely letting our fingers brush. He was frigid.

"Are you not cold? Your fingers are like icicles." Storybooks never explained how the internal body mechanisms of Pookas worked—just that they changed forms.

"Are you concerned for my well-being, Sunshine?" His eyes darkened. He knew damn well that I was. *Jerk*.

His playfulness reminded me of the first day we met. He knew all the right buttons to push, and I'd let him. Like a kid in an elevator, lighting up every button on the switch panel for the fun of it.

CHAPTER 32

"You *are* concerned. I know that look. *Intimately.*" Fearghas beamed as he raised an eyebrow at me.

"You are insufferable." I couldn't help my eye roll when he added the word intimately.

"I don't feel cold like humans do, if that is what you're wondering. It has to do with the shifting and magic. Our bodies are unaffected by the surrounding climate. I may be cold to the touch but internally, my body remains a constant comfortable temperature."

His eyes narrowed at me, a smile remaining plastered to his face.

"Did you not know this as you sent me into the depths, Ciara?"

Okay, noted. That was pretty badass, though.

Moments later, he was engulfed in darkness and his clothes were back on. I wondered why he was changing again if we were the only ones out here.

"Well, I didn't exactly, but...you agreed!" I had to call his bluff.

"I'm joking. I did agree to it, and I'd do it again. I'm completely unharmed, don't worry your pretty little head of yours. So, what would you have done if you hadn't found me out here?"

His question lingered for a bit, swirling in my mind's abyss. Before he arrived, I was about to turn around and call Ronan to pick me up. Accept my defeat.

Then, Fearghas had arrived, and he was there for me when it mattered.

I searched his eyes for any tell that he knew it too, and had come to my aid. My silence said everything I couldn't admit aloud. His hand brushed my cheek, and I leaned into it.

"Thank you," was all I needed to say for him to understand.

"Always. I'm happy I could be of service." He planted a kiss on my forehead as he held me in his strong arms and I clung to him. Such a simple yet intimate action. I realized this was what I had been missing since the funeral. Where words failed, actions spoke volumes. Sincerity wasn't words wrapped in silk ribbons passed off as thoughts and prayers; it was truth and understanding. Understanding that the pain was so great that any combination of words would be insufficient. When there was a hole in the heart, you must smother it with affection.

When he released me, his expression turned somber, as if something else lingered in his mind that he was holding back from me.

When he finally spoke, his words were softer, with a touch of melancholy. He only broke our embrace to say them to me directly:

"I've got you, Sunshine. Throughout any darkness that smothers you—"

Suddenly, his nostrils flared as if he was back to his animal form scenting a nearby predator.

"Ciara, you have to leave here immediately. I can smell that Uallas is nearby and I cannot allow him to harm you like he did your father. If you were ever to not be breathing because of him..." He shook off the thought, hardly missing a beat. "Let's just say it would be his last breath, too... no matter if we were cut from the same cloth. Please, *run*."

His pupils were wide and dilated with pure fear—either from Uallas or the fact that he had let slip a vital, damning piece of information. He confirmed what I had known to be true, but I was just as stunned as if I was learning it for the first time.

I might as well have been transformed into the crying statue from my gardens, as I stood there in silence as tears flowed down my cheeks. Every stage of grief enveloped me. Especially denial over the fact, that Uallas had not only betrayed, but also *murdered* my father.

Did Fearghas know about it the entire time, and this had all been some twisted way to protect me?

I'd sell my soul for my father to be alive, so I wouldn't be in this predicament right now. I'd have to accept the fact that nothing I could do would change the fate that Uallas so maliciously bestowed on him. My father wasn't coming back, ever. He'd only be alive in my fondest memories.

A cool wind stung the salty tears on my cheeks and brought me back to the moment, to Fearghas. He had been calling my name to bring me out of my stupor for who knows how long.

What was it that he said again?

Oh—he begged me, urged me to run. So I did. Picking up the sword, I ran back toward the forest clearing where Ronan had dropped me off.

My aching muscles went as fast as they could take me. I hadn't gotten far before I noticed an obsidian stallion galloping next to me, nostrils flaring like they had that night behind the tavern.

Steam erupted from them like my kettle.

He whinnied for me to get up on his back. He'd be much faster than my legs could carry me. I somehow made it up onto his back with my one free hand. Pure adrenaline coursed through my veins now, tears still leaking, freezing my face. I held on for my life, gripping onto his luxurious mane, but an invisible force held me in place, relaxing me. We raced along as if we were catching the setting sun along the horizon.

"Where are we going?" I asked and gripped his body tightly with my thighs just because I could.

I could have sworn he smirked at that. He sped up, the sound of his hooves striking the ground was in perfect pace with my heartbeat. Thunderous and fast.

The edge of the forest was in sight. I eased up when we finally hit the clearing. He still maintained his speed to lead me to safety, so I dared a glance behind me. I tried to conceal the sword as best as I could so Uallas couldn't see it.

"Hurry!" I yelled at Fearghas. Uallas, in his rabbit form, was gaining on us.

I thought for sure Uallas would be an absolute idiot to follow us into territory where any eyes could be on us. I had underestimated him before, but I doubted even he was dumb enough to risk a stand off with his brother out in public.

If Uallas found out that I took the sword from where he'd hid it in the lake, I'd be in trouble. I didn't want his wrath directed toward me. Knowing he was capable of killing a person who trusted him was terrifying.

Of course, I missed my father immensely, but I would not be greeting him at the holy gates today. No—I still had so much more to live for. There was life I had yet to experience.

So not today, and not until my body is withered and my hair fades to a shade of white. Only then will I be ready to tell him all about my life.

The moments here in Ireland that I cherished. Meeting Finn, Norman, Fearghas and even Conor. I'd leave out the spicy parts, of course. I'd tell him about my future husband and any grandchildren we may have. Or maybe I'd tell him about how The Agency was doing and about my future role in the company. Wherever my life may take me.

But my story couldn't be cut short. Not today.

"I will not stop until you are back at home, inside with me, doors bolted, and I can assure your safety." He sneered, irritated at Uallas for intervening.

To my horror, Uallas was not slowing. I wrapped my arms tighter around Fearghas's neck; despite his magic holding me in place. It felt right to be close to him when I was terrified.

It was ironic, being chased by a killer in the form of a pure white rabbit.

I didn't look back until we arrived at the estate, so I didn't notice the slight flicker of Fearghas's ember eyes or Uallas halting abruptly by the roadway.

CHAPTER 33

In a matter of minutes, we arrived at the castle. Fearghas told me that Uallas had stopped chasing us after we left the clearing because he had invaded his emotions and sensed the intensity of Fearghas's threat. What a coward Uallas was.

As soon as we arrived at the front entrance, I unlocked the door and entered. Fearghas followed closely, after swiftly changing form and we bolted the doors behind us.

I went over to the sitting room and turned on the fire, as usual. Fearghas sat in the chaise next to me. His eyes appeared to cast no reflection against the light of the flames.

"Fearghas, care to explain?" I cut the silence.

The adrenaline of the chase was starting to wear thin. I

wanted to have the conversation we should have had before I ran for my life.

"Ciara, before I start, no matter what I say, I know it isn't going to make it better. Fuck, I never wanted it to come to this, but damn the code to hell. I realize that now. I was wrong to hold all this from you," Fearghas fiercely apologized.

"But"—I paused, trying to wrap my head around the previous events that occurred—"how did he do it? If you knew of it, tell me everything. I deserve to know. Now that it's just the two of us."

My eyes had no more tears to shed. I had nothing left to give. Asking the question triggered the memory of that one devastating phone call, leaving me feeling numb.

Fearghas hesitated before answering, carefully brainstorming his next set of words. His shoulders sagged as he spoke. His elbows rested on his knees as if his body was heavy.

"Ciara, when Uallas learned that your father had acquired the Solais Sword, he became feral, obsessed with taking it from him by any means necessary. Any logic or sense went out the window. He ignored the code of our kind. When he went after him, your father, even stealing it from the armory, it would have been sufficient to prove his lack of ethical conduct. Sure, we are notorious for being mischievous, but even we have our limits. One day your father met with Uallas just outside these walls to confront him about the theft. Your father tried to reason with him peacefully, probably using the tactics he'd acquired from The Agency, but Uallas was having none of it. Uallas stabbed him with the sword, straight through his heart. I have reason to believe your father knew that if he was the one to obtain the sword, that it would protect you. With his last dying breath, he was looking after you, Ciara. Despite it all, I'm glad that I could be the one that retrieved it for you because even though it took his life, it also represents what a strong man your father was. I cannot attest to my brother's actions; in fact, he is on my list of fuckers to bring down, but I want to do right by you in any way that I can."

His eyes held mine for minutes after, not daring another word before I had my say.

His words wrenched my heart, squeezing almost every last ounce of happiness and hope from it. Fearghas was my silver lining to it all, in some strange way. He was my saving grace. My thoughts stuck to his mention of how strong my father had been for me.

His last moments must have been absolute torment before the blade struck. An intended heirloom representing free will and heroism and righteousness, stolen by Uallas who was the opposite of all it offered.

The sword was only intended to be wielded by a hero, and so my father was, in many respects. In my studies at the library, it was highly regarded in legends as a weapon to slay the gods with. From the people I've met here that knew my father, they spoke highly of him, as if putting him on an altar. It was close enough in my eyes. The very idea made my broken heart start to heal.

I gave Fearghas a tight-lipped smile before my lips began to quiver. I went over to him and squeezed in next to him in the chaise, wrapping my arms around him and burying my face into his chest. He stroked my head and kissed my hair. It was all too much for words to be spoken, so we sat together like that until it was time for bed and the fire was long gone.

After I got up, I asked Fearghas to stay. I thought it might be best to have him here in case Uallas had any mind to pay me a visit in the middle of the night. I led him upstairs to my room and closed the door behind us. I walked over to the bathroom and began undressing for the shower.

"Fearghas, I wanted to thank you for retrieving the sword and being there for me today when I needed you the most. In probably more ways than you can imagine," I said through the crack in the door.

I caught Fearghas watching me undress and letting my hair down. The look he had on his face when I caught him made me smirk. He didn't look away; he seemed to enjoy that I was watching him admire me.

"You are delicious," he said darkly from beyond the bathroom door, eyeing my bare figure. "May I come in?"

I nodded as I turned on the shower and hopped in, silently extending the invite for him to join me there. Fearghas's tall stature made the space feel so small.

He undressed and entered the shower with me. He took it slow this time, starting with his shirt. The rise and flex of his chest and abs was a sight to behold. Next came his slacks. He expertly unbuttoned them with one hand. I kept that maneuver buried in my thoughts for later. I ogled the way his body and horns took up most of the room in the shower.

I let the hot water cascade down my body as I continued to admire him, only blinking when I allowed it to run down my face and over my eyelashes. I completely lost sight of my initial goal to wash myself. I just stood there stupidly, mouth agape like a fish out of water.

He simply beamed at me, holding my chin between his thumb and forefinger.
"Would you prefer for me to wash you, Ciara?" he said, one singular dark brow raised.

I licked the droplets of water still falling from my lips and agreed.

I nodded to my lavender soap and loofah. I'd never had anyone offer to wash me before, but after today, I'd earned it. He motioned for me to turn around and started scrubbing my back first, the circular motions feeling more like a massage. Then he moved to my shoulders and arms before progressing to my lower back.

The action was pure. I was too exhausted in every capacity to make anything sensual of it and, to curiously, he didn't explore that option further during the wash. Not everything intimate had to be a sexual experience with him, though I certainly preferred when it could be.

After, we toweled off, and I dressed for bed.

"Sleep next to me," I proposed to him. "Please?"

Even though I wasn't certain how his head would fit on the pillow with his spiraling horns, I wanted him to lie next to me like we had on the chaise downstairs.

"Of course, Sunshine, I know it's been a rough day for you," he replied affectionately as he slid onto the other side of the bed.

I had a feeling he would have stayed anyway, even if I hadn't asked.

It took him a while to adjust to the bed, attempting to find the perfect angle for his horns so as to not be too much of a nuisance. When he found his sweet spot, he enveloped his arms around me, our bodies flush again at last. I hummed in pleasure at the touch of him against me in all the right places. He ran his hand along the curves of my body and the sensation was my last thought before I fell into a deep sleep.

CHAPTER 34

FEARGHAS

Ciara was so exhausted that she fell asleep in an instant, as if under a spell. A real Sleeping Beauty. I didn't blame her after the day she had endured.

My little fighter. Always having to stick it out even when she's going through absolute hell.

She wouldn't be suffering alone in silence much longer. I brushed a tendril of her hair away from her face. Who could have guessed this radiant woman would transform me into something so soft-hearted?

My makers would be dumbfounded to see that their little prince of nightmares was *cuddling*. I suppose even the devil was once an angel. The notion of it had me smiling.

I would never again be the evil they had planned for me. Not with Ciara in my life.

However, I'd burn the world down if it meant she could find peace again from the ashes. That was my only quest now: to let her find peace. Whatever hole was missing from her soul after Sean passed, I would do my best to fill it.

So I started with what I knew best. I shut my eyes and let my mind drift into hers, seeking out that passage that separated the real world from the realm where dreams were created.

I opened the door into her mind and I was greeted with a pitch black room of nothing. A blank canvas for me to do as I wish. So, I created a paradise of birds chirping and waterfalls cutting into mountains. I painted the many hues of purple and yellow wildflowers lining the banks of a secluded forest, with cotton candy colored skies in the distance.

A warm wind played with her hair as she dipped her toes in the water, disrupting the bioluminescence of the deep turquoise. Glowing specs in varying shades of greens, blues, and purples took the form of fireflies above, dancing around her. I allowed her to play as long as she wanted in the magical space, until her mind drifted.

Soon, the landscape I had created for her began to transform into Lough Guinness and I could tell that she was about to spiral into the terrors of today.

Fuck, what was I thinking, showing her a body of water? Of course, it would trigger where her mind was headed.

I filed through the happier memories I had of her father. Most were in a secluded field of rolling emerald hills and patchwork shrubbery, similar to the area where we had our first kiss. I thrust the new scenery into her dreams quickly, as every second counted in this realm. This time, I added her father. They were together walking alongside each other down a gravel path. It was from one of my own memories of Sean and me.

Next to me in bed, her lips began to twitch, attempting a smile from the new dream. A good sign. I had never played around with dreams and the recently deceased in this manner, as the dead could usually walk in this realm of their own accord.

So, I decided I'd try something I never had before. I briefly left Ciara's mind to seek out Sean. Maybe being so near to her and planting this new vision, I could invite him personally to walk beside her, allowing for a more natural interaction. One that I knew that she needed, if at all possible.

When I reached back into the depths of my own mind and sought the dream passage, I had to dig a little further into the expanse of the realm. A blindingly white door with filigreed golden handles answered my beckoning. The gates to the afterlife.

Sean was somewhere in there, but I had to tread carefully. The last thing I wanted was to be stuck in the afterlife for an eternity. The deepest sleep one can have. I'm not sure even my immortal life would stand up the those laws here.

I did the only thing I could think of and knocked.

"Sean Driscoll? Are you there? Ciara needs you," I said into the light before me.

A familiar voice echoed back through the door. "Fearghas, my man! A million thank yous to you for looking after my daughter. I'm surprised you made it all the way over here from your dreamland, but I suppose that's where I'm needed. Goodbye, old friend."

Sean's words were muffled but it still sounded like his typical animated self, as if in the afterlife he'd managed to continue being just as cheerful as in life. When there was a lull from the other side, I knew he was where he was meant to be. I didn't dare linger any longer than I needed to.

Back down my familiar passage, I reentered Ciara's dream just to make sure he made it safely and that she was still there as well, walking the path.
The dangers in the afterlife were just as perilous as on

earth, only multi-dimensional.What I saw when I returned would thaw the coldest of hearts.

Ciara and Sean laughing and walking together. Ciara was catching up her father on everything she had experienced while in Ireland, and I saw the similarities in their personalities then. Undeniably one in the same.

One day, that happiness would come back to her, even if I couldn't bring her father back physically. I'd still pulled off a damn near miracle, and witnessing this was the best reward. I found a nearby alder tree to sit under while they had their time together.

I found Sean glancing over his shoulder at me to offer a nod of gratitude, and I smiled broadly in return. I gave him back something he hadn't been able to have since I'd known Ciara: *time*. An extra moment together of a life that had an abrupt end.

I have taken advantage of this life as an immortal being I'd come to realize.

When your lifespan has an expiration, every moment matters. Giving them back time to express their love and gratitude for each other was such a delightful gift.

As young as Sean was when he departed this world left everyone baffled, but none as much as Ciara. I can speculate that she had perceived his expiration date to include another thirty or so years or so. About another third of his life, according to the average lifespan of humans. The devastation of missing out on that amount of time left me gobsmacked.

Time was just a blur when you had forever to live. When you lived forever, there was no need to end every conversation with an I love you, just in case it was the last time you'd see that person...The thought of it left my head spinning.

A sudden movement caught my attention. I couldn't believe my eyes. Was that Ciara showing off her stances for—sword fighting? I chuckled silently to myself. My little fighter indeed. I was no longer needed here.

I chased sleep but still kept our link open, just in case.

Once sleep had finally found me, it stayed until morning. I slept through the night peacefully for the first time in who knows how many years, still embracing Ciara.

I carefully got out of bed, silent as the night so as not to wake her. She looked so peaceful laying there and I didn't want to disturb her. She deserved to have any extra moments of serenity. I walked over to the window, cracking the curtain open slightly to see if I could spot any sign of Uallas nearby. The dew on the grass from last night was frozen again, shimmering like a million diamonds against the rays of the morning sun.

It made the garden look like one of my dreamscapes and

I pocketed the sight for later on. Nature was beautiful, always changing. Every day painted a new picture.

I hoped Ciara could feel the beauty of it all without an ounce of pain left, though I knew it would always linger in the depths of her soul.

When she woke, I told her of the dreams and we tousled in the sheets. It was a perfect start to a new day, her mouth deliciously around my cock. My mind was still reeling. She was my everything—I had to make sure she knew that. I'd been distant lately, but I'd rather be dead than leave her side, regardless of whatever came our way.

Afterwards, I left to make my way down the stairs and search the halls. I had barely gotten to the far side of the castle before a splitting pain in my temple brought me to my knees. It was excruciating. I thought for sure my head was cleaved in two, but when I screamed to warn Ciara of the potential danger, my voice was stolen.

No noise came out—just ragged breaths. When I opened my eyes wide in fear, there was a white fox bastard staring at me from outside the stained glass window. I was utterly helpless.

Uallas had his talons gripped deep in my mind. I was losing this battle. Simply looking away would have no effect on his powers.
He was always the more powerful of the two of us. My

creators made it so that any possible evil I could do, he would outweigh it with the balance of all that is good and light.

Except for this terror. They hadn't guessed that the tables would be turned and I was royally fucked.

CHAPTER 35

When I woke, I wiped my crusted eyes and scoured the room for Fearghas. Last night was the best night's sleep I had gotten since my father was alive, when I could hear the cicadas symphony outside my window in the Florida summers.

My father. We walked side by side in my dreams last night. It was almost as if I was given back a few of the moments that had been stolen from me. It felt so real, as if I truly had those moments back. It was bliss.

I figured Fearghas also had something to do with the extravagant dream I had when I first fell asleep. As stunning and picture perfect as it was, it was absolutely nothing compared to those moments walking alongside my father on that old dirt path. Hardly the gorgeous landscape of the waterfall with its glowing waters, but that wasn't what made the dream perfect. It was the person I shared it with.

I saw him standing by the bedroom window, his eyes glued to the world outside. I figured he would be double checking all the doors and windows and every inch of the castle for my safety, but still remaining here, within eyesight, never leaving my side.

"Fearghas? I have something to ask you..."
The dreams from last night replayed in my mind over and over again. It was rare that I was able to remember most of my dreams, except for a select few. My voice broke his reverie, and he turned to face me.

"You can ask me anything, Sunshine." Affection coated his words, but his eyes darkened at the sight of me in bed, the glow of the morning sun trickling in from the windows.

His Sunshine.

"The dreams I had last night. Were they from you?" I asked.

It had been so long since I'd had Fearghas as the puppeteer of my dreams. I had to know, especially about the one of my father. Fearghas walked over and sat on the edge of the bed next to me.

"Yesterday was a rough day for you. I simply wanted to offer you peace and tranquility, so I gave you a dream as close to paradise as I could muster. To keep any of the nightmares at bay. I hope it was okay, Ciara," he said as his callused hands stroked my cheek tenderly. I leaned into his warmth, nodding my approval.

"And the one with my father?" I looked up at him with hope in my eyes. He inhaled steadily.

"That was... more of a team effort. I had to enter the depths of the dream realm to talk to him. He went without a second thought. It was the next best thing I could do aside from bring him back for you, Ciara. I could see the pain etched on your face and I knew that, while my initial dreams helped, it wouldn't be enough for you. Nearly trapped myself there, but it was worth it as I stayed back and watched you two for a moment. You were genuinely happy, and that alone was worth it."

Fearghas's testimony left me stunned. An ache growing in my chest.

The butterflies he'd trapped there started fluttering. He had not only given me those dreams, but he had given me back the gift of time with my father. A gift that, up until now, I thought was an impossible task. But somehow, he pulled it off. That was why it felt so real. It wasn't just a dream—it was my father's spirit walking side by side with me.

Without a second thought, I pulled him close and my lips

were on his. I wanted to show him what he meant to me. I'd give him everything I had to give. *Everything.*

I found an opportunity and let my tongue slide into his mouth, tasting him further. My hands roamed down his abs and we were soon entangled in a flurry of tongue and teeth. I bit his lip gently as I played with the waistband of his pants, feeling his hardening cock in my hand. I groaned at the size, imagining the feel of it inside me. I freed it of its clothed cage and stroked it from the hilt to the tip.

"*Mmm.*" He moaned at my touch, and I wanted to be his undoing. To bring this immortal man to his knees would make me the happiest girl in the world. I flipped us over so I was now on top of him, ripping off my shirt and tossing it to the floor.

My breasts peaked in the morning air, the daylight illuminating my best features.

"You are beautiful, Sunshine." He reached up, gripping my breasts in his hand, toying with nipples between his middle and forefinger. The sensation drenched my panties as I straddled him. He leaned up to suck on my other nipple, gently biting and teasing. I kept working his cock with my hands before I slid down lower and replaced one of my hands with my mouth.

His hands gripped my hair, pulling slightly on my roots as he guided my motions. My head bobbed up and down, licking his most sensitive areas before moving back down his shaft. My free hand massaged his balls while my other hand held him down.

I kept my gaze glued to his while he watched my every move. The way he was staring at me turned my insides into molten lava. I somehow managed a smile while I had him in my mouth as he watched me work intently.

"*Fuck* me," he gasped. He was unraveling, allowing himself pleasure and I fucking loved the sight of it.

"I thought you'd never ask." I know he said it because he was in ecstasy, but I took it as an invitation. I only paused to say those words before sliding my panties over and inserting his cock into me slowly, savoring every thick inch. I moaned at how delightfully he stretched me, pleasure humming throughout my entire body. I wasn't going to stop until I was riding him into oblivion.

Licking my lips, I began to move, grinding him into me deeper. I'd been waiting for this moment with him since that rainy day, and the build up just made it that much sweeter. He whimpered beneath me and the sound put me on the edge of orgasm.

"*Fuck,* you feel like heaven," he said breathlessly.

I held him down, hands planted on his chest as I got into a better angle that allowed me to slide up to the tip slowly before slamming down on his entire length over and over again.

He felt absolutely *perfect*.

"Take me to oblivion, Fearghas."

He moaned at my words and his eyes grew darker. The sound of him made me wet again.

"Get on your knees for me," he growled. The timber in his voice made me obey his command. I did as I was told and he slid into me from behind. The familiar stretch of him was absolute ecstasy. The sound of our bodies smacking together on every thrust thrilled me. His balls tapped my most sensitive areas as he kept his pace.

He got impossibly deeper this way, and I knew I was on the verge of my release. A few more thrusts and I screamed with pleasure, my body shuddering. His release came shortly after, trickling down my thighs. The aftershock of it all left my body numb and spent with satisfaction. My arms and legs crumbled back down on the bed as he lay next to me, playing with my hair. He was so beautiful. His face flushed from our tousle, lips swollen still, eyes searing into my soul in a way that told me I'd be screwed forever. We stayed like this for a few moments after, just admiring each other silently.

He finally cleaned me up and planted a kiss on my forehead before he dressed.

"I'm going to go downstairs and make sure everything is

secure while you get ready here. I love you, Ciara. You are my anam cara, my soul mate."

He gave me a long, tender kiss, and before I could reply, he walked out the door.

I turned on the shower, staring at myself in the mirror. My hair was an utter mess, but I had a glow about me. While I waited for the water to heat up, memories of us cuddled on the chaise from the previous night rushed into my head. I smiled at the memory, even though I was still coming off the high of us in bed this morning. I wanted to tell him everything my body said instead. That I was eternally grateful for all he had done for me and, most importantly, that I loved him too.

I stepped in the shower, letting it wash away the musk of the sex and sweat coating my body. He had called me his *anam cara*. His soul mate.

I knew he was mine, too. My body and soul were made for him, and I was foolish to just let him walk away without making sure he knew it. I quickly washed my body and hair, not letting any more time pass before I got out and dressed for the day.

After I had dried my hair with a towel, I carefully styled it into two classic French braids. Feeling refreshed, I beamed at the thought of telling him everything on my mind over breakfast.

CHAPTER 36

When I finally made it downstairs, the castle was eerily quiet, only the groans of wind against the windows cutting the silence. If I listened intently enough, I could hear the thumping rhythm of my heartbeat, like a drum ready for battle.

The silence was so very wrong. It wasn't the type of silence I'd grown accustomed to. There wasn't even the sound of another pair of footsteps to grace the inside of these castle walls, though there should have been. Now was the only moment when I resented how many the rooms this castle contained.

Suddenly, the electricity in the air shifted into something much darker, warning bells ringing loudly in my head to turn back around and lock myself in my room upstairs.

As I rounded the corner, I halted dead in my tracks.

Before me was the husk of Fearghas, eyes enraged. He held a double-headed war axe in his hands, sneering at me. The muscled arms and sculpted abdomen that had just given me pleasure and comfort was now transformed into unadulterated horror.

Every lean muscle in his body was poised and ready to fight me until I would inevitably meet my own demise. His nostrils flared as he scented my terror. His fixed glare glazed over, without the empathy that I'd grown to love, made me nearly soil my pants. I was now on the receiving end of his wrath instead of his protection, and the only explanation I could think of was that Uallas was behind it—meaning he was close by.

The measly sword lessons with Finn would barely allow me to put a papercut on this immortal being whose brain had been warped to hunt me down. No matter the progress I was making with my practicing, it was nothing in comparison to his centuries of honing his skills and his clearly planted ill intent towards me.

Fearghas snarled at me, yet an unseen force within him hesitated to move toward me. His body was rearing up like a wolf ready to attack. He was a warrior and I was the enemy. He continued to peer at me through his lowered gaze, brows scrunched and a menacing glare burning into me like the sun setting on the ocean.

His heaving breaths reaffirmed his massive stature, accentuating every veined muscle in his arms and every single well-defined ab muscle on his torso. Even his horns made him look evil in this light. I hated to admit that I'd be turned on if he was looking at me like that with passion, instead of the fury from Uallas's curse.

As if summoning him by simply thinking of his name, Uallas, in his human form, burst into the arched window behind Fearghas. Rainbow-colored stained glass shattered around them both like dangerous confetti. Neither one of them flinched, though I suppose it couldn't harm them—not really.

I carefully backed up a few steps as Uallas put a cordial hand around his brother's shoulders, as if they were thick as thieves. Fearghas was now more like a puppet than that of kin. I had to find a way to snap the strings Uallas had bound to his mind.

The familiar truth set in, that time wasn't on my side. I had to make a plan for my protection soon or I would be killed by the subjects of my own childhood stories, in my father's castle, no less. What a poetic end to my life. To find everything I had ever wanted to be true in this world, love and fairy tales, only to have it ripped from my grasp. I'd no longer be walking with my father in my dreams; I'd be walking alongside him in the afterlife. We'd talk about all the other things we had envisioned for my life, but I never would get the chance to experience them.

I was my father's daughter. I was smart and passionate and I'd fight like hell for this life I was honored to have. I supposed I hadn't thought too far ahead about what type of danger I could be in. Not one but two Pookas were out for a taste of my blood, instead of wanting to be a friend or lover.

How the tables had turned.

The sword they were seeking was still up in my bedroom, safely tucked away by Fearghas. I knew that if I ran, Fearghas would catch me in no time. He knew where the sword was hidden and would hand it over to Uallas while under his spell. Who knew what malice Uallas had in store for me with Fearghas out of his way and on his side.

The best I could do at this moment was put enough space between us to grab whatever weapon was hanging on the wall and strike Uallas with it, creating enough of a distraction to break the curse and give Fearghas his mind back. I needed him. I missed *him*, not this shell of a being that Uallas had molded him into for his own agenda.
I slowly backed away, keeping my hands up, begging them

both to not harm me. Playing the fool that they wanted me to be. If Uallas wanted the Solais Sword to have me as his own, then I couldn't be harmed. I'd be of no use to him dead. I was just in the way. That's possibly why Fearghas was just a threat and my guts weren't already on the floor right now.

They both had no idea, but I had the upper hand here. I wouldn't dare show my hand until I was ready. I slowly inched back another step, out of the den of the lions before me. I would sooner die than be a prisoner in my own home. My father didn't raise a coward. A memory floated into my mind.

"Patience, Ciara," my father said. "The woods will still be there by morning and all the dangers lurking there will be asleep. It would be foolish to enter a predator's territory when they are built for the night and you are not, right? We'll go in the morning after breakfast. In the meantime, how about a story?"

I nodded my head and grabbed my favorite book, 'The Tale of the Pooka,' from my bookshelf on the wall. He lay down in my bed next to me, far too big for my twin size bed, and started to read to me theatrically. It was my favorite tale and he read it to me nearly every night, but I didn't care. I longed for the adventurous stories of the shape-shifters who thrived on chaos. Who could transform into any of my favorite woodland animals on a whim.

My father only stopped reading when I fell asleep. He would kiss my forehead and tuck me in tightly, saying, "Sweet dreams, my dear. Your adventures can wait until morning. I love you always and forever, Ciara."

I remembered those nights as vividly as the dream from last night. Looking back now, he was right, of course. It wasn't cowardly to wait until morning, it was the smartest option: to use my senses to their full capabilities in the light of day.

The mornings were full of great blue herons and white egrets waiting by the river's edge for their next fish of the day, turtles sunning themselves on logs to the melody of the birds in the trees. Coyotes were asleep in their dens and as far as the wide variety of reptiles Florida had to offer, at least during the light of day they could be seen and avoided to respect their territories.

I hadn't known what other perilous, mythical creatures could have also been lurking in the woods at night, but I'm sure my father had—hence, the warnings I eventually gave into.

I continued slowly backing away from Fearghas and Uallas, as if I had entered an alligator's nest. Territorial and lethal. I noticed the shimmer of a sword on the wall from the open window, but I didn't dare break eye contact to look. Finally, I stopped moving when I was within reach of the sword on the wall. Far enough away now from either Pooka that I was at least out of a claws reach from Fearghas, giving me the perfect time to strike.

Uallas took my stillness as an invitation to get closer, so I let him, falling into my strategically placed trap. Fearghas followed close behind, like he was tied to an invisible leash. Even though my plan was slowly coming to fruition, I was still terrified.

What ifs plaguing my mind about if it didn't work out. I was well aware that I was still unevenly matched, as if I was venturing into the Florida woods long after the sun had set. This time I had a plan, though. I wasn't a little girl anymore who needed to have her hand held.

"Hello there, *dear* Ciara," Uallas purred devilishly, the sound like nails against a chalkboard to me. He knew full well how much I despised that word, yet said it again, completely disregarding my wishes on purpose to irritate my nerves.

"I believe you have stolen something from me, and I've come to ask for it back." He said the words like I supposed he would have many centuries ago, as if formally requesting it from royalty. Demanding it was a more accurate statement.

The words cut like a double-edged sword. I bit my tongue to refrain from scoffing at his request. This asshole thought that *I* stole from *him*? He had another thing coming if he thought that was the truth.

"Breaking into my home doesn't exactly feel like *asking*. What have you done with Fearghas?" I demanded.

"Fearghas? Oh, he's just *finally* acting like the brother he was always destined to be. Isn't that right, brother?" Uallas said eerily animated as Fearghas grunted in forced agreement at his side.

Keep him talking, Ciara. Distract him with the sound of his own voice before you strike, I thought to myself. I could do this. I *had* to do this. If not for my sake, then for Fearghas's. I needed him back to tell him that I loved him.

I had to break the brainwashing Uallas had placed on him. He wasn't himself. It was a kind of sick warfare, to infiltrate someone's own mind and make them act beyond their own natural thoughts and wishes. To remove all sense of one's control was an unthinkable act. Something I would never wish on my enemy.

"So, this is what you do, Uallas? You terrorize people from afar so you can weave your web of lies before you sink your fangs in?"

The comparison to the daddy long legs spider and the way they hunted was uncanny and fitting, especially as that subterranean corridor was where I found the missing sword in the first place.

I thought of how the spiders I found there were able to catch their venomous prey by shooting their webs from afar before feeding on them alive.

The thought alone made my skin crawl. Uallas was no better than them, and he inflicted the same reaction from me. A shiver slithered its way down my spine.

I ripped the sword off the wall and pointed it toward him, remembering my stance and the few moves that Finn had taught me.

Slash, slash, stab.

When I got close enough to Uallas, I did not hesitate. I was not like the spider, and I surely was no coward. It all happened so fast that I barely had time to think of the stance I'd practiced with Finn and in front of the mirror.

My first slash missed, but my second one sliced through his arm, almost through to the bone, hitting my mark.

I didn't hesitate on my next sequence as I stabbed straight into his stomach and then leaned into it.

"You fucking bitch!" he howled. His screams of pain echoed throughout the halls like a wounded animal. My initial reaction was to run, but I couldn't help the smug smile of satisfaction from the pain I had caused him, from my blade no less.

CHAPTER 37

I shouldn't have been surprised that I'd severed Uallas's forearm straight through to the bone. It was a well-executed plan to disarm him, though gravity and a sharp blade were a great help.

Uallas had grossly misjudged me, which I used to my advantage. He mistakenly thought me to be frail and scared.

Instead, I'd held onto hope.

Hope that I would avenge my father. Hope of survival, both physically and emotionally. Lastly, the hope that my plan would work and it would be just enough of a distraction to free Fearghas from the grip Uallas had on his mind.

Fearghas blinked rapidly and furrowed his brows, confused by his actions and how he'd gotten there. He immediately looked up at me, scanning my body for any signs of injury. Realizing that he'd been aware of what was going on but could not do anything about it absolutely devastated me.

"Ciara," he breathed as his body relaxed knowing that I was free from harm, his mind apparently his own again. There was no time to spare. Uallas was raging next to him.

I'd be damned if I let my plan go to shit due to taking precious moments to celebrate Fearghas being himself again. I couldn't risk him not being in control of his emotions again, or worse; dead. That tormented look on his face cut into my heart like a knife.

"Fearghas! Help! Get the sword!" I screamed.

The sword that I happened to grab in the hall was made of steel and not iron. Uallas's wounds were starting to heal. Just my luck. Of course, of the many iron swords my father had planted around for my safety, this was the one I would grab. It would only inflict temporary damage, but nothing life-threatening to Uallas. He'd be healed in little to no time at all.

In a clouded flash, Fearghas was gone. Uallas was cursing my name and screaming about his arm half falling apart.

Everything that happened next moved in slow motion.

In my ears, there was just a ringing sound where Uallas's screams echoed in the halls. My vision blurred, but I could still make out my steel blade dripping with dark blood in front of me, and the splatter that now coated the velvet emerald curtains.

I felt my hand shaking from the heaviness of the steel in my hand. The first time I truly wielded a sword, and there was blood. Of course, I knew this was what it was meant for, but my lessons were precautionary. At least that was what I'd told myself.

Despite using it for my own safety, I was not a violent person. I never wanted it to come to this.

Breathe in, breathe out.

You were protecting him. You were protecting him. You were protecting him…

My sword arm was growing heavy as I held my fighting stance, yet I was unable to drop my weapon in case I needed to use it again for my own protection. I was growing weaker by the second and the evil grin on Uallas's face said that he knew it, too. I was frozen in place as beads of adrenaline-filled sweat clung to my forehead and trickled down my back.

I couldn't blink, because if I blinked, if I looked away from Uallas for more than a second, I would become vulnerable. I didn't want to think about the possibility that executing my plan had been sheer luck. Fearghas appeared in my peripheral vision and I eyed him with a terrified gaze.

Help, I'd told him earlier. The plea was still plastered all over my face and fear probably laced my scent as well. In an instant, he knew exactly what I meant by the look on my face when my words failed me.

He rushed upstairs in whatever was his fastest form to retrieve the sword.

I repeated the mantra over and over, like a broken record, until a gust of wind ruffled my hair.

Breathe in, breathe out. You were protecting him...

Fearghas was back and the breath I'd been absentmindedly holding was released. A familiar sharp and pointy thing rested in his rugged hands. The Solais Sword.

He stood in the middle of me and Uallas, shielding me. But now the situation that lay in front of him was a battle of heart and head. He lowered the Solais Sword, pointing it directly at Uallas's cold beating heart. He pressed it into his chest, just enough to prevent him from charging at me.

"Uallas, this is over," Fearghas said to his brother. "This is what you have forced me to do. You were supposed to be the good brother, not me. Look at you now. Stealing, killing, lying. You want the *Claídheamh Soluis* so bad?" He paused for a moment, almost hesitating, before he pressed the sword to his brother's heart and rammed it farther into his chest.

The sword squelched straight through his heart and Uallas

began to gurgle blood.

"It is yours, brother." Fearghas moved closer to him, mere inches from his stunned face. "May the afterlife serve you well in hell."

A single tear fell from Fearghas's eye. Just one.

A gasp escaped my mouth as I finally dropped my sword. Steel clanking on the wooden floor reverberated throughout the castle.

Fearghas said he would not hesitate to ensure my safety, but I had previously thought that there would be certain stipulations. Hard lines even he wouldn't cross, given he had been devoted to the code of his kind. Family, I guessed, was one of those lines. Whatever kind of fucked-up family they were to each other. I guess doing the right thing overturned the ill deeds of being blood or made in likeness.

Being an only child, I didn't have a secondhand account as to how sibling relationships worked. My friends back in Florida would tell me that no one loved you more than your sibling, but they'd constantly be at each other's throats, then making up the next day as if nothing had happened.

Fearghas hastily removed the sword from his brother's chest, Uallas's artery shooting blood from his body. I winced at the gory sight. Faint smoke from the chemical reaction of iron and Pooka flesh caused the rest of the blood to bubble in his wound. It was utterly grotesque.

Fearghas held me, allowing us to step back as Uallas bled out, fell to the floor, and withered. I hid in Fearghas's muscular chest, one eye remaining on Uallas, closely watching him in his last moments to see if there was any semblance of regret on his face. I found no such thing.

I was so grateful to have Fearghas back as my protector.

Killing Uallas in the same manner as he had killed my father was meant to be a message to him: that evil and good must have a balance in this world, like all things in life. Both left imprints on our hearts—one meant to scar and torment, and the other meant to heal and love.

Nothing could take away the fact that my father no longer walked this earth with me, but by ending Uallas's life, it meant that no one else's life would be at risk in the future.

I should be rejoicing at Uallas's demise, spitting on his rotting corpse, but I couldn't bring myself to feel the hate that he so easily carried with him. Instead, I felt sorry that he had an eternity, an immortal life, to choose to do what was right and good, and he chose this path for himself instead.

I felt the ache for Fearghas having to kill him. He knew it

was the best option to keep me and his world safe and at peace.

Only after I was fully certain that Uallas was no longer alive did I allow myself to fully lose control in Fearghas's arms. I sobbed for everything. For the grief; for the family lost, both physically and morally; for the innocent little girl I once was. For everything I held onto that needed release. For my love for Fearghas, and how I could have lost him today without ever saying how I felt.

It wasn't a cure-all for everything wrong in my life, but it felt better. Someday, I knew I'd learn to be grateful for those parts of me too, the ones that made my heart hurt.

It was powerful to be so broken but so hopeful for a great life, regardless of its trials.

Once my tears dried, I needed to let Fearghas know how grateful I was to him and how much he meant to me, too. For having every tool in his arsenal to be bad but always choosing to do good. It was one of the many reasons I loved him. We would be there for each other, through any force of nature or magic.

So I leaned up and kissed him passionately. I opened my mouth slightly, inviting him to taste me deeper, not out of a need to bandage any wounds to my soul but as a need to show him that he wasn't alone in this world. That he was all that was as good in my life and deserving of the love

I had for him. The kiss said that he was important to me without having to say a word, but I did anyway.

"I love you, Fearghas. You mean everything to me." A tear trailed down my cheek.

It was a raw moment and I was lapping up every second of it. His strong hands gripped my ass and I wrapped my legs around his waist instinctually. Without breaking our kiss, he held me there, pushing me against the stone wall. The rough wall bit into my back delightfully as I yelped at the pleasure of him slowly unraveling from my kiss.

He growled deeply at the sound of my satisfaction and we blocked out the rest of the world around us.

CHAPTER 38

"Fearghas, you are everything good in my life. You are my everything. Don't ever forget that I love you." I smiled at him softly. It was the truth, I realized; I just had never said the words out loud before, reinforcing the fact that I was in love with him.

"But, you look terrible. Let's get washed up." I added with a smirk.

It was my turn to take care of him and toss in a little banter to lighten the load a bit. I shot up off of the bed and grabbed his hand to lead him into the washroom, turning on the shower. I removed his blood stained shirt and loosened the belt around his pants, letting them drop to the floor.

I was always a bad liar. He looked far from terrible, despite the blood that soaked through his shirt and onto his skin underneath. He looked powerful and handsome and rugged, but emotionally, he'd been dragged through the mud. It softened his rough edges and made me want to put a smile back on his face. I found myself wanting nothing more than for that banter of his to return. For my Fearghas to fully come back to me. I knew it may take some time, but I'd be a good girl and be patient.

I led him into the shower, letting him embrace the hot water washing away the grime that he carried, both physically and mentally. Slowly, I saw him feel this relief of the water washing him clean. When he closed his eyes, I got down to my knees and massaged his cock with my hands.

"Ciara," he breathed. It was a plea, either to start or to not start. He deserved to have this release, though. I wrapped my lips around the head of his strength and I started to bob my head to my own rhythm. I kept moving my hands and wrapping my lips around him until he was deep into my throat. Water was raining down on me like our first kiss in the field. I'd hold that moment in my heart forever.

Now, my focus lay on my tongue and lips, and his pleasure. I wondered how my mouth must feel on him. I hooked my fingers onto his well-sculpted ass to allow myself to go deeper.

His head fell back as his hands gripped my hair to help guide my mouth. I sped up my movements. I wouldn't stop until I could taste his delicious release. He briefly removed his hands from my hair and began massaging my head. It took me a moment to realize what he was doing as I licked up the side of his shaft and watched his expression through my wet lashes.

A hint of a smile tugged at the corner of his tempting mouth and I realized he was shampooing my hair. Moans escaped my mouth at the feeling of being taken care of while simultaneously taking care of him. I strengthened my grip on him as my hands and mouth worked in tandem for him to find his pleasure. I wanted to show him how very appreciative I was for him, since I couldn't tell him at the moment because, well, my mouth was full.

"*Fuck*, Ciara, you feel so good," he grumbled, watching me work his shaft. I knew he couldn't hold on too longer. Moments later, his salty essence spilled into my throat.

I swallowed his cum and the satisfaction of making him come undone from my mouth and got up from my knees. I rinsed any remaining shampoo from my hair, and when I finally opened my eyes, I found his eyes searching deep into my soul.

"*Tú mo ghrá,*" he said under his breath. I could barely make out whether the words were in English or Gaeilge.

I tilted my head slightly, trying to understand what he had said to me and if I had heard correctly.

"What did you say?" I asked.

"Tú mo ghrá," he repeated more confidently, holding my body flush with his.

My breasts pushed up against his chest, his cock pressed up against me.

"You are my love, Sunshine. I *love* you," he reaffirmed for me. The shower hid my happy tears by washing them away.

For the first time in a long while, I felt hope within my grasp. I could have it all with Fearghas, though I knew it would take time. The best things in life weren't rushed.

We both finished up in the shower as the hot water began to run cold. Fearghas summoned a new outfit while I changed the human way.

It was well past morning now, closer into the afternoon. I still hadn't eaten today and Uallas's cold body remained downstairs. Romance would, unfortunately, have to wait.

"Not to ruin the moment, but you need to eat and I need to take care of my brother's body downstairs." He definitely ruined the moment, but as I already knew, the romance would have to wait.

"Okay," I said. "After I eat, I'll help clean up with you. You shouldn't have to do it alone, Fearghas."

He planted a firm kiss on my lips and we went our separate ways once reaching the bottom of the stairwell. I was nervous to be separated from him, given the nightmare from the last time he walked away, but there were no more threats now.

It's okay. Everything is okay, I told myself.

I made my way into the kitchen as Fearghas walked to the horrific scene from this morning. Upon opening the fridge, I found it was fairly sparse. My kitchen staff was on holiday so I was low on eggs and completely out of bacon. *Great.*

As I prepared what was now brunch with my limited supply, my mind drifted toward Conor and our conversation the last time he was here. How Uallas had manipulated him into holding vital information from me regarding my father.

The whole conversation made me uneasy, even though I told him I'd have to think it over. How could someone justify betraying someone who had helped him out in a time of need? For so many years, nonetheless. If you respect someone enough, you would do anything to defend their honor, no matter the cost.

Plus, it would be a little awkward having him around once I'd moved onto Fearghas, because I didn't think Conor had fully moved on from me.

People's eyes were the windows into their soul. You could read someone's intentions through a simple gaze. That's what I was reading in his eyes that night, too. Hurt beyond just his mother. A potential love he let slip through his fingers. He also didn't seem to be in a good place, mentally. He was barely holding it together and it was apparent it caused his sense of control over his life to spiral dangerously low.

I couldn't, in good conscience, just throw him out on the street, knowing he didn't have a job or a place to stay other than the hotel. It wasn't something my father would do, no matter the situation.

But would it really be in Conor's best interest to come back to this place and be haunted by all those memories every single day? It would be another kind of torture for him—I knew it would be.

I wondered if Norman would be opposed to having him as a manager there at the Black Horse. Norman would still own the pub, of course, but maybe he'd like to retire to Florida as a snow bird instead of freezing his bones over here in the winter.

If Conor could run this castle as a steward, then the tavern would be a breeze, especially with his familiarity of it from his earlier years. His expertise as a whiskey sommelier made it the perfect option for him.

It had been a while since I'd seen Norman. A visit to him would be comforting. He was a good soul. Plus, I could put in a good word for a friend while I was there.

Breakfast was made quickly, just a sunny-side-up-egg and two pieces of buttery toast to dip the yolk into, paired with my usual morning cup of tea.

After I cleaned my plate and washed the dishes, I made my way to where Fearghas was with a rag and cleaning supplies in hand.

When I arrived at the scene, Fearghas was sitting on his heels on the floor, his hands wrapped around the back of his head, sobbing.

He had already rolled Uallas up in the stained runner carpet, and now appeared to be coming to terms with the fact that he was the one to kill his brother.

My heart cleaved in two for him, stuck between his own moral identity and reality. I put a reassuring hand on Fearghas's back so he knew I was there with him, through whatever peril life threw at us.

I dropped the cleaning supplies and got down on the floor next to him. I wrapped my arms around him, letting the silence speak.

He would talk to me when he was ready. He needed this moment of release, too.

CHAPTER 39

FEARGHAS

Almost every ounce of my being told me that killing my brother was the right choice.

The other part of me, the *made* part, told me I had just committed the betrayal of a lifetime. It told me that I'd broken one of our codes. Was I no better than Uallas himself? I had *killed*. I couldn't bury that voice that said I was wrong to think that way. That he was my brother, and that counted for something. That there was another way to save him, and I had chosen not to take that path. I chose to end it with death and destruction instead. I chose brutality and wished him well in hell.

Did he truly deserve that?

Regardless of what he did or didn't deserve, it would only

be right to give him some kind of burial and eulogy. I'd take him to the cliffs and send him off into whatever afterlife awaited him via the waters below.

A water burial was meant to wash away the sins of the living. Once it became time, their souls would be welcomed at the gates. That was, at least, how the ancient legends went.

I'd bring him to the whimsical cliffs of Howth. They were secluded enough that we wouldn't be bothered there, as long as we stayed away from curious tourists. Though I doubted many humans would make the trek up there this late in the winter.

Ciara came over to me and rested her hand on my shoulder. It broke me from my reverie and I looked up at her, my salvation. With watery eyes, I had no words. The silence just seemed right at that moment.

She was holding a rag and a bottle of something I could only imagine would clean up the terror of what remained in the hall.

"I'm going to give him a proper water burial at Howth today," I finally told her while my eyes remained fixed on the carpet that contained his body and masked my deed from earlier. I knew once I told her where I planned to take him that she wouldn't allow me to go alone, like I had originally planned. Maybe some small part of me wanted her by my side while I sent him off to the afterlife. She would go only to help put together the pieces of me that had slowly started to crumble, as I had done for her and would do over and over again.

She wrapped her arms around me in an embrace, the feeling as comforting as a warm blanket, and asked if I would like her to accompany her to the cliffs. The fact that she asked, even though I knew she wanted to be by my side, spoke volumes of her love. If being alone was what I needed for the grieving process, no doubt she'd allow me that respect, too. Though the cliffs may be too far for her to walk by my side, I had wanted her to accompany me for the part of it that mattered. To walk with me metaphorically through my grief—*our* grief—together.

"You are more than welcome to accompany me, Sunshine, but I need to walk him there alone. By foot. It would be too far for you," I said as I lifted his limp body onto my shoulders. I gave her a nod as I walked out the door toward the Howth cliffs. It would be a long, grueling walk, but it would allow me some time to process everything.

Everything Uallas was to me, everything he actually represented. With every footstep, I thought of him. Our younger years in this life that we were given. Memories—that was all they were now. Of when Uallas was good and pure, but that was ages ago. I think even he had forgotten about those days too, by the end of it. We didn't grow up as humans do. We were always shifted and formed from the world around us.

Where I was destined to study the chaos of the world and be the prince of mayhem, Uallas was always meant to be like a moth. Attracted to the light of the world. I was trying to remember when it occurred to me that our roles had become intertwined, switched even.

It was a blip in time and I couldn't pinpoint exactly when it started. Sean's presence was a catalyst for the switch, though. Ironically, for both of us. Uallas was the unholy balance of whatever Sean was not. Uallas had acted like every positive quality that Sean radiated was mocking him.

Jealousy. That was where his ugliness came from.

It was a slow release, our switch of fate. Uallas studied the wrong type of humans and aimed to be a carbon copy of them. I saw their mistakes and lack of values, and I discovered that it would only lead to a dead end. That with betrayal came fear and power, and those who had that power became lonely. Those false kings and rulers only had the biggest castles and the fanciest of jewels due to horrific acts, but had no one to fight for them.

The best rulers of the lands were compassionate and honest, and while their castle walls weren't as thick, they had loyal armies at their backs who would fight to the death to protect them. Their stories would remain throughout history, untainted and told throughout the tests of time.

Uallas only saw the grandeur of material objects and what had to be done to achieve such things. He never understood the power of what honesty could bring him. Friendships and love.

We were born alone in this life. What did it matter after all was said and done? He always had me and he must have figured it was enough—but in the end, it wasn't. The choices he made had ultimately led him here.

Dead and on the way to his own burial.

He had executed a compassionate and honorable man, a friend of the supernatural, and with that, he was the designer of his own fate.

That type of evil and wrongdoing would never prevail. The world needed more compassion, so here I was, doing my brotherly duty despite being the reason behind it all. It was destiny that the same blade to cause such wickedness had also put a stop to it. Ciara and I made sure it was so.

The same blade that, for centuries, represented light triumphing darkness had fulfilled its destiny, time and time again. I still remember when it was forged for Aelia's suitor, but she had sought it out instead for herself. She later became the land's most cherished queen. I never wanted to be part of quests such as those that her many suitors had been bred for.

That was probably why I was always observing from the sidelines and deciding on my own what was most important. I could only have hope for my brother that he may finally learn empathy and find its peace in the hereafter.

I was slowly approaching the edge of Howth, where the lands crumble into the sea hundreds of feet below. I paused to take in the scenery, the final resting place for Uallas.

The bitterly cold air and snow-dusted landscape muted the hazy mountains behind me. In front of me, the land dropped off into razor-sharp rocks miles below as the sea crashed and foamed along it—having nowhere else to go.

The scenery represented what Uallas had become at his core. Cold and sharp, a bottomless pit of violence. It was the perfect resting place for him.

I placed him a mere few feet away from the edge and heard footsteps crunching on the earth, approaching from behind me.

"Fearghas!" a familiar voice called out before I had the chance to turn around.

The sound was like the first sight of dawn after a long, restful night. I turned toward it and welcomed Ciara. She must have had someone drop her off out of sight for privacy.

I hadn't heard any motors running nearby. It was then my turn to shed tears in her arms as she consoled me. If anyone knew this feeling, it was her.

We held each other for a while until I stopped leaking from my eyes and the moment had come to send off Uallas officially and properly.

"Ciara, thank you for being here." I smiled at her through a sodden face. "I've had a lot to think about on the hike over. I don't regret my actions, just my brother's, which has led me to realize my motive for...stopping...him today. He was built for good and had as much time as me to use it for his own benefit. Hell, he's had as much time as the mountains had to grow tall, *but he kept choosing wrong.* Every decision kept digging him deeper and deeper into an abyss of corruption. I couldn't allow him to continue along his path. I am eternally grateful to have you here by my side, and I can only hope that his send off will grant you some modicum of peace and justice for your father's life."

Every word I spoke was the truth, and it was enlightening, even though a dark cloud still hovered over my heart. Now was the time. I picked up Uallas and brought him to the edge of the cliff, holding him in my arms as I told him my goodbyes. I said in our mother language that he would always be my brother, even at the very end. How I had wished I could have saved him from the darkness before it consumed him—but, in a way, I supposed I had. It was difficult for me, but I still forgave him.

Forgiveness would help heal this wound instead of having bitterness taint my soul. I made sure he knew that, even though hell would welcome him with open arms, he could still seek redemption in the afterworld. I also sought atonement for my soul for taking his life to whatever god would listen.

Closing my eyes, I connected my feet into the earth as I tossed his body over the cliff and into the churning depths below.

I whispered, "Suaimhneas síoraí air," into the wind to honor him, a misplaced soul.

Eternal peace on him. It was the only sentiment I could offer.

After lifetimes of violence and heinous acts, it was my last request to him. To find peace. It took a few moments before I witnessed his body finally sink under the churning tides below, then I turned away. He was one with the earth now, sins cleansed and forgiven, finally able to rest.

I walked back to where Ciara waited, further away from the cliff's edge, and wrapped an arm around her again.

"How are you feeling, Ciara? Today was not only a difficult one for me. It was rough on you, as well. Care to talk with me?" I asked softly, almost purring.

She had witnessed me kill my brother in the same manner that Uallas had killed her father. The trauma of witnessing what Uallas did to Sean must have weighed heavy on her mind all day, but instead, she chose to make sure I was alright.

"I won't lie to you, Fearghas, and say that I haven't mentally replaced Uallas's face with my father's in that scene, picturing his death on repeat since you left today. But the real damning thing is that I don't feel anything at all for him—for Uallas. My father was the real loss, but after today, Uallas can't hurt anyone again. You know what else I think, Fearghas? Whether you realize it or not, that makes what you did the bravest and most selfless thing anyone can do. You did the right and honorable thing, though the pain from it can feel sharp and cutting. You made the world a brighter place. You gave me a peaceful future, one where I won't be looking over my shoulder every minute of every day. Who knows how many others you could have saved from him, as well? We're here for each other, Fearghas, and I love you."

I said nothing, but pressed my lips onto hers. The action said everything I couldn't form with words. I loved her, too. If we could get through this together so seamlessly, then there was nothing that could stand in our way.

My *anam cara*. My Sunshine.

CHAPTER 40

After Fearghas and I went our separate ways leaving the cliffs, I decided it was due time for me to pay my friend Norman a visit at the tavern. I could definitely go for a pint and our usual shot together, toasting to good fortune or whatever sentiment Norman was feeling particularly fond of that evening.

I wish Fearghas could come with me to the tavern, but a muscular six-foot-something man with horns might be a bit out of place. Fearghas wanted some time alone after the funeral, anyway. He had killed and sent off his brother on the same day, after all. I could only imagine what was going through his mind.

I wouldn't be terribly long here anyway. Maybe an hour or two.

The heavy red door was a familiar sight. The distinct smell of a fire burning in the hearth filled the room, greeting me on arrival. Its crackling was drowned out by the laughing and shouts of today's customers. The place was packed with locals that had nothing better to do except get drunk and talk about themselves.

I scanned behind the bar to find where Norman was and see if he was busy serving anyone. He was multitasking, of course: pouring a perfect Guinness from the draft and laughing with an older gentleman in a beige tweed flat cap. I envied his gift of gab, how natural it was for him to easily turn patrons into regulars and, eventually, friends.

I supposed I fit into that last category now.

"Hi, Norm! It's been a while. How are you?"

As soon as he saw me, his face lit up with a smile. It gave me a warm and fuzzy feeling to elicit such an emotion from him, my friend.

I ordered my usual, Guinness and pie. He filled me in on everything that had happened in his life since the last time we spoke. How the mysterious horse had stopped appearing and that business had picked up because of it. I fought the smile tugging at my lips, thinking of Fearghas.

Norman's uptick in business couldn't be a more perfect opportunity for the purpose of my visit.

I took the occasion to ask Norman if he could use any extra hands with the tavern.

"Who's askin'?" he replied.

"Well, I am asking for a friend. Would you be interested in possibly hiring Conor for a management role?" I cut straight to the point.

I knew Conor would be too full of pride to ask for himself, if he had even thought of it as a possibility. For him, I considered it a second chance to excel in life. To grant him an opportunity, as my father had done with him in the past. The irony that he'd be back here in a more suited position made it feel like destiny.

Of course, Conor could deny the offer if he so chose, but I felt like getting Norman on board first would help the case. Norman usually manned the bar by himself, and while he excelled at it, everyone could use a helping hand from time to time. Hopefully Norman wouldn't be too proud to accept the help, either.

"I thought he was working for you at the estate. What happened?" Norman asked.

It was a valid question, but I'd have to give him my famous bubble wrapped answer. There were still some truths that were not my story to tell.

Catherine or Finn probably wouldn't take too kindly to me divulging details about the Pooka who took up residence here. How could I find the words to say everything that had happened these past couple of months, anyhow?

It would be easier to just say that after his mom passed away, it was difficult to go back to his old life at the estate, and that it would stir up too much emotion.

Most people danced around the topic of death, probably because everyone handled it differently. It was easy to be there for someone through it all and not ask unwanted questions about the process. In my experience, however, that wasn't always the case. If Conor was ready to talk about it to anyone, he would. There wasn't a set timeline of when that would be, or if he ever wanted to. He'd let me know.

Norman was good about not poking the bear when it came to difficult subjects, and I respected that about him. I knew Conor would be in good hands working here with Norman as his boss. The worst that could happen would be Conor rejecting the offer, but that would be his choice to make, ultimately. Norman and I would lay the offer out on a golden platter for him, but you could only bring a horse to water...

When Conor had come to me asking for help with housing, he seemed like he had exhausted all his options, or perhaps he was just mentally spent from making more decisions than necessary. The second seemed like the more logical explanation of the two.

I explained to Norman that I believed Conor's time at the estate had come to a close and that I didn't want to send him off without having another opportunity lined up. My father wouldn't do that, and I couldn't either, in good conscience.

I told Norman that if he hired Conor as a manager, it would make his life at the tavern easier—especially with the added perk that Conor was a sommelier of whiskey and it would give the place an edge to have one in house for recommendations.

Maybe they could even add a whiskey and food pairing on the menu. I sweetened the deal with the idea that it would give Norman some time back to himself so he could live his dream of seeing palm trees during the winter months while Conor held down the bar.

Norman really liked the idea of vacationing somewhere tropical, and I knew I had him sold. The only other person I had to convince had no idea I was here trying to do him a favor.

"Excuse me for a moment, Norm. I need to make a phone call."

I tilted my chair against the bar to hold my spot and I stepped out to call Conor. I took a seat on the curb and dialed the number I had saved to my contacts long ago. He answered after a few rings.

"Hi, Conor. I know it's last minute, but could you meet me at the Black Horse Tavern?"

"Alright, Ciara. I'll head over in a few minutes. Everything okay?"

Conor was always looking out for others, so the question shouldn't have caught me off guard like it did. One of the first things he told me was that he'd taken care of his mom from a fairly young age. I guess when you spent most of your life looking out for others instead of yourself, questions like that become second nature. The realization made me a little sad, but I also thought that taking care of customers here would help him to fill that void.

"Yes, everything is fine." As fine as it could be, but the last thing I wanted was for him to worry. "I actually have a surprise for you."

"Color me intrigued. I'll see you soon. I was hoping we could have a chat soon anyway," he said before hanging up the phone.

I ordered another pint and had cleaned my plate when Conor walked in. He looked like he hadn't shaved in about a week, auburn and blonde stubble shadowing his jawline. I called him over to the empty spot next to me at the bar and gave him a friendly hug, because I knew he could use one.

"Ciara, I just wanted to start off by saying I'm sorry for everything. I'm sorry for letting Uallas manipulate me into betraying your father when he's been so important to me. I'm also sorry about how I left things between us. I realize now how wrong I was and I would understand if you didn't want me back at the estate at all. You deserve better."

Conor said it as though he'd been practicing the speech in a mirror, sighing with relief after he got it off his chest.

"I appreciate your apology, Conor. I know it wasn't easy to say. Please know I don't fault you for your decisions back then. As for us, you were what I needed to fill a void at the time, and if I'm being honest, I think we served the same purpose for each other. You deserve something real and to be happy. You're a good guy. But, I actually invited you here because I've been talking to Norman about you. Don't worry—I've only said good things. We think it would be a good opportunity for you to become a manager with him here at the tavern. I told him you've been a whiskey sommelier since working for my dad, and I think he could really use an extra hand around here, with doing more than just wiping glasses and counters. I'm doing okay at the estate and I thought maybe this opportunity could do you some good. I just know you'd thrive here. What do you think?"

Conor was at a loss for words. We both had changed so much since the first day I landed here in Ireland. I was no longer the girl who was so numb to feeling anything that she would take anyone to bed who looked at her for more than a minute, as a replacement for real love. A void to fill. I grew into the carbon copy of my dad's aura and someone I knew he'd be proud of to carry on his legacy.

Conor turned into a shell of himself after his mom passed, which made me sad to see, as I knew the brighter, smiley version of him. I'd love to see that version of him come back.

Norman came out from behind the bar to greet Conor with a pat on the shoulder.

"So, what you say, Conor boy? You ready to take over the bar again with me? Ciara has given you a glowing recommendation, and it seems I'd be a fool not to hire ya." Norman smiled up at him in anticipation of his answer.

Conor looked from Norman to me and took inventory of the liveliness surrounding us. Patrons were laughing amongst each other, pints were clanking and spilling on the bar. The room had an energy to it that made it feel as though joy were built into the very bones of the place. Happiness and cheer attracted people here like a magnet.

Conor considered the offer carefully, then spoke: "Alright, alright. When do I start?"

An amicable smile broke his lips, a hint at the old Conor cracking the surface. I physically relaxed after his acceptance, a contagious smile now plastered on my face as well.

"How about as early as next week?" Norman answered.

"Sounds excellent! Thank you both for the opportunity. I know ma would be proud," Conor said, a hint of sadness creeping over his features again.

I felt so sorry for him. He didn't have anyone now, except for me and Norman and this place. I was eager to see him in his element here. With the support of this community, I knew that sadness would ease up in no time.

"She would be, Conor. You have us to lean on if you need it. Don't be a stranger, okay? I gotta run though. See ya around!"

I gave them both a hug, chugged the rest of my beer, and paid my tab. When I walked out the door, I saw the figure of a black horse prancing in the distance, its mane and tail billowing in the wind, and I smiled.

CHAPTER 41

As I spotted Fearghas in his stallion form in the field outside the tavern, butterflies danced inside my chest. He looked so carefree out there after his time to himself.

The sun was inching its way toward the treelined horizon, backed by clouds resembling the colors of pink and orange sorbet ice cream.

Rays of sun simulating an amber spotlight shone down over Sugarloaf in the distance, as if to honor Uallas' life.

The sky always seemed to be painted extra beautifully after a loved one's passing. As if God himself were saying, "All is well up here—let me show you."

Though I felt indifferent to Uallas's demise, I knew it was difficult for Fearghas. I wanted him to spend the night with me again, even though I didn't need the protection anymore. Once our eyes met, I nodded for him to follow me down the street, away from prying eyes. His nostrils let out a tendril of steam when he caught sight of me and he started off in the direction I had indicated.

I picked up my pace, knowing full well he'd still get to the meeting point first.

I finally spotted Fearghas under a massive oak tree further down the road, past the hustle and bustle of the city. He pawed the earth impatiently, awaiting my arrival, and I rolled my eyes.

"You know, I only have two legs, and you currently have four," I said pointedly to him as I approached. I pushed his mane away from his eyes and pet his neck. He whinnied happily at the affection, or at the satisfaction of seeing my eyes roll at him. Quite possibly both.

At that, he shifted back into my favored form of muscled chest and horns, his shadows dancing lightly with the shade from the tree.

"Am I more to your liking now, Sunshine?" he purred as he pulled me close to his sculpted body.

"I *suppose* I could work with this," I teased, giving myself an excuse for my hands to wander idly over his sculpted arms and stomach, inspecting his hard muscles thoroughly. I moved my hands up and around the back of his neck and leaned up to kiss him. He deepened the kiss, claiming my mouth while his hands found their place, cupping my ass.

He lifted me up and my legs instinctually wrapped around his waist as he pressed me onto the rough bark of the tree. My winter coat cushioned its bite against my body. Part of me wished it wasn't there so I could feel the sting on my back while the rest of my body hummed with pleasure from his touch. I loved how my body reacted to even the slightest hint of him. Every pore on my body awakened as he bit my lip softly.

"Sunshine, we should get you back home. Naked in bed would be preferred," he growled next to my ear, his breath and the huskiness of his voice sending shivers up my body and settling low in my stomach.

I rested my hand on his chest to steady myself.

"Okay, but can you shift back? I'm tired of walking." I let loose a breath.

"So, you'd like to ride me, Sunshine?" He smirked at me and his pupils dilated at the thought of what we'd done this morning. I smiled back coyly as I nodded, pink heating my cheeks.

Of course, I wanted a ride on Fearghas, and not in the innocent way. We broke our touch for just a moment as he shifted back into his stallion form and I hopped on his back. Moments later, we were back at the estate, entering through the gardens in the back.

The statue of the crying woman looked beautiful, her tears now frozen in place from the cold. Bark from the birch trees that lined the property was peeling away, resembling torn sheets of parchment paper. The rosebushes shed their colorful blooms and were now various tones of glazed browns from the ice that coated them, pruned for the season. The orange and purple glow from dusk was the only color that remained here. Its sight was a beautiful reminder that growth needed time, and that we could always try again tomorrow. The outcome was colorful and full of life.

I jumped off Fearghas's back and headed toward the garden doors leading into the estate.

"No pets in the house, Fearghas," I sang as I walked up the stone steps.

He shifted into his human form, shadows swirling behind my back.

"So I'm a *pet* now, Sunshine?" he chimed in, and a shit-eating grin appeared on my face. Before I could turn around, he pounced on me, kissing my neck.

He sucked the sensitive spot next to my collarbone and I melted, wetness already pooling in between my legs. He inhaled sharply at the change in the air, giving me away.

Slowly, he unbuttoned my jeans and slid his fingers in, circling my wet slit.

I moaned at the warm contact mixed with the coolness of the air outside.

Fearghas was finally opening up with me, unafraid to claim me whenever and wherever, and I savored every ounce that he was willing to give me. He chuckled in my ear and it made my body tingle everywhere.

"I believe there was somewhere for you to be, Ciara," he whispered, referencing his mention earlier of me being naked in bed, and it did nothing except inspire my current situation down there.

He released me so I could go inside the house. As he followed, he checked the locks and drew the curtains behind us. Always my protector.

I smiled, grasping his hand and leading him upstairs. We didn't even make it to the bed before Fearghas was removing my clothing. I backed up into my desk and he lifted me up so I was sitting on it, arms braced behind me for support.

He knelt before me, spreading my legs to get a better view of me.

"You are exquisite, Ciara," Fearghas hissed. He trailed his rough hands up my thighs, marveling at the smoothness of my skin. Drinking me in. It made me weak with anticipation, but I just watched as he marveled at my curves.

I ran my fingers through his black hair and up his rough horns.

He groaned at my touch. It was an opportunity for us to both slow down and take inventory of each other.

I knew that would be short-lived, however. He planted soft kisses all the way up my thighs, teasing over my hips, before his expert fingers began to massage my wet and ready center. My hips bucked off the desk at his touch. With his other hand, he held me down and inserted his fingers, pumping me slowly.

"You are *mine*," he growled.

I dropped my head back and moaned at his touch and the baritone of his words. The need for more of him overcame me. He added his tongue, rotating figure eights along my bundle of nerves. I couldn't keep myself upright at the instant pleasure, finally giving in.

I lay back on the desk fully, disregarding the papers that fell onto the floor. He kept working me with his fingers while his tongue played, sending waves of ecstasy through my entire body. He lifted his hand off my stomach to play with himself as he watched me writhe in front of him. I watched him rub his thick length as my orgasm came closer. When he sensed my arousal, he picked up speed, sending me over the top in waves of lust.

As I let myself go, I was nearly seeing stars. My chest rose and fell rapidly, trying to gain its equilibrium after my orgasm.

He carried my body, limp from passion, over to the bed. We laid together with my head on his chest and him twirling my hair around his fingers. I was struggling to keep my eyes open, and before I realized it, I had drifted off into the most calming sleep I had experienced in months. Fearghas placed a tender kiss on my head and it was the last thing I remembered before falling asleep.

It took a moment for Fearghas's dreams to find me. It was a replay of that day in the rainy field during our first kiss. Except this time, I was able to hear his inner monologue. I could've sworn I felt a smile creep up on my lips as I slept.

"Sweet dreams, Sunshine. Tomorrow is a new day," he said.

CHAPTER 42

It was about eight in the morning when I woke, feeling well rested.

Today, there were no obstacles I had to face. No shadow lurking in the corner, waiting to pounce. Everything felt calm. Even the birds outside my window sang a different song.

I surveyed the room, assessing the aftermath of our coupling the previous night. The desk was a mess. Papers were still strewn about on the floor.

I got out of bed to clean it up before we started our day. I shuffled the papers around in my hands before setting them on the corner of the desk, next to the stack of portfolios. But then one of the papers I picked up off the floor had grabbed my attention.

It was another article from the *Malahide Craic*. I turned it over to find a black-and-white photo of my dad at the Black Horse Tavern.

He was in the center, dressed in a suit, surrounded by a group of smiling people I'd never seen before. Alongside them were Conor and Norman. They were all raising their pint glasses in a toast together. The paper was dated just after his passing. It made my lips start to quiver, and tears pooled in my eyes.

The article, titled *"Remembering Local Hero, Sean Driscoll,"* read:

Today we remember the life of our favorite local hero, Sir Sean Patrick Driscoll.

As honorary mayor of the town of Malahide, we celebrate his life and legacy. Throughout his years here, Driscoll was solely responsible for keeping the peace of our proud town with the terrors that live at its borders. He died unexpectedly Saturday, the thirteenth day of July, at his twenty acre estate in Malahide.

Sean was a loving father. He is survived by his daughter, Ciara Driscoll, who resides at his second residence in Florida, which he visited on a regular basis. He worked for the Irish government's private sector and was a staple to his community. Sean was a passionate philanthropist. He was the founder of multiple charities for displaced children, homeless families, and women. He was an honorary member of the Dublin library, funding a majority of the upkeep and maintenance of its most valued works of original literature. Driscoll was a generous and magnetic man who had a love for original works of mythology and lore. You could find him befriending anyone at the Black Horse Tavern or at the local cafe when he was in town on business.

His celebration of life will be held at St. Patrick's Cathedral in the Dublin town square this upcoming Saturday, the twentieth day of July. All are welcome to attend in honor of his life. We will all greatly miss you, Sean Patrick Driscoll. May you live on in our hearts as well as in our community

The obituary should have been a small article in the back of the paper, along with all the other lives lost, but the paper had put him front and center. The town and its residents clearly loved and adored him as much as I had. It warmed my heart to read the article and the kind words it contained. He was a much bigger part of this community than I could've ever imagined. To see him happy with friends, familiar faces along with some I have yet to meet—that was how I wanted to remember him.

The friendly, loving guy that had taught me so many invaluable life lessons. Maybe one day I'd be able to meet those other friends from the picture and we could share our stories about him. I had never been more proud to call him my father than I was after reading it.

Fearghas stirred in bed. He reached out an arm to where I would have been, but found the bed empty. Once his eyes finally landed on mine and he noticed my tears, he came over to me.

"What is the matter, Sunshine?" he asked sweetly. He bent down so we were eye to eye, his hand cupping my cheek, wiping away my tears.

"I found my father's obituary in the papers. The town loved him. They called him their 'local hero.' He was always so secretive with me because of his job. I had no idea he was so loved over here in Ireland, too. I was worried about how others may have seen him, but now I know."

I showed him the paper I had just read. The tears that lingered in my eyes still blurred my vision before falling down my face again. Fearghas took a few minutes to look it over to see what I was crying about.

"Oh, Ciara. He was that and more to us, too. He was our protector. He was the one we could not harm, according to our code. I will be forever sorry that my brother took him from you. Your father was also my greatest friend. He saw the good in me when I could barely see it for myself. Now, I have you, my anam cara, the sunshine of my life." His words made my tears flow like rivers, but he wiped away every single one.

"I love you, Fearghas," I said through a quivering grin.

If I had just gone through the papers on the desk the day I arrived, I wouldn't have had to wonder. I wasn't ready for the truth then, and I was barely holding myself together now. Despite my tears, I felt comforted.

Maybe my tears were a mixture of love, relief, and sadness.

Healing. I was healing.

I knew the emptiness I felt in my heart would never go away fully because my father was gone, but if I focused on all the good he had brought into this world, it would make it hurt a little less every day.

Good really can triumph over evil, no matter the cost. People will remember what you do for them and that is what makes you immortal through memories.

Fearghas was right. He had me and I had him. Together, we'd continue the legacy my father had started: to bring more light into this world and snuff out the darkness. We didn't need the Solais Sword for that, just the message that it represented.

I was my own strength, and Fearghas by my side made me unstoppable. Just in case he was listening, I looked up at the cobalt sky and said, "I love you forever, dad."

EPILOGUE

THREE MONTHS LATER

I walked up the steps to the red door of the Black Horse Tavern, looking over my shoulder to see Fearghas in stallion form behind me. As usual, I rolled my eyes and smiled before I entered. A chalkboard A-frame sign advertised the whiskey and food pairing menu for the day.

The bar was teeming with locals and tourists alike. I had to squeeze through the crowd to find a spot just to say hi. Conor and Norman were working in sync together behind the bar.

Conor was clean shaven except for a mustache. He was smiling and conversing with tourists at the bar, suggesting places to visit nearby. Norman was buzzing around, pouring beers and asking regulars how they enjoyed their meals.

They had also hired more servers because the whiskey pairing menu was such a hit. The Black Horse Tavern was now a tourist spot for delicious fare as well, as a vital part of the town's history.

Among the hustle and bustle, I spotted a painting of a black horse with glowing eyes against a mist covered backdrop. The paint strokes were wispy, giving it an air of mystery. Its color palette was done mostly in varying shades of black and grey. The only brilliance that stood out was the horse's fearsome eyes. Below it, a plaque explained that this was the horse that inspired the namesake of the tavern many years ago, and while it barely comes around anymore, it is no longer seen as an omen, but rather a sign of good luck.

Memories from before I met Fearghas flooded my brain. I remembered being frightened of him that night, and Norman calling him a bad omen. I knew even then that it wasn't the case, despite my fear of the unknown.

I butted my way through the crowd to order a shot and a Guinness. I'd come here every week since Conor got hired to check on his progress and make sure he was settling into his new role properly. It fit him like a glove and I was happy to see his growth.

"Hey, Ciara! Nice to see you! How are things going?" Conor asked.

"Can't complain. The place keeps getting busier and busier every time I come here! How are you holding up?"

It was true: word of mouth about the tavern had seemed to spread. There was a new crowd every time I visited.

"Going great! We're thinking about adding a beer garden—a place for people to gather outside and enjoy fresh air during the warmer months. We were also thinking of adding a few benches to honor your da and my ma. Been deciding on the color of rose bushes we'd plant out there. I got a flat in town here, and have been settling in the past month." Conor seemed to light up at the thought of the new developments in the bar and his personal life.

It reassured me I had made the right choice those months ago to not hire him back. Growth took a little discomfort before you could feel the fruition of reward. It seemed that this place and this community had rewarded him greatly, and I was happy to stand on the sidelines and watch his new life unfold.

"That sounds excellent, Conor. I know they both would be proud of you," I said, and I meant it, too.

I turned my attention to Norman.

"Hi, Norm! The place looks busy. How are ya holding up?" I shouted over the crowd, looking around at all the people mingling.

"Never better! I wanted to say thank you for giving me

Conor. He's really made something of himself and the bar here, and I could not be more proud of him. Oh! That reminds me—I have a surprise to show you, Ciara!"

He went into the back for a moment and brought out a sleek black frame.

Inside was my father's 'Local Hero' article from the Malahide Craic, with the picture of him toasting with them all. I realized it was taken a while ago, here at the Black Horse Tavern.

"I've been doing some redecoratin' and I wanted to hang it up behind the bar here, but I wanted your approval first. That's us here, and Conor, with some of your da's other friends from the government agency he worked with. We were just over there when it was taken." He pointed to a spot in the middle of the bar next to a wooden pole where a couple was talking.

"Thank you, Norman. It's perfect. He would love it," I said through the tears starting to form in my eyes—but the tears welling up weren't sad, they were happy. Happy that my father had found friends within this community. Happy that everyone loved him here.
Happy that I had found them, and they had become like family to me, as well.

"I miss him every day, Ciara. He will always live on in our hearts. Sláinte!"

We clanked our shot glasses together, tapped them on the bar, and threw back one final shot of whiskey in my father's honor.

Acknowledgements

I am so grateful to my team at DBWP, from the moment I said that I had the idea to write this book, all the way up to publishing it. You all were the best supporters and accountability managers a girl can ask for. Thank you for helping to see my vision through to publishing day.

To my editors, Blue Line Co and Clarity Copy Co. I could not have made this book without you. You all were a vital part of making my dreams happen and I hope that you never forget that you make so many authors dreams happen with your literary talents.

To my friends and family, your support means the world to me. Thank you for listening to me rant about a chapter, a character or just the process of it all.

To my book artists, you all are so talented and I appreciate the time and dedication you took to bring this book and its characters to life with the vision we created together.

To my found friends from Island Vibes and Elevate, thank you for providing a safe and creative space for me to write a significant portion of this book and being so supportive to this stranger who walked into the cafe one day.

To my readers, for which this book has given life to, thank you for reading and supporting an independent author.

Finally, to my father. I miss you all the time. After you left this world about 2 years ago, I started to get lost in fantasy books again and that was the catalyst for me writing this book in hopes that maybe someone going through loss could find solace in this book. Sorry for the smut, dad.

ABOUT THE AUTHOR

Alison Tuite is a central Florida based author of her debut novel, *Sharp and Pointy Things*. As a hairstylist for fifteen years and counting, she has shared countless stories behind the chair with her clients throughout the years. She has always been a lover of writing as another creative outlet, starting with diaries as a child. When she isn't writing, you can either catch her snuggling with her pitbull (Fred), kayaking or reading a fantasy book or two.

Stay up to date with my newsletter and follow me on instagram @alisontuiteauthor

www.ingramcontent.com/pod-product-compliance
Lightning Source LLC
Chambersburg PA
CBHW031514010826
48973CB00013B/1273